Dead Rules

Rules

RANDY RUSSELL

HARPER TEEN

An Imprint of HarperCollins*Publishers*

HarperTeen is an imprint of HarperCollins*Publishers*.

Dead Rules
Copyright © 2011 by Randy Russell

Library of Congress Cataloging-in-Publication Data
Russell, Randy.
Dead Rules / Randy Russell.—1st ed.
        p.   cm.
Summary: When high school junior Jana Webster dies suddenly, she
finds herself in Dead School, where she faces choices that will determine
when, she, a Riser, will move on, but she strives to become a Slider
instead, for the chance to be with the love of her life—even if it means
killing him.
ISBN 978-0-06-198670-3
[1. Dead—Fiction. 2. Future life—Fiction. 3. Schools—
Fiction. 4. Supernatural—Fiction.] I. Title.
PZ7.F915937De   2011   2010032452
[Fic]—dc22

Typography by Torborg Davern
11 12 13 14 15   LP/RRDB   10 9 8 7 6 5 4 3 2 1
❖
First Edition

THIS BOOK IS DEDICATED TO STEPHANIE
MACLEAN, WHO GAVE ME WINGS.

CHAPTER ONE

JANA HAD THE JITTERS.

It was her first day at her new school and everyone on the bus looked distinctly peculiar. She felt her face with both hands to be certain she wasn't dreaming. The inside of her mouth tasted like strawberries. She didn't remember eating breakfast.

Her hands lingered upon her face. Her fingers felt cool.

"It's the back of your head," the girl sitting next to her said. "Not your face."

"What's that?"

"Your hair's messed up in back. Did you fall down?"

"I guess I did," Jana said. She was beginning to remember.

"I'm Arva Davis." The girl choked out her name in a harsh whisper.

"Jana Webster."

Of Webster and Haynes, Jana wanted to add, but didn't. Everyone at her new school would soon learn that Jana wasn't alone in this world.

"Oh, I know. We're roommates. I'm here to help with your orientation, first day and all."

If Arva was trying to be cheerful, it was difficult to tell. She spoke in a strained whisper, like the bad guy in a movie after he's been shot.

"There's a school guidebook in the library," Arva said. "But if you have any questions, you can just ask me."

Jana gazed out the window. The houses on the street seemed to slide by, as if they were moving instead of the bus. It wasn't a street she had seen before.

"Where's Michael?" Jana asked. It was the most important question she had.

"Which one?"

"My boyfriend. Michael Haynes. We're never apart."

They were famous at her school for being together, for being a couple. Jana felt undressed without him. With Michael, she was the perfectly content Jana, the confident and talented Jana. Without him, she fidgeted.

"He's at your old school, I guess. Are you feeling homesick? Everybody does at first."

Something was stuck in Arva's throat, Jana decided. Nobody could talk like that on purpose. Jana wanted to pound Arva on the back until her voice turned normal.

"He won't leave me here alone," Jana said. "He'll be waiting for me in the parking lot when we get there."

"Closed campus," Arva said. "No visitors."

Jana turned around in her seat to look out the back window of the school bus. Michael was probably following in his car. He couldn't live without her.

The students in the seats behind her stared at Jana. There was something odd about every one of them. Even the cute guy sprawled out in the backseat of the bus looked a little crazy. He smiled at her.

He had beautiful blue eyes and perfectly arched

3

dark eyebrows, but Jana knew his kind with one glance. Every school had them. They acted tough and talked dirty. Michael could scare them off with a wave of his hand. So could Jana.

She held up the back of her left hand to the boy at the rear of the bus, the hand with Michael's white-gold senior-class ring on it. Jana waved her fingers at herself.

The boy at the back of the bus nodded and grinned. Then flipped her the bird. A tall guy with his leg stuck out across the aisle laughed.

Jana turned around in her seat.

"Don't look at them," Arva warned her. "The guys at the back are Sliders. They're dangerous. They'll get you into real trouble. That's all they're good for."

Jana's new roommate sounded like a frog trying to talk.

"If I strangle you right now as hard as I can, will you quit talking like that?" Jana asked.

Arva giggled. It sounded like car brakes squeaking.

Jana looked for her cell phone and noticed her clothes. They were the same clothes that Arva wore: a pleated plaid skirt of dark greens and a white button-down blouse with a man's collar. Knee socks and black loafers. These weren't clothes she'd owned before. Ever.

They didn't smell like her clothes. They didn't smell like her fabric softener or like her perfume—the one Michael had given her for Valentine's Day. Jana wrinkled her nose. Her new clothes smelled like Ivory soap. And so did she.

She slid her bottom forward in the bus seat and checked her new clothes for pockets. There was one on each side of the thick cotton skirt. Both were empty. She checked the top of her socks.

"Are you looking for cigarettes?" Arva asked.

Jana shook her head. "Cell," she said. "I need to text Michael." He would meet her wherever she said. Whenever she said. He would leave class if he had to.

"Can't," Arva told her. "Cell phones don't work here. Not on the bus, not at school, not in the dorm."

"Oh," Jana said. "Really? That can't be true."

Her white blouse had a chest pocket. It was empty.

"Definitely true," Arva said. "If you had one on you when you came here, it will be back in the dorm with the clothes you were wearing, but it won't work here. There's no signal."

"Purse?" Jana asked, startled that she might have lost so many things by transferring to the new school. Not the least of which was Michael. "Where are my books? My laptop?"

"Purses and bags are not allowed on campus. Your books and notebooks for each class will be at your seat when you get there. You just leave them where they are and then they will be in the dorm room when school is over. It's one of the things they do. And there's a computer in the dorm room, but you won't like it."

Jana didn't care whether she liked the computer. Email would save her life. She'd just have to wait.

"What time do we go home?" Jana asked, her thoughts shifting.

Arva laughed again. Or at least Jana interpreted the two harsh squeaks as a laugh.

"It's a boarding school, of course," Arva said. "You'll get out for a funeral and field trips, things like that."

Jana looked out the window again.

Nothing made sense, really. No one should be plopped down in a new school in the middle of the year. Especially not her junior year when she was dating a senior. Jana touched the back of her hair. It felt messy. Her brush was in her purse, wherever that was.

"We're almost there," Arva told her. "We'll be in homeroom together. But if you have any more questions, you should ask them now. When I talk in class, they know it's me."

Jana was puzzled by a girl who sat at the front of the bus. Everyone else wore school uniforms. She wore a shimmering white gown. It looked like satin.

"Okay, then," Jana said. "The girl in white. What's her story? Is she in a cult or something?"

"Shhh." Arva held her finger to her lips. "Don't make fun."

"I'm not making fun," Jana said. "She just looks so pale. Except for her lips and eyes, she's the same color as her dress."

"I know. It's like you can see right through their skin. She's a Virgin. They're diaphanous. Ethereal."

"Why is she wearing a gown? Is she in the choir or something?"

"Sort of," Arva said. "Virgins sing. Otherwise, they don't do much at school. They aren't in classes with the rest of us. They're not allowed to talk to us either. They're almost angels."

"How do you get to be one?" Jana asked. She wouldn't mind skipping class for a year and a half.

"A Virgin?" Arva grinned. "Think it through. You start out as one."

"Well, crap, then. I'm a virgin!"

Arva shook her head slowly, looking directly into Jana's eyes. "Fingers count," she said.

Jana stared at her new classmate in disbelief. That wasn't fair. You've either had intercourse or you haven't. Jana and Michael hadn't. They'd made a unanimous decision not to. They were going to, but not yet. Jana was almost an angel too. Almost.

"Anything else?" Arva asked.

Jana shook her head.

"You want to know his name, don't you?"

"Whose name?"

"That guy in the backseat. He's beautiful, really. I look at him all the time when it's safe. But don't let him see you doing it. He has a smile that can melt the buttons off your blouse."

"No," Jana said. "I don't care what his name is."

He was rude and crude and that's all she needed to know.

"Mars," Arva said. "Just like the candy bar they used to have when we were kids. His name is the only good thing about him. Those boys are poison, Jana. Pure poison."

Jana turned in her seat. She was on a school bus with an almost angel in the front seat and pure poison sitting in the back.

She looked hard at Arva. Her orientation adviser's lips were tinged slightly blue at the edges and they were quivering. There was a small feather in the corner of Arva's mouth. It looked like pillow down, except for the color.

Arva noticed her stare. She touched her mouth and pulled the little black feather away. "Happens," Arva said.

Jana had fallen.

She remembered it now. That's what messed up her hair in back.

When Michael told her that Nathan Mills wanted to double-date, Jana wasn't happy with the idea. Nathan was a jerk. Michael was only best friends with him because they'd grown up across the street from each other. They had walked to school together every day in junior high, before Michael and his father moved to a better part of town.

"We see him all the time," she said. "Does he

have to go out with us too?"

"It's special this time, Jana. He wants to impress this girl who has a crush on him. He thinks this could be the real thing, the one who waits for him to come home from the Navy."

Michael had that look in his eyes. The one that promised Jana the world. How could she say no?

"Why is he joining the Navy?" Jana asked. "He doesn't know anything about boats."

"To get away from here," Michael said. "To see the world. Just like us."

"But we're not going to float around in a boat, Michael. We're moving to the city where there's *real* theater." She had explained this a hundred times.

"We can go to Hollywood right out of college," he reminded her. He'd learned the easiest way to get along with Jana was to keep her dream alive. College came first in Michael's world.

"Or New York," Jana said. "Denzel Washington started out in New York."

Webster and Haynes were destined to be famous actors. They had won regionals in Duet Acting last year. And this year they were going to win state. Everyone said so. Jana had also qualified in Solo Humorous Interpretation with a reading of *Horton*

Hears a Who, while Michael had taken a regional in After Dinner Speaking. They were that good.

"Okay," she relented. "Who wants to go out with Nathan, anyway?"

"Sherry Simmons. She's a sophomore."

Jana groaned.

"Do you know her?" Michael asked.

"Does Nicole know Kidman?" Jana said.

"Does Sandra know Bullock?" Michael countered.

"*Practical Magic*," Jana answered. "Too easy." It was their private game. It made her smile.

"I should have said Stockard Channing."

"You should have told Nathan no. You know he gives me the creeps. And Sherry Simmons is a slut. Nathan's not going to marry Sherry Simmons. Nobody in this town is."

"She just wants to be liked," Michael said. "And doesn't know how to go about it."

"Oh, she knows how to go about it. And she's already been liked by half the boys in school."

Sherry was short and round. She wore hickeys on her neck like they were jewelry. She got a fresh set every weekend. Her father was a locksmith. The only thing Jana had ever heard Sherry talk about was how to break into stores and people's houses. The guys in school ate it up.

Sherry was always watching Jana in the halls. When Jana looked back at her, Sherry would make a face like she and Jana were supposed to be friends. They weren't.

"Come on, Jana," Michael said. "It's not going to kill you."

"Okay. But they go home early and I mean it. I'm not riding around in the car all night while Nathan drinks beer and giggles until he throws up."

"Nathan asked her out for Thursday. So we're booked?"

"You owe me one," Jana said.

"You can decide what we're going to do. I was thinking maybe a movie."

"Movies are just for us, Michael. You know that." Jana considered their options. "I'll come up with something," she said.

And she did. Jana wished now that she had thought of something where you couldn't fall down so easily and so hard.

CHAPTER TWO

ARVA TUGGED JANA'S ARM.

"Homeroom," she said in her creaky voice as she led Jana inside. Bluish faces were the trend here. And more.

"Your desk is next to mine," Arva croaked cheerfully. "See, your notebook is already there. Pencils and pens. You can take notes, but you leave your notebook here when class is over."

Jana sat slumped in her desk. She leaned her head over her notebook, letting the fall of her dark brown hair hide her face. One wall of the classroom had windows. The seats along the windows had been taken by boys, except the first desk. It was empty.

"Hi," someone said to Arva. Jana didn't look up right away.

She barely wanted to look at anyone. There were things about some of these students she didn't want to see twice. Disfigured faces. Bodies damaged in odd ways. The bus had been bad enough. The hallway was worse. With Arva, it was the little black feather in the corner of her mouth and that muffled rasp and croak of her broken voice. But with others . . .

"This is Beatrice," Arva was saying.

"What's your name?" Beatrice asked.

"Jana Webster," Jana answered, still slumped forward, still hiding her eyes from the classroom.

"Of Webster and Haynes," Arva hoarsely choked out. Jana had told Arva all about Michael on their way to class. She couldn't help it.

"Oh, sounds juicy," Beatrice said, catching on quickly. "How hunky is he?"

"Big-time," Arva said.

With that, Jana lifted her head and pulled her hair behind her ear to look at Beatrice. Jana had her smile in place, the one she used when she met new people at speech and acting tournaments.

Jana looked once at Beatrice, then quickly looked away.

"I'm sorry," Jana mumbled. She held her hand to her mouth then dropped it. "I'm so sorry . . . but there's something . . . there's . . ."

Beatrice apparently was accustomed to an initial gasp or two when being introduced. She grinned at Jana. Beatrice had a wide mouth that pointed downward when she grinned. She looked cute when she did that. Jana would have to practice the technique. It was a look she could copy when there was a reason to smile about something you weren't really happy about.

"Something sticking out of my head?" Beatrice asked. "Looks like a hat, doesn't it? A clown hat or a big fake flower."

"What is it?"

"Yard dart. Church picnic."

"I didn't know they still made those."

"Oh, they don't," Beatrice told her. "They're bona fide collector's items."

Jana nodded like an idiot. Beatrice sat in the desk behind her. Jana faced forward and slumped into place, letting her hair fall again to hide her face. She tried not to shiver, wondering whether Beatrice had tried to pull the thing out of her head. She had such pretty brown eyes, but no one in the world was going to notice with a metal rod and three bright yellow plastic fins sticking out the top of her skull.

A new sound caught Jana's attention. Three kids on gurneys with squeaky wheels were brought into homeroom by attendants wearing gray. The students on gurneys were placed in a row, heads along the wall without the windows, toes pointing at the class. Jana, apparently, had been transferred to a magnet school for the critically lame.

She peeked over her shoulder at the back of the class, her eyes shielded by the fall of her hair. Boys talking in low, chiding voices were punching one another in the arm.

Sliders. That's what Arva had called them. A couple of them wore jeans instead of the black school uniform slacks. Mars was right in the middle of the group. He caught her looking at him.

"Roll!" a male voice boomed from the speaker mounted next to the institutional clock above the blackboard. The students' names were read in alphabetical order. His last name was Dreamcote. Mars Dreamcote. It sounded like something you wore to bed if you wanted to meet Martians in your sleep.

Their teacher appeared. He stood at the front of

the room, peering over their heads, looking at none of them. Jana didn't blame him.

"All present," he said. He glanced at the empty desk at the front of class and added, "Vacancy noted."

Jana opened her notebook and saw that someone had already written on the first page in dark pencil. It was one simple word, followed by a short notation in smaller, carefully printed letters underneath.

The word was *Murder.* The notation below said *From a Friend.*

Murder. What was that supposed to mean?

"Jeff Bridges," Jana said.

She was on the phone with Michael. Jana had spent the evening searching online, finding just the right activity for their double date with Nathan Mills and Sherry Simmons.

"And?" Michael asked.

"Sam Elliott."

Michael stalled. "That's not an easy one," he said.

"It will be when I give you one more."

"No, I'm getting it."

She waited.

"Okay." Michael gave up. "One more."

"John Goodman."

"*The Big Lebowski*," Michael said, then swore for needing three actors' names to get it. "One of my favorites. I should have had it at Sam Elliott."

"Fart, fudge, and popcorn," Jana said in return, laughing. It was her catch phrase, the one she used in place of cursing. "You didn't."

"I guess we're going bowling?"

"Yep," Jana said. "The perfect double date. I've already reserved a lane."

Jana didn't like bowling. It was too loud, for one thing, and she felt utterly wretched when she rolled a gutter ball. But bowling would save her from having to do anything the least bit romantic with Nathan and Sherry along. More importantly, it would keep those two from doing anything romantic in front of Jana. The idea of watching them kiss made her shudder.

"I didn't know you liked bowling, Jana."

"I hate it," she said brightly. "But I'll live. And the next time we go on a double date, it's going to be with people I choose. Okay?"

"Woody Harrelson," Michael said in reply.

"*Kingpin*," Jana said, nailing it. "Way too easy, Michael." Then she added quickly, "Bill Murray,

Randy Quaid." She earned ten bonus points for naming the movie and two additional actors in the cast. The more actors who had to be named before you guessed the right movie, the more difficult it was to come up with additional cast members.

"Bonus noted," Michael said reluctantly.

"Don't you just love me?" Jana teased.

Of course he did. Of that, Jana was most certain. Webster and Haynes loved each other dearly, deeply, and for all of time.

One of the Sliders wrote it, Jana decided.

Murder. From a Friend. The printing was so precise. She glanced at the back of the classroom to see if they were watching her, waiting to laugh when she read the spooky note.

Mars caught her looking at him again. He let one corner of his mouth smile. There was a dimple.

She quickly turned her head around. The teacher was writing on the blackboard. He had greased hair parted high on one side. Nearly two inches around his ears had been shaved. He was in his early forties, she guessed, but his face looked more tired than his age. His hands were too large for his sleeves.

The instructor's name was at the top of the

blackboard: Mr. Fitzgerald. He didn't wear a ring on either hand. After writing *Today's Assignment* on the chalkboard, he turned around to check his notes. He wore a twill jacket with a small checkered pattern and a funny knitted tie. It had perfectly horizontal contrasting stripes and was too short. It was also cut flat across the bottom.

Jana liked watching older people. She worked hard to figure out what motivated them. It was part of being a good actor. Mr. Fitzgerald, however, didn't seem motivated by anything. He had tired eyes and the flesh of his face sagged. She bet he drank. He was an alcoholic and she wondered why.

Failed romance, Jana concluded. He had loved and lost. And he was still obsessed by it. Not everyone could be Webster and Haynes.

Thursday night, Jana and Sherry had gone to the restroom to check their makeup.

"Do you like him?" Jana asked the younger girl. Sherry's hair was thick and straight, cut far short of reaching her shoulders. It was plain brown hair, but Sherry wore it with fat, cherry red streaks dyed from the part across both sides. Each red streak had a narrow yellow stripe down the middle. Her head look like a piece of striped candy.

"Huge crush," Sherry said. She was telling the truth, but it had nothing to do with Nathan.

"Be careful," Jana warned the younger girl. "He's a senior and you're a sophomore."

Jana's hair was simply dark brown without natural or unnatural highlights. When she wasn't performing, she wore very little makeup. Her mother said Jana was born with bedroom eyes. Her eyelids were well defined, but Jana believed her eye color was dull and boring. Hazel. Almost green, but hazel. It was just one of the reasons Jana wasn't as pretty as her mother. And never would be.

She knew all her faults and could live with them. Her eyebrows weren't dark enough. Her chin was a bit too prominent. Her mouth was too big. When Jana smiled for real, it took over her face.

Jana's mother was a spectacular beauty, a once-famous cover girl model. She'd told Jana time and time again that being beautiful was dangerous. That Jana was lucky to be a little on the plain side, because just look at what being ravishingly beautiful had done to her mother.

"When you're beautiful, everyone sees a different story for you, but it's not your story," her mother explained. "Be glad you get to go through life being plain old Jana. You can define yourself rather than have someone else do it for you."

Jana wore waterproof mascara because she was on a date and didn't want to smudge Michael's shirt. Afraid that the bright lights of the bowling alley would wash out her features entirely, she carefully applied a new coating of peach lip gloss. It felt like silk on her lips. It made her feel pretty, even though she would never be as pretty as her mother.

Jana smacked her lips in the mirror and smiled. But not too big a smile.

"Sometimes, you have to make up your mind who you want and not worry about the little things that might get in the way," Sherry said. "I'm not perfect, like you are. So I have to try harder."

Jana laughed. She wasn't perfect. She caught Sherry's stare in the bathroom mirror and saw the seriousness in her eyes. Sherry stared at Jana with a funny little pout that made her eyes look mean.

"Little things?" Jana asked.

"You know, other people." Sherry shrugged. "Little things like that."

Strangely Jana found herself agreeing with the sophomore's assessment of getting what you wanted in life. Other people wouldn't get in the way of Webster and Haynes. Ever.

"Also, I'm not perfect," Jana said. "You want perfect, you should meet my mother. And just wait till you see me bowl."

Sherry grinned. This time it was for real. Her mean eyes twinkled.

"And neither is Michael," Jana continued. "We just happen to be perfect for each other."

Sherry's purse was open on the vanity counter. Jana glanced at it and saw an aerosol spray on top of her other stuff.

"Is that hair spray?" Aerosols ate holes in the atmosphere.

Sherry closed her purse with a snap. "Pepper spray," she said. "My dad's paranoid. He won't let me leave the house without it. I have enough to take out an entire football team."

"Well, if you have any trouble with Nathan, just let me know. Michael will make him behave."

Sherry stepped back from the mirror and did something Jana had never seen another girl do before. She tugged her T-shirt down in front and lightly rubbed the palms of her hands up and down over the points of her breasts. Jana had to turn around to keep from saying something rude. No wonder she needed pepper spray, Jana thought.

They joined Michael and Nathan at the bowling carousel.

The sound of heavy balls hitting the floor and rolling down the alleys echoed from wall to wall. The crash and fall of pins sounded almost like a war going on. People whooped and hollered. They jumped up and down and screeched.

Michael sat behind the electronic scoreboard. As Jana walked toward him, she was overcome by a keen sense of déjà vu. She saw him twice in a row, sitting, entering their names on the tabulator keyboard. Jana wanted to tap him on the shoulder and ask him to leave with her. There were butterflies in her stomach that shouldn't be there. Something was wrong tonight.

Jana shook off the tickling of dread. Michael was with her and she was safe.

Nathan and Sherry sat together on the half-circle bench behind Michael. Jana sat down next to Sherry to put on her bowling shoes. She carefully and evenly tugged the laces of her bowling shoes and tied them tightly. Then she tied each of the loops into a knot on top.

"What are you doing?" Nathan asked. "Crochet?" Nathan laughed at his own joke. His laugh sounded like a motorcycle trying to start. That's what he did when he drank beer. He laughed. He would laugh all night. It was so boring.

Sherry bent forward to watch Jana tie the second knot in each of her shoelaces. Nathan accidentally kicked Sherry's purse and the pepper spray rolled out. The sophomore must have been embarrassed by it, because she immediately got down on her knees in front of Jana and reached under the seats to retrieve the canister before anyone else could see what it was.

While Sherry was bent over, Nathan made a face at Jana, bouncing his eyebrows and letting his tongue loll out of his mouth like a panting dog. Nathan was such a creep.

"Jana, your turn," Michael said. He turned around and winked at her. "Break a leg," he added for good luck.

CHAPTER THREE

JANA WAS UP.

She stood and straightened the legs of her capri pants. They were light blue with vertical cream stripes. They made her legs look longer.

Jana picked up her marmalade-colored house ball and her foot slipped out from under her on the polished-wood floor. Bowling was slipperier than she remembered. She caught herself on the carousel with her free hand and righted herself. Then she slipped again. Her right shoe slid out from under her like it had wheels or she was trying to stand on ice.

She lifted her foot high to keep from falling.

Jana's left shoe caught sideways and she did a

goofy dance. She leaned too far forward, then propelled herself upright as hard as she could. She raised her marmalade bowling ball over her head to try to keep her balance.

It was no use. Her right foot slid away from her on its own.

Jana heard Nathan's laugh start up as she fell backward, the weight of the ball pulling her arm back over her shoulder.

She held on to the eight-pound bowling ball like it was a life preserver. The ball hit the floor first. Her fingers were locked inside it. Jana's head landed on the bowling ball when she finally fell. Her elbow stuck up in the air.

Michael was nearby, but she didn't see him when she fell. Her skull was cracked just a little, with her skin barely broken over it. The pain was instantly unbearable. Just as quickly, it went away.

Air rushed inside Jana's brain. Her dreams rushed out.

She was three years old, sitting naked in a two-ring plastic swimming pool in her backyard in the middle of summer. Her mother wasn't there.

Then she was seven. There was a pony at her birthday party. Her mother wasn't there. The pony had long white hair that fell over the front of its face.

In the third grade, a boy called Jana a bastard child. She chased him until he tripped and fell. Then she kicked him because she didn't know what else to do and the other kids at school were watching.

Jana bought belted cargo shorts and flip-flops for her Ken doll.

A picture of her mother stared at Jana from the cover of Vogue. It didn't look like anyone Jana knew.

Jana danced at her junior high prom. The boy she danced with took large steps to the side. Jana could smell the corsage of white carnations on her wrist.

In the school parking lot, she choked on a cigarette and thought she was going to die.

"Ye wouldn't never leave me, would ye?" Jana asked Michael in the funny accent she had learned in order to play Abbie for a competition cutting from Eugene O'Neill's Desire Under the Elms. Michael was Eben. They'd had a baby together in that play.

Jana's mother sat on the edge of her bed and wept. Her mother was beautiful even when she cried.

In the back row of the movie theater, Jana removed her bra without taking off her sweater so Michael could feel her breasts. She had practiced for weeks.

The memories were gone in a flash. Was someone

kissing her? Air came in and her life ran out, sweeping away her question. Every sensation she ever felt evaporated. Except for the lasting taste of strawberries in her mouth.

Fart, fudge, and popcorn. She was already dead.

The girl at the desk in front of Arva said, "Ouch."

She had very pretty hair. It formed a lustrous fan across her shoulders and seemed to lift slightly as if held on a summer breeze.

"Ouch." Then in a minute, again. "Ouch, ouch." Each time she said it, the girl's hair and shoulders bounced.

Mr. Fitzgerald continued writing on the board. Jana turned her attention to the boy in front of her. He had three inches of thick black hair that stuck straight out. It made his head look like a dark dandelion puff. When he held his head to the side, she could almost see his eyes. His cheekbones were prominent.

He had looked at her when she first sat down and she noticed then that his dark brown eyes were round and wide, as if he had just been surprised. He had a smooth, round face to match.

"Ouch," the girl in front of Arva said.

Jana shut her eyes and fought to concentrate. Mr. Fitzgerald sat at his desk. He opened a book to read. Their assignment was on the board.

"That which doesn't kill you makes you stronger," he had written in barely readable cursive. *What about that which does? Answer in 250 words by the end of this period: Leave your notebooks on your desks. Have a good day.*

Jana recognized the initial quote. It was from the writings of Nietzsche, the German philosopher.

"That which doesn't kill you makes you stronger." What about that which does?

She was thinking it over when the round-faced boy in front of her turned in his seat and placed a note on her desk. He grinned at her in a shy way and turned back around. Jana opened the folded piece of paper. It read *Hi. I'm Henry Sixkiller. Come here often?*

Jana couldn't help it, she laughed. She put her hand to her mouth. Her fingers felt cold on her lips. She ducked her head over her open notebook, hoping no one had noticed the chortling sound she'd made.

"Ouch," the girl sitting across from Henry said quietly, with her peculiar little shoulder jerk.

Jana worked on her essay.

Love, she wrote, *defeats death*. She and Michael were as in love with each other as they had ever been. And one of them, it was now apparent, was dead.

She hadn't seen Michael when she fell. But he was there. He was so near. Still, she had died alone. That's what troubled her now.

Once she'd met Michael, once they'd kissed and she'd felt a magical, warm-blooded life move back and forth between them, Jana knew she would never live alone again. Like she had with her mother.

It wasn't fair that Jana would die alone. It just wasn't.

Romeo and Juliet died together. Old grandmas and grandpas in nursing homes died within days of each other. The plane went down and killed everyone on board, Jana and Michael locked in each other's arms.

Jana returned to her essay, adding a few paragraphs, and concluding, *That which kills you doesn't kill love. The philosopher who said suffering short of death makes you stronger is critically flawed in his thinking because death doesn't end how strong you are.*

I am still here. And I am still strong. I am strong because I am in love. What Nietzsche should have said is that love makes you strongest of all.

Jana liked her essay. You didn't get straight As through your junior year if you couldn't write a couple hundred words that made sense. Jana only wished she could have read her work out loud. She was a whiz at dramatic interpretation.

Sometimes she even made herself cry.

Jana looked at the clock. The hands of the clock hadn't moved since she first sat down at her desk. She rubbed her arms for warmth. The room was cold. She thought to check her cell phone for the time, then remembered she didn't have it. Jana hoped it was in the dorm.

She opened Henry's note. At least he'd found a way to say hi. That was nice of him. Jana wrote a reply. She leaned over the top of her desk and tapped Henry on the shoulder with her pencil. She liked the way his hair stuck out all over and wondered how he got it that way. When he turned around, she handed him the note.

Once in a lifetime, she'd written. Then she had signed her name and added *of Webster and Haynes.*

• • •

Time sat still. But Jana couldn't.

If she was really dead, Jana decided, then this wasn't going to hurt. She jabbed her arm with her pencil.

"Ow!"

It hurt like crazy. Jana felt stupid. There was a spot of blood on her arm. She glanced at the back of the room to see if Mars was watching her.

He was.

Arva caught her eye as Jana turned from looking at Mars. Her roommate shook her head and silently mouthed the word no. Arva drew her index finger across her throat.

The door banged closed and everyone in class looked up. Three Virgins had come into homeroom. They stood shoulder to shoulder at the front of the class. They wore their translucent white gowns over their nearly see-through skin. They glowed.

The Virgin in the middle was a boy. He wore the same gown as the girls did. The three Virgins sang three notes in turn. It sounded like bells. Everyone in class closed their notebooks. The door opened and the Virgins walked into the hall. Mr. Fitzgerald was already gone.

Jana glanced at the clock, surprised to see that

the hour hand had finally moved. It was an hour later now than when she'd sat down. There were no minutes in Dead School, she thought. Only hours. It was the first time Jana had thought the words *Dead School*.

But that was it. She was dead. And she was in school. They should put the name over the door so you didn't have to guess when you first got here.

CHAPTER FOUR

SECOND PERIOD.

It was just like first. There were the same students sitting in the same places. This time there was a textbook along with a new notebook on her desk. The teacher was named Skinner. He wore glasses and was busy drawing boxes on the chalkboard, muttering to himself.

Beatrice still wore the yard dart in her head. Henry said hi and then turned around in his desk in front of Jana. The girl who sat in front of Arva had quit jerking her shoulders and saying "ouch" for a while. Mars stared at Jana from his desk at the back of the room.

Jana opened her notebook. She caught her breath when she saw the note on the first page. This one read: *It was murder.* The words were in pencil, in the same precisely printed letters as the message in her first-hour notebook.

She turned quickly around and glared at Mars. Their eyes locked. Jana's eyes were daggers. Mars tilted his head to one side, as if he didn't know what daggers meant.

Arva reached across the space between their desks and touched Jana's arm. Jana jerked her arm away and stared angrily at Arva.

"I will if I want!" she said to Arva. "I don't need a mother." If Jana wanted, she would march to the back of the room and tell Mars to stop writing in her notebooks.

She had spoken too loudly. Mr. Skinner stopped talking and turned from drawing boxes on the chalkboard to look over the class through his thick glasses. Students at the front of the class turned in their seats and stared at Jana.

Jana ducked her head over her open notebook and doodled. She traced her hand on a blank sheet at the back of her notebook. She drew in the lines of her palm and wrote *J. W. + M. H.* on the line that represented her heart. Then she cried. Jana couldn't help it. When she read her palm, her future didn't look so good. Her life line was blank.

She was very quiet about crying, letting the tears fill her eyes, forcing herself to breathe evenly. Her fingers trembled. She placed her hands in her lap. She kept her head down with her hair covering her face from both sides. She hoped no one would notice.

Jana cried because she was alone. Not because she was dead. She could get along with being dead if only she weren't so alone. Without Michael, she would always be alone.

He had left her in this awful place.

He was half of her and he was gone. Just like that.

Teardrops made wet circles on the pencil outline of her hand. Jana put an end to it by biting her lower lip as hard as she could stand. It was her first day of school and so far all she had to show for it was a sore dot on her arm where she'd jabbed herself with a pencil, an empty heart, and trembling fingers. And she still couldn't get the taste of strawberries out of her mouth.

Jana blinked rapidly, trying to bat her eyelashes

dry, when the Virgins came in and sang their three-bell song that signaled the end of class. She'd cried in class. Other students must have seen her. She might as well have thrown up on herself.

The Sliders from her class walked down the hall between second and third period in a group.

Arva and Jana stood still as they passed. Some of their faces were a mess. One of them limped severely. His left leg barely seemed to work at all. There were two girls with them. They were Sliders too. Jana absentmindedly smoothed the front of her plaid skirt with her free hand as they walked by.

Jana held her second-period notebook in her other hand, wanting to show Arva what was written on the first page. Maybe Arva could tell her who was doing it.

"You have to believe me," Arva said urgently. "You can't talk to them." When Arva was excited, she sounded like a duck, quacking out one word after another. "Don't even look at them. If they see you looking, they'll try to talk to you. And you can't do that."

A thin boy wearing a wrinkled school shirt showed up from nowhere and stood in front of Jana with his hand out. He kept his eyes on his shoes. The boy looked gray to Jana. His shirt was grayish instead of white. His black school tie was faded and knotted wrong.

He didn't say anything. Just stood in front of Jana with his hand out.

"Oh," Arva said. "Your notebook. You can't take them out of class. You have to give it to him. He's a hall monitor."

"But I wanted to show you . . ." Jana began. She fumbled the notebook open, to show the first page to Arva, to show her how precisely the letters had been written. As Jana moved the open notebook toward Arva, the boy reached out to stop her.

"Leave the girl alone," a male voice said. "It's her first day,"

Arva froze, her mouth open to speak. Nothing came out.

Jana looked up to see Mars Dreamcote standing behind the boy, his hand on the hall monitor's shoulder. Mars had on an old pair of jeans without a belt. The collar of his white shirt was unbuttoned. The knot in his tie was two or three inches lower than his collar.

Mars studied Jana's face. His blue eyes sparked

like matches being struck. A lock of dark hair had fallen across his forehead. The side of his mouth dimpled one cheek when he smiled.

Jana was embarrassed. She hated her clothes. She tried to think of her school uniform as a stage costume. It didn't work. She looked stupid and she knew it.

Mars wore a small teasing smile that Jana had thought of as a snicker when she saw him on the bus and in class. This time the smile felt different. He was trying to be nice to her. He must have seen her crying.

She closed the notebook. Jana gave him a little smile back and leaned her head to one side. His eyes followed the movement.

Mars reached around the boy and slipped the notebook from her hands. She barely noticed he was doing it. He gave her notebook to the hall monitor and turned the smaller boy around with both hands on his shoulders and gave him a push to get him started.

Mars glanced at Arva, daring her to speak. Arva's mouth closed. He turned and walked away.

Arva let out a long breath. It sounded like a sigh being squeezed out of a balloon. "Oh no," she said in her usual foggy rasp. "He likes you."

Arva had said on the bus that Mars had a smile that would melt the buttons off your blouse. Jana realized that she had felt warmer while he was standing there, when he looked at her. When he reached his hand toward her to take away the notebook, heat from his hand moved across the top of her fingers. Jana checked her buttons. They felt hard and smooth between her fingers. Maybe Mars wasn't so dangerous after all. Or maybe he had used only his little smile and not his big button-melting one.

Jana and Arva stood in the cafeteria line.

Hospital gurneys lined the walls. Occasionally one of the students on the wheeled stretchers would raise a hand and wave at someone coming into the cafeteria. Many of the tables in the room were already occupied. The room was filled with voices.

"First, second, and third period," Jana was saying, "they all have the same students in the same seats and the one vacancy."

"That's our class," Arva told her. "There are four junior classes. Mornings are the same courses for all of us. Afternoons, the Sliders aren't there. Fourth hour is your elective. Fifth and sixth periods you're back with your homeroom class again."

"I get an elective?"

When Arva talked rapidly, Jana had to listen closely. Some of her words were barely whispered, while others were sharp little croaks.

"You know, art, music, journalism, gymnastics . . . whatever you want. Today you go to the library for fourth period and choose your elective."

Drama would be Jana's elective, of course. Drama or speech. They had to have one or the other.

The two girls picked up trays as they reached the service counter.

"What's your elective?" Jana asked.

"Journalism," Arva said. "I'm on the newspaper and yearbook staffs." She coughed, then added in a hoarse whisper, "It's easier for me to write than talk."

"Does it hurt to talk like that?"

"Not at all," Arva croaked. "I just can't get enough air out and my vocal chords are jammed. Anything that happened to your body before you got here doesn't hurt now."

"But you're stuck like that? For all time?"

"Pretty much," Arva said. "And I guess you

figured out what you do to your body once you're here can hurt like crazy."

Jana nodded. Arva must have seen Jana jab her arm with a pencil.

Two of the grayish-looking students stood behind the service counter in the cafeteria. The first food bay was filled with bottles of water. The girl behind the counter set three bottles of water on the countertop without looking at Jana. The girl had dark circles under her eyes. She wore the same school uniform blouse that Jana did, only instead of the blouse being clean and white, it was gray and wrinkled.

"You have to take three," Arva told her, urging Jana along. "You don't have to drink them all right now, but they want you to take three."

The next station at the counter had decks of cards and stacks of board games instead of food. Arva picked up a deck of cards and placed it on her tray, then stepped away from the line and started walking toward a table. Jana quickly caught up.

"Why are those students gray?" Jana asked.

"Suicides," Arva said. "They're depressed. We call them Grays."

Beatrice and the girl who said "ouch" were already seated. Arva and Jana joined them. Jana tried not to stare at the yard dart sticking out of Beatrice's head.

"This is Jana Webster," Arva said, introducing Jana to the ouch girl.

"Hi. I'm Christie. Wow, you're pretty."

"Me?" Whoever this girl was, she had been dead too long. Or maybe, Jana thought, you looked better when you first got here.

"What color are your eyes?" Beatrice asked. "They're just gorgeous. The right shade of eye shadow and I bet they'd look turquoise."

"Hazel," Jana said.

"Not quite hazel," Christie said.

"Smoky green," Beatrice offered.

Olive drab, Jana thought.

Arva unscrewed the cap from one of her bottles of water and held it carefully to her lips. Tipping the bottle just so, she let a trickle of water run into her mouth.

"Jade!" Christie concluded. "Your eyes are jade. Absolutely, perfectly jade. Now that that's settled, I hear you have a boyfriend."

"I do," Jana said. "Michael Haynes. Everyone calls us Webster and Haynes. He's a senior. We're in drama together and he's district student council president."

"Sounds like he's going places," Christie said. "I

mean, he's not here, is he? You didn't die together in an accident or anything like that?"

Christie wore a delicate silver chain around her neck and a narrow dark pink ribbon tied across her forehead. The reddish ribbon was at a slant, high on one side and nearly touching her eyebrow on the other.

"No, he's not here."

"Oh, that's good," Christie continued. "I was worried he might be one of the Stretchers. Or you know . . ." Christie let her words trail off as she watched the Sliders come into the cafeteria. Beatrice and Jana followed her gaze.

Arva made disturbing noises in her throat and the three girls turned their attention back to their own table.

"Did you have your purse with you when you died?" Beatrice asked Jana.

"No," Jana said. "I left it in the car."

"Too bad," Beatrice said.

"She just wants your makeup," Arva told Jana. "You can use what you have with you when you die but when it's gone, it's gone. You're not supposed to loan it to anyone else or give it away. Makeup here is contraband."

"It is not," Beatrice said. "You're just making that up because you don't have any."

"You can get demerits for contraband," Arva insisted. "It's a rule."

"It's an Arva rule," Beatrice said. "Not a real rule."

It took Jana a moment to realize the girls were fighting. Thankfully Christie was quick to change the subject. "Were you wearing cute underwear when you died?" she asked Jana.

Jana shook her head no, puzzled by the question. She realized the pink-red line across Christie's forehead wasn't a ribbon, after all. It was a scar.

"Too bad," Christie said. "You get to keep the clothes you died in."

"Have you looked at your school underwear yet?" Beatrice asked.

"Granny panties," Christie said.

"Maximums," Beatrice countered. "You can sleep a family of four in these things. And I think they put starch in them. It's like wearing armor."

Christie giggled, which only encouraged Beatrice to continue. "I swear, the boys in this school don't want to get in your panties. They just want to pull them off you. As a community service."

Everyone laughed. Arva even squeaked a little.

"My mom's a beautician," Christie said. "Her shop was in the house. I think I can do something with the back of your hair, if you want me to try."

Jana raised a hand to her hair. "Thank you," she said, wondering if it looked that bad. That's when Jana noticed that she wasn't hungry.

She'd been hungry since the seventh grade, when she first realized that all famous actresses were thin. She hadn't eaten anything but a piece of celery with peanut butter on it before going bowling. And now she wasn't hungry even a little. If it wasn't for the taste of strawberries in her mouth, Jana wouldn't have thought of food all day.

"Okay," she said to the three juniors sitting with her, "tell me this. Why is there no food in the cafeteria?"

"Dead people don't eat," Christie said.

"But you have to have water or else you dehydrate," Arva said. "Better drink yours now. You can take only one bottle with you when you leave. Sliders drink out of the fountains, so it's best to consider those one hundred percent contaminated. You don't want to get what they've got."

"If you don't drink water, you'll crack," Christie added. Jana wanted to reach out and straighten the ribbon of scar that crossed Christie's forehead. She had such pretty hair. It flowed over her shoulders and fanned out gorgeously to either side of her face. The scar line ruined the whole effect.

"Sliders eat," Beatrice said in a hushed tone. "When Sliders sneak off campus, they get something to snack on. They smoke too, if they want to. They can do all sorts of things we can't."

Christie nodded in agreement. Then she jerked her shoulders and quietly said, "Ouch." Jana decided Christie had hiccups that went away for a while, then came back. She must have been nervous when she died.

"Don't listen to her," Arva said to Jana as if Beatrice wasn't there. "All that stuff is just stupid rumors. Besides, she has a dart in her head. You can't believe a thing she is saying."

Beatrice turned quietly and picked up the deck of cards. She opened the flap on the box and slid the cards out. Jana could tell her feelings were hurt. It showed in her eyes. Jana set down her half-full bottle of water and rubbed her arms with her hands. The cafeteria thermostat was set too low.

"The dart's partially my fault," Beatrice said, placing the deck of cards in the middle of the table.

"How could it be your fault?" Jana asked.

The plastic yellow fins leaned in closer to Jana as Beatrice began her story. "It was summer and I wanted to be in love," she said.

CHAPTER FIVE

BRAD HAD HIS OWN CAR AND A TATTOO. *He was everything Beatrice wanted in a boyfriend.*

She invited him to her church picnic. He said he might make it.

Beatrice was surprised when he showed up. She was in the pool. Brad stood at the chain-link fence and watched her until she finally noticed him. Her hair was soaked from swimming. She smelled like chlorine and coconut butter.

The picnic was at one of the park pavilions. The charcoal was lit, but they wouldn't put on the hot dogs and burgers until everyone was out of the pool.

Beatrice stood at the fence. It was too noisy at the pool to talk.

Brad asked her if she wanted to go for a ride somewhere. Beatrice couldn't leave the picnic. But they could go for a walk.

The two of them walked through the part of the park that had swings and a slide. They walked around an open sloping area where some guys were throwing a Frisbee. Four kids were off to one side, near the woods, throwing yard darts high in the air.

Summer was when girls could snag a boyfriend for the rest of the year. Beatrice had come close last summer to going steady, but it fell apart just before school started. This summer would be different.

"Let's go to the river," Beatrice said. There was a path through the trees, she told him.

They held hands on the walk to the river, except when they passed through a spiderweb and had to brush it away.

It turned out there was nothing romantic about the river. It had been raining and the water was brown. It smelled like fish. Small swarms of gnats hovered nearby.

It was now or never, Beatrice decided. If they came out of the woods without kissing, they weren't going to.

Beatrice wanted to kiss Brad hard and long enough that he would have to ask her out.

She stopped walking. Brad turned to look at her. She took his other hand in hers and kissed him. It was an easy, simple kiss. To get things started. Then she pressed up against him and his hands went around her back. When they leaned back from each other, Beatrice realized that the left strap of her swimsuit had slipped over her shoulder.

Beatrice kissed him hard this time. When they broke for air, he kissed her neck.

"Wait," she said. "My top is falling off."

"It's okay by me," Brad said.

He hadn't asked her out yet. He should any time now.

Beatrice brought her fingers to her fallen strap. Instead of pulling it back into place, she pulled the strap down to her elbow, until her breast was exposed. Then she pressed herself against him again and kissed him the best kiss she had.

His hand found her breast almost instantly. He pressed her pliant flesh with his palm and fingers. Beatrice had to stop. It was a church picnic, after all. She stepped away from Brad and pulled her swimsuit top into place. She blushed.

"If you want to keep doing this," Beatrice said, "you have to ask me out."

"Okay by me," he said.

Beatrice was pleased. She took his hand in hers again and they continued along the path from the river back to the park.

"Friday?" she asked.

"Okay."

Beatrice stopped walking. They were at the edge of the woods. "Wait," she said. "Didn't we already say that?"

"Say what?" Brad was puzzled by the question.

"What we just said," Beatrice tried to explain. "Did we say that twice?" She had the feeling that the last half minute had happened twice in a row.

"I don't know what I said," Brad replied.

"Oh yes you do," Beatrice said, smiling broadly. "You said you were taking me out Friday night."

They were at the edge of the park, just coming out of the woods, when a large steel dart with three bright yellow fins fell from forty feet above them. Miraculously missing the trees, the dart gained speed as it raced through sky toward earth, seeking impact. Beatrice stood in the way. She wasn't going to go steady with anyone this summer either.

Jana gulped down the last of her second bottle of water.

"It was just like in those slasher movies," Beatrice said. "I let a boy see my breast and the next thing you know I'm dead. When a girl in one of those movies takes her top off, you know she's going to be the next one killed."

Beatrice showed Jana her upside-down smile.

"Does it get heavy?" Jana asked. "I mean, do you feel it there when you walk and sit down and stuff?"

"I'm used to it," Beatrice said. "It's the way things are. You just live with your body the way it is when you get here."

"And you still have to take showers or you'll stink." Christie wrinkled her nose at Jana.

"I'll bet that Brad guy thinks twice before going around and grabbing a boob at a church picnic," Arva said in her harsh, throaty whisper.

She screwed a cap back on one of her bottles of water. A small black feather was in the corner of her mouth again. Wet from her drinking water, the feather looked like a fat spider leg reaching out of her mouth.

"Don't look now, but someone is watching us," Christie said.

Jana turned around to see who. That's what you do when someone tells you not to look. But she didn't see Mars Dreamcote's blue eyes staring at their table from across the room. Instead, she saw a girl walking behind their table carrying her head on a cafeteria tray.

"Fart, fudge, and popcorn!" Jana gasped and turned abruptly back to the girls at her table.

Beatrice and Christie laughed.

"Freshman," Arva said, shaking her head. "She should be wearing it when she's in the cafeteria. She has to wear it in class."

"Show-off," Beatrice added.

"She can put it on anytime she wants to," Arva explained. "If she couldn't keep her head on, she'd be a Stretcher."

"They're all over the place," Christie warned Jana. "Your first day or two, you have to be careful where you look. Then you get used to it."

Arva noticed the wet feather on her own lip and plucked it from her mouth.

Christie involuntarily jerked her shoulders and said, "Ouch." Her hair bounced. "Wait till you meet Pauline," she added.

"Who's Pauline?" Jana asked.

"One of our roommates," Arva said. "She's a senior. Her cafeteria break is on another rotation from ours. And there's Darcee. There are four to a dorm room, and we have our own bathroom."

Jana didn't want to meet more dead people. But she figured she was going to.

CHAPTER SIX

JANA STOOD ALONE.

The Dead School library was grim. It had only books. She'd never been in a library that didn't have computers.

Long bookshelves stood against the back wall. Tables and chairs were arranged in the middle of the room. The outer wall was a row of windows that looked into the hallway. A group of Sliders occupied the far table, elbowing one another and giving her the eye. They were kind of cute, but scruffy. Like lost dogs.

Jana approached two gray students who stood behind a counter just inside the door, their heads bowed.

"I'm Jana Webster," she said. "I don't have an elective yet. I was told to come here."

One of the Grays handed her a piece of paper. Her named was typed at the top in all caps. Below was a list of elective classes. An elective called Speech & Drama (Acting) was highlighted in yellow, along with the teacher's name and a room number.

"You start tomorrow." The Gray who had handed Jana her elective registration took back the sheet of paper.

"Okay," Jana said. "So what do I do now?"

Without saying a word, the Gray reached under the counter and brought out Jana's notebooks from her first three class periods. He slid them toward her across the counter. He set two sharpened pencils on top.

Jana sat at the nearest table, her back to the gawking Sliders.

She looked at the first page of each of her class notebooks. She opened all three and placed them side by side, overlapping the pages so that the hand-printed notes were across from one another.

Murder. It was murder. And from third period, *You were murdered.*

Nope, she thought. It just wasn't so.

Still, someone had taken the time to write the notes in that precise lettering. Jana figured it was a game the Sliders played with new students. She ran her fingers across the words of the third note and felt the penciled letters smudge under the press of her skin.

Jana decided to make a list. She opened a new page in her first-period homeroom notebook and titled it *Things to Do.*

Under that she wrote: *1. Talk to Michael ASAP.* She wanted to write it a hundred times.

Then she wrote: *2. Mom.* Jana probably needed to check on her mother. No doubt Jana's death was reason enough for her mother to double down on drinking and pills again.

Jana's list was too short. There had to be more to her life she cared about. But what could she write down? Get a job. Travel. Neck, cuddle, and kiss. That stuff seemed unimportant now. Finally she thought of another thing and added it to the list.

3. Transfer.

This was the wrong school for Jana. She didn't fit in here. She didn't fit in anywhere without Michael.

Thinking it over, Jana crossed off item 2. Her mother had never checked on her, after all. And there was a neighbor who was paid to take care of her mom when Jana couldn't.

Her mother owned the house Jana grew up in and that was about it as far as mothering had gone. Until her retirement a year ago, Jana's mother had never actually lived there. Instead, her mother lived a glamorous life in glitzy apartments on one coast or the other. Throughout Jana's life, it seemed, she had had no mother at all.

Jana had never known who her father was and, apparently, neither had her mother. When Marilyn was twenty-two, the year Jana was born, she was already famous and had briefly dated any number of musicians, tennis handsomes, and pro-ball players. During the time Jana was conceived, Marilyn often woke up in the mornings after dazzling parties not knowing the name of the man sleeping next to her.

Jana had been raised by nannies, overnight babysitters, and neighbors. When she was thirteen, one of them had tried to take her home for Christmas so Jana wouldn't be alone.

She declined the invitation. They waited in silence for the overnight sitter to show up. So what if Jana didn't have a family to spend Christmas with? It didn't mean she wanted a fake one. Besides, she was accustomed to being alone. It's what she knew how to do.

And she had something secret in mind for Christmas Eve. She'd bought her Ken doll a complete ski outfit, had wrapped it, and was going to throw a little party for the two of them. You couldn't do that in front of other people. They wouldn't understand a thirteen-year-old playing with a doll.

Before Jana met Michael, Ken and the people in movies had been her only friends.

A Slider walked behind her and bumped Jana's shoulder. She turned in her chair. He was already walking back to his kennel of shaggy brethren. He had touched her back lightly with his hand, just above her bra clasp. His touch was warm, as warm as Mars's hand had been when he had reached for her notebook in the hall.

It must have been a dare from the others.

"What is this, third grade?" she said out loud. As a practiced dramatist, Jana knew how to project her voice without shouting, without turning her head.

The table of boys snickered. Jana studied her list and wrote one more thing to do.

4. *Find out why Mars Dreamcote stares at me.*

There was something different in the way he

looked at her. It was like he'd known her before and was waiting for her to remember. Or like he was waiting for her to catch on. Catch on to what?

She'd ask him. First chance she had. Mars didn't scare her even a little. As far as Jana was concerned, she was still Webster and Haynes. She had backup.

Michael must be thinking about her constantly.

He likely couldn't sleep. He would use the extra time to think of a way to find her. She was still here, after all. She was right here.

Jana didn't want Michael to kill himself instantly. But the sooner the better, she supposed. For both of them. He would live an empty, mournful life until then. He'd find a way to be with her somehow. He had to.

She finished her list:

5. *Come on, Michael. Find me!*

Mars stood poised at the edge of the swimming pool in the school basement.

Two Risers loitered nearby, watching him. They were waiting to use the high dive. Once Mars had spent his time in the water and climbed out, they'd turn on the pumps that circulated water from the bottom of the pool into power surface jets to either side of the diving board. This kept the surface of the water roiling in the diving area. Hitting the flat surface of water just right could break your neck.

Just jump in! Mars wanted to say. *You can't be afraid of everything. You're already dead.*

Most Risers, though, didn't have the courage to break the rules. They wouldn't even leave campus. They wanted to know what would happen before they did anything. Not knowing was the point. Finding out what would happen was the adventure. Curiosity may have killed the cat, but the cat learned something first.

What kind of life did you have if you never found your way around a few fences? Okay, Mars thought, *life* wasn't the right word. But just because you were dead didn't mean you were supposed to stop using your brain to figure out something new. That's why Dead School existed in the first place. You had to see some things for yourself. You had to touch them, to figure out how they worked.

Mars dove in from the side of the pool. He pushed himself underwater with powerful kicks for as long as he could, pushed himself further than his breath would allow. Mars was stronger than they were because he worked at it. "Anything worth

doing," his father had said, "is worth doing harder."
Then he'd taken the belt to Mars.

Touching the far end of the pool, he came up for
his first breath. Mars lifted his head through the
surface of the pool and let the water run from his
eyes. He swam to the middle. Two quick breaths,
and he slipped underwater again. Allowing the air
to escape his lungs in a rapid ascent of bubbles, Mars
dropped to the bottom of the pool and sat there.

This was his one place to be entirely alone. No
one could touch him here. No one could talk to
him. He could cry underwater if he needed to and
no one would know. Today he didn't need to.

Today, he was remembering the last time he'd
seen the new girl. The girl with dark brown hair, a
killer smile, and beautiful jade green eyes. He'd seen
her on the Planet. He'd seen her in real life. Mars
thought it was planned that way sometimes: to have
you cross paths with a stranger you would meet in
the afterlife. It had to mean something when that
happened. Didn't it?

Jana wrote a new list.

This one was a rapidly growing number of
questions she had for Arva. She started slowly, then

pushed herself to write quickly so she didn't forget anything. Halfway through, she took a deep breath and paused.

Jana didn't have to ask Arva anything right now, she realized. All she had to do was read the guidebook. Arva had said there was a copy in the library.

Scooting her chair back, she smoothed her skirt. Her hands felt cold as she touched the skin of her legs at her skirt's hem. The Sliders were talking a mile a minute at the back table. She ignored them. Jana returned to the checkout counter.

"It's at the tutoring table," a Gray told her. "First-day students have priority. They'll give it to you there."

"What's the tutoring table?" Jana asked.

"Where they're being loud," he said.

It was time to confront the bad boys. Jana strode to their crowded table and stood in her best posture in front of the Sliders. Michael would have been proud.

There were five of them. They all looked messy but one. The one in the middle wore his student uniform clothes correctly. He had thick-rimmed glasses and very straight brown hair that was combed forward to form bangs. There was a prominent cowlick in back. A large open book was on the table in front of him.

He stared awkwardly at Jana, while the others jostled and joked under their breaths. Standing in the immediate area of the Sliders, Jana felt warmth, actual heat, radiating from the group.

"The guidebook, please," she said firmly. "It's my first day." She tried out her version of Beatrice's upside-down smile on the boys. It was a great way to smile without flirting, or being nice at all, when Jana did it.

"Hey, it's Webster, the girl who pokes herself in class," the tall one with the mangled leg said. The others went quiet when he spoke. She'd seen him before, limping in the hall, sitting at the back of class with Mars. He kept one side of his face turned away from the table. The boy in glasses closed the book in front of him and started to push it across the table toward Jana.

A Slider's hand fell on top of the closed book and held the volume in place.

Jana opened her eyes wide, arched her brows, and tilted her chin up slightly to the side.

"It's ours for the hour," a Slider said. "Our tutor is reading us bedtime stories."

The boy in glasses grinned stupidly. He was the tutor, Jana realized. He was the object of ridicule with these guys, but seemed happy to be accepted among them at any level. Jana was the outsider now. He was no longer the bait.

"We need this more than you," the tall Slider said. Jana could see a portion of the side of his face he kept turned from the others. It was scarlet and rough. Brow to chin, that side of his face was badly disfigured. It looked as if it had been rubbed across a cheese grater. His death must have been painful.

Jana brought her hand to her neck and made a circle of her mouth. She was acting.

"My oh my," she drawled. "But I do have only a few minutes remaining and I'd like the book to while away my time." She batted her eyelashes.

The tall Slider snickered. The others stared. She had them locked in place. They knew she was messing with them, but they were unsure how.

"I don't think so," the disfigured one snarled, using only one side of his mouth again. "We *need* this right now. You just want it." The others mumbled a few words, agreeing with the pack leader. The only one she heard clearly added, "She *wants* it." They laughed.

If they knew Michael, they would have given her the book already. As Jana considered her options, the Sliders suddenly turned quiet. They dropped their arms and sat upright. They were staring obediently at something, or someone, behind Jana.

She turned to see two Virgins, side by side, as translucent and simultaneously white as ever. They sang two perfect notes each, in low alto voices. One note up, then one note down. It was a warning.

The boy in glasses stood abruptly, pushing his chair back. He picked up the book and leaned across the table, offering it to Jana.

"Here," he said. "Please."

Jana accepted the book from him. The Sliders looked elsewhere, not at one another and not at Jana. When she turned around to walk back to her table with the student guidebook in her arms, the Virgins were gone.

The book was large and heavy, bound in covers that looked like dried sheepskin. It seemed ancient, its pages written by hand in faded brown ink. The florid lettering looked like that of one of those religious books that monks copied and hid from authorities hundreds of years ago. The writing was large and clear, but each letter was crafted with a pattern of flourishes that made it very difficult to read. Some of the writing looked upside down.

Jana thought she'd been given the wrong book. She looked at page after page and couldn't make sense of it. The words weren't English. The writing was full of funny-looking Js and far too many letters were topped with tailed dots and little caret-shaped thingies.

Her concentration was broken when Jana felt a warm breeze at her back. A Slider was close to her. She didn't look up. He sat down in the empty chair on her side of the table and pulled close to her.

"Okay, what?" she finally said. She gave him an icicle glare.

It was the tall Slider with half a face. Jana could see him clearly now. The scalded red side was missing an eye. That side of his mouth had no lips. She could see his teeth and gums. Even when his mouth was supposedly closed, the bad side wasn't. His eyelid was red and shriveled and looked like it had been sealed shut with glue. He kept his crooked arm in his lap, under the table. He nodded down to his hands.

He held a small narrow knife. It looked as sharp as a razor. His sleeves were rolled up.

"This is from Mars," he said.

The Slider leaned in close to her. The warmth from his face touched hers.

He pressed the knife blade against his upturned lower arm and she watched in horror as blood appeared. He pushed the blade deeply into his flesh, then drew it away quickly and slipped the knife inside his clothes. She watched him tense in pain. The Slider placed his hand over the deep cut to stem the blood as much as possible. The red liquid poured from the cut, bubbling up between his fingers. It looked sticky and thick and hot.

Standing up, he leaned over Jana, still clutching his bleeding wound. He held his cut arm turned up. From the corner of his mouth, he said softly, "See you in homeroom tomorrow, Webster. Make sure you say hi."

The Slider walked away, limping on his bad leg, bent slightly at the waist. He listed to one side and back with every awkward step. Jana took her first gasp of air since seeing the knife. As her pulse raced to her temples, she felt her heartbeat at both sides of her neck. Jana lowered her head and stared at her hands. They were shaking worse than her mom's.

CHAPTER SEVEN

ARVA WENT ON. And on.

"I can't believe they let Sliders use the library," she said on the bus after school. "And they shouldn't have given you that old guidebook. There's a newer one."

Her croaky, breathless voice was weaker at the end of the day, but it didn't keep her from informing Jana about the evil of Sliders and why it was crucial that she have nothing to do with them.

"I should have gone with you, Jana. I can be with you every minute of the day if you want. For a week or so, I can go to your elective instead of mine. New students are so fragile."

Jana wasn't listening. Henry had passed her another note in sixth period. It said *Where are you from?* And he had added a smiley face.

She'd started to write it down for him, but couldn't remember the name of her town. She must have hit her head hard enough to forget some things. It would come to her, she was certain.

She waited.

It didn't.

She finally wrote *Tell you later* on the note and passed it back to Henry.

As the scenery moved by the windows, Jana glanced toward the back of the bus. Mars was there. She tried to watch him without his knowing it. But every time she looked, he was staring right at her. His friend with half a face kept his leg stuck across the aisle. The tall Slider was never looking at Jana when she looked at him. Then again, he had only one eye to hide.

There were no Sliders in Jana's fifth-period or sixth-period classes. Arva had told her that some of the Sliders were in vocational training classes in the afternoons. Others were in basic math and English courses designed for Sliders alone.

"They're like GED students," Arva had said.

"Sort of pass or fail. Some of them are here for a year or two. Others, for a couple months. If they do something bad enough, the school kicks them out. And then they go, you know, down the slide."

"Down the slide?" Jana asked.

"Yeah, that's why they call them Sliders. It doesn't really matter what grades they get. Sliders don't graduate with the rest of us. If they finish at all."

"Why are they here?"

"I don't know, really," Arva said. "They're one hundred percent hopeless. They're given an equivalency test at some point, then they slide on by."

Jana thought about it. She was catching on to Arva. There were a lot of things her roommate didn't know.

"Okay, then," Jana said. "If they're Sliders, what are we called?"

"Oh, we're Risers, silly. Didn't anyone tell you? We're on the way up when we graduate. We're going places. Sliders aren't. They're earthbound. That's why they're dangerous. You don't want to have anything to do with them. They were doing something bad when they died."

Arva paused to look at Jana solemnly.

"You can become one," Arva warned her. "If you break the rules once you're here, you can become a Slider. So for us, Sliders are against the rules to start with. If you hang out with them, you can be on your way down too. Do you understand me?"

Jana nodded that she understood.

"They're poison, I swear they are," Arva went on. "Sliders should come with a skull-and-crossbones label on their foreheads so you know to stay away from them."

Jana thought of the poison apple in *Snow White*. She giggled at herself when she thought of Mars as a poison apple. Forbidden fruit.

"Think of this," Arva continued. "The vacant desk in homeroom used to be somebody. Somebody just like you and me. It can happen to any one of us. Expulsion. You can be expelled, Jana. You can't take a single step in that direction or . . ."

Arva paused to find enough air to choke out her final words on the subject. "Or," she said, "it can happen to you."

The bus of dead kids rolled on.

When she thought Arva wouldn't notice, Jana looked at Mars again. He looked tired, but he was still smiling at her, his blue eyes lit up like twinkle lights. His hair was tussled and disarranged. Mars seemed radiant and messy at the same time. He should comb his hair, she thought.

"Let them off first," Arva said when the bus came to a stop in front of a building that reminded Jana of an old three-story motel. "They won't bother you on the bus," Arva added. "The driver is watching them."

The Sliders stood from their seats at the back and filed forward. Like prisoners. They didn't look as cocky as they had in the morning. Maybe their vocational training involved heavy lifting or endless hammering on things. At her old school, one of the vo-tech classes built an entire house each year.

As he walked by, Mars touched the back of the bench seat she shared with Arva. His fingertips brushed across her shoulder. Jana felt a radiance of warmth pass over her then drift away. A part of her wanted to follow the warmth of Mars, to keep it close to her. The part of her that was an animal, she thought. That part of her hadn't died either.

Darcee was as pretty as a Virgin, but without the ephemeral glow.

She lay on a gurney against the far wall, her hands crossed over her chest.

"Coma," Arva said. "Broken brain stem or something. They say the coma Stretchers can hear, that they listen to everything you say, but no one can really prove it. I talk to her sometimes, when I'm trying not to fall asleep. Beatrice put makeup on her once. She was really pretty that way, but we washed it off."

Jana imagined herself unable to move, unable to open her eyes. She wondered whether it was better to be able to think about things or not to think at all when you were in a coma.

"Why is Darcee here?" Jana asked. "People in comas aren't dead."

"Not officially, I guess. She's caught in between. She doesn't go to class or anything." Arva made a face.

Jana thought of *Snow White* again. There should be a prince to come kiss Darcee and wake her up from her sleep to live happily ever after. Jana went numb at the thought of "happily ever after." This was Jana's ever after. This place, this room, these people. She wasn't happy at all.

There was only one way Jana could be happy

again. And that was to be with Michael.

"If Darcee does wake up, she'll be out of here. Just like that, back to the Planet she goes."

"The Planet is real life, then?"

"I shouldn't call it that, I suppose. But everyone does."

"Where's the Planet?"

"Oh, it's all around us," Arva croaked cheerfully. "We're right in the middle of it. There's a boundary between us and the real world. The fences around the dorm and around the school. But it's more than fences. When they let you leave the campus, you become a spirit. You'll think you have your body just like you do here, but you don't. It's pretty scary."

"So we're right here on Earth?"

"Yeah, that's the cool part. Dead School is in a real school building and the dorm is a real building on the Planet too. They have Dead Schools all over. Around the world, I imagine. They're vacant buildings. But we get to use them. When a new student shows up, they try to find you a vacancy near to where you live. Your town could be very near, you see. Or maybe we're right in it."

"Who are they? You said 'they' try to find a Dead School near to where you live."

"The regents," Arva said. "There's a Council of Regents. They oversee everything. They're like a board of education. I have to find you the student guidebook, don't I?"

Jana realized Arva didn't really want to show her a copy of the student guidebook. In fact, Jana decided, Arva was probably keeping it from her on purpose. She enjoyed getting to explain her version of things to Jana.

"Let me get this straight," Jana said. "The building is real. But it has people and books in it only when we're there. Same with the dorm. And we're real too. Our bodies are real while we're here. But we have bodies only when we're on campus, when we're at school, on the bus, or in the dorm."

"Yes. For Risers, of course. We're the ones who matter, Jana. Sliders are closer to Earth than we are. And some of them do things on the Planet the rest of us can't. But you wouldn't want to do that."

Arva changed the subject in the middle of her reply.

"That's the other thing," she said. "Your body is different here, Jana. If you lie down, for instance, you'll go to sleep. It's lights out for you for the rest of the night. The next thing you know you're on the bus heading to school the next day."

It was clear to Jana that Arva was uncomfortable talking about the world off campus. In that world, she and Jana were also real. They were real dead. Arva could manage being in Dead School easier than she could manage being dead.

"What about the vacancy in homeroom?"

"She was a Riser," Arva said. "Kind of horrible, isn't it? I mean, you would expect it from a Slider."

"I don't know what to expect," Jana confessed. "So, what happened, did she date a Slider or something?"

Arva paused.

"Okay, you'll probably hear it somewhere else," Arva said. "There's a rumor she just left. That she walked away from campus somehow and stayed away overnight. If a student goes off campus and isn't back in time for classes the next day, they're expelled. Being expelled is a vacancy."

"Risers can walk off campus?"

"Oh no. Well, I mean, that's against the rules. I know all the student rules by heart."

Jana nodded. She wasn't sure she trusted everything Arva said. Just because something was against the rules didn't mean you couldn't do it.

"I wouldn't believe the rumors, Jana. What happened was probably worse. But unless someone was there to see it, we don't really know what she did. Maybe it was suicide."

"But we're already dead," Jana said.

"Remember, your body is still here. If you hold your breath long enough, you'll pass out. If you want to end it all, if that's your goal, they'll let you. If you get hurt some other way, they fix it for you. Every day here you wake up with the body—"

"I know, I know," Jana interrupted. "The body you died with."

"So, yes, you can smother yourself or something. Or hang yourself or . . . I don't know what all." Arva wheezed out a sigh of air. "Any more questions?"

Jana had enough rules to consider for one day. As soon as she could, she would talk it over with Michael. They'd come up with something.

"You'll meet Pauline soon," Arva croaked along, without missing a beat. "She's down the hall somewhere or in the common room. It's the lobby, actually. This used to be a motel before it was closed down. Pauline hangs out with other seniors after school. She's always half one place and half somewhere else."

Jana looked around her new room. It was larger than she thought a normal dorm room might be. Besides Darcee's hospital gurney, there were three beds, each in their own little area, and three desks with chairs. Just as Arva had said, Jana's notebooks from class were stacked on her desk.

Her street clothes were laid out on one of the beds. Jana recognized her capri pants.

A pair of rental bowling shoes sat on the floor at the edge of her bed. Jana made a stink face. Talk about adding insult to injury, she thought. She was supposed to walk through the afterlife in bowling shoes.

Jana would wear her black leather school uniform shoes day and night instead. At least they were all one color. For now, though, she took them off. She switched her school socks for her pair of shortie cottons that were tucked inside the bowling shoes. She picked up her blouse. There was a bloodstain at the back of the collar.

Arva pulled off her plaid skirt, left on her school granny panties, and wrapped herself in a dark blue silk skirt.

"My prom dress," she said. "Beatrice cut it down for me."

"It's pretty," Jana said, then changed the subject. "I tried to read the original guidebook in the library. But I couldn't make heads or tails of it."

"Nobody can," Arva told her. "Don't worry about that old thing. It's in a bunch of ancient languages. It was written a thousand years ago. They just keep it there so we know there is one. Risers put together their own guidebook. We pass it around among ourselves."

"There's not one copy for each student?"

"No," Arva said. "You only need it for a day or two. I thought it was right here. I'll ask around and make sure you can see it by the end of the week. Until then, if you have any questions, I can tell you everything that's in it."

Arva went into the bathroom. She quickly stuck her head back into the dorm room to say, "Remember, don't lie down while I'm gone. If you do, you'll go to sleep."

Jana unbuttoned the waist of her school skirt. The skirt was new and the buttonholes wouldn't relax. She almost pulled both buttons off working them through the holes, then spied the computer on a small table against the back wall of the room.

She was there in an instant. Jana could email Michael.

A keyboard was attached to a large television screen. A small printer was connected to the computer. It was an old-fashioned daisy wheel printer, the kind that actually typed each letter to print out a page.

Jana sat down and turned on the computer. To her horror, fat green letters appeared on a blank gray screen. There were no icons to click, and for that matter, she couldn't find a mouse. She hit the keyboard and watched letters and then words appear as she typed.

The computer was nothing more than an antique word processor. There was no internet connection. Without the internet, it wasn't a computer at all. Jana turned it off, remembering her cell phone. Holding her skirt closed, she rushed to her bed and found her cell in the pocket of her capri pants, along with a tube of peach lip gloss.

Jana flipped open the phone. No signal.

So that was it. She looked over her stuff from real life. Lip gloss, bowling shoes, and a cell phone that wouldn't work. If she had advice for anyone in high school, it was to die with your best stuff in your arms. Have your pockets full and carry a backpack of the things you care about most at all times. Just in case.

It was silly of her to think about it, but Jana's secret wish, if she had to die without Michael in the first place, was to have died with her Ken doll. It was someone to talk to when she felt alone. Ken had been her best friend since she was six and she told him everything.

It was Christmas 2001 and her mother wasn't home. She sent gifts to Jana instead. Same as every Christmas.

Jana's mother had been hired by Mattel to appear in places around the world as Barbie for the fortieth anniversary of the original Ken doll. Marilyn wore a striped one-piece bathing suit in all the pictures Jana had seen of the international promotion of the new Ken doll. She had her hair tied in a ponytail. The model playing Ken wore a tuxedo with a silver, glittery cummerbund.

Inside one of the Christmas packages was the perfect American couple in washable plastic. A new Barbie, dressed in a formal gown, and a Ken dressed in a tuxedo. Jana fell in love with Ken. He was a man, not a boy. And he became her best friend overnight. Two days later, Jana threw away the Barbie. It looked too much like her mother.

Ken could do no wrong.

Jana bought herself small gifts when she was a little older, for her birthdays and for Christmas. She wrapped them and put tags on the boxes that read *To Jana, From Ken.*

She guessed she wouldn't be getting gifts from Ken anymore.

"You have your own shelf in here," Arva said, coming out of the bathroom. She had combed her hair and her face looked freshly scrubbed. "The school gives you a brush, comb, toothbrush, and toothpaste. Things like that."

Jana was struggling not to cry. There had to be someplace she could get a signal. She wondered if anyone had tried using a cell phone on the roof.

Someone knocked on the door to their room. Arva answered it without opening the door widely enough for Jana to see who it was.

"No," Arva said in her froggy voice. "You can't be here. Go away."

A hand pushed the door open from the outside. In a flash, there stood Mars, grinning. The tall Slider with half a face stood behind him.

"Shut up, Davis," Mars said. "I'm here to see Webster."

CHAPTER EIGHT

"LET'S GO FOR A WALK."

Mars glanced briefly at Jana's clothes from the Planet spread out on the bed, then motioned for her to come outside.

"I don't think so," Arva said, speaking for Jana.

Jana had already had an entire day of Arva telling her what she should not do. It was time her roommate learned that Jana had a mind of her own. She left the room to go with Mars.

The Sliders walked down the hallway. Jana followed. Mars's thick dark hair was shaggy in back. His jeans fit too tightly and were practically worn through at the seat. There was a hole in his rear pocket and a corner of his wallet peeked out.

Guys had an advantage over girls when they died, if they died with their pants on. They got to bring their wallets with them. Photos, IDs, driver licenses, and all sorts of things. It was like a memory book for them. She couldn't even remember the name of her town.

At the end of the hall, Mars pushed open a metal door under an Exit sign in red letters. The tall Slider stepped outside.

Mars stood back a half step and held the door open for Jana. He started to smile, then dropped his eyes. She slipped by him, feeling an aura of warmth. Heat radiated from the Sliders, Jana was learning. Especially from Mars.

They stood under a dull yellow light mounted on the brick wall above the door. Jana's feet were cold. They were on a second-story fire-escape balcony. The stairs that led to the railed landing above had been taken away. Maybe third-floor dead kids didn't catch on fire, Jana thought.

The breeze was chilly. Jana got goose bumps.

"Three things," Mars said without looking at Jana. "First, this is Wyatt."

The tall, disfigured Slider now had a name.

Mars kept talking. "Wyatt's here to apologize, aren't you, Wyatt?"

"Yes," he said. "I'm sorry about the thing in the library. I didn't mean to scare you."

In the dying sunlight, Jana could see how his face might have looked before half of it was scraped away. She felt sorry for him.

"Show her your arm," Mars directed his companion.

Wyatt held out his forearm toward Jana, the one he had sliced open in the library while sitting next to her. There was a red mark where the blade had pressed against his flesh, but no wound from a cut.

"It's okay," Jana said. She put her weight on one foot, then the other, feeling the cold iron grate through her socks. She worked her toes to keep them warm.

"Did you tell anyone?" Mars asked.

Jana shook her head.

Mars nodded to Wyatt and the tall Slider hoisted his good leg onto the railing. Teetering on his bad leg, Wyatt reached high over his head until he grabbed the bottom rail of the third-floor balcony. He pulled himself up.

She watched his legs disappear above her head.

The Sliders were obviously practiced at moving between the floors of the dorm this way. He was gone in seconds.

"I have a question for you," Jana said now that she and Mars were alone. "Did you write those messages in my class notebooks?"

She stepped toward him as she spoke. The taste of strawberries grew stronger in her mouth.

"What messages?" Mars seemed confused.

Jana decided not to give away too much information. "Just messages," she said. "Did you write them?"

"Ask Henry. He writes notes all the time, Webster."

Clever, Jana thought. Mars had dodged her question.

She waited. She breathed in slowly. It was an actor's trick, a purposeful pause intended to make Mars speak. As she breathed, her head swam with the smell of ripe strawberries. Her mouth tasted like sugar.

"Do me a favor," Mars finally said. He stood between the railing and Jana.

Mars was deadly handsome this near. His eyebrows were perfect dark arches over blue eyes.

His eyelashes were dramatically dark and swept down, then back up like delicate wings. Just for a second, Jana wished she was as beautiful as her mother.

"What's that?" she asked.

"Don't tell anyone what Wyatt did. He could get into trouble. Real trouble."

So could I, Jana thought, if Mars moved one inch closer. She was cold on the iron fire escape. Mars was warm. His breath smelled of mint. When he smiled, his face created that disarming dimple near the edge of his mouth.

"I won't tell a soul," she promised. "If . . ." Jana raised her eyebrows and held them there.

"If what?"

"If you help me get my cell phone to work."

"There's no signal here or on campus," he said. "Your battery goes dead trying to find one."

"The roof?"

"Won't work," Mars said.

"But there is a way, isn't there?"

"Yes."

"Then we have a deal," Jana said, smiling brightly.

"I guess we do. When you're ready, Webster, I'll show you how. It's risky."

"I'm ready." Jana was filled with new hope. She could call Michael. She could tell him everything. They'd find a way to be together.

Mars considered it, then shook his head no.

"Not now," he said. "It doesn't work the way you think. It doesn't work the same way it used to. Nothing does here. Give me a day, okay? I'll fill you in on everything, but we can't stay here long. The Grays walk a circle around the dorm every so often."

"Okay." Jana gave in.

"The Grays are snitches," he added quickly. "Never tell a Gray anything you don't want the school to know, Webster. And be careful when you talk to other students in front of them. They have no choice. They tell."

"Okay."

"And don't tell Arva either. She's scared of everything. She'll rat you out too. Not on your first day or anything. But later, once you've been here awhile."

Jana listened intently. Mars spoke with such quiet urgency that she believed everything he told her. She moved closer to him as he spoke. With every inch, the warmth increased.

"Risers who rat are worse than Grays," Mars

said. "Grays have no will. Risers make a choice to do you in. They think it keeps them safe."

Mars leaned back against the balcony railing. Jana felt his warmth being pulled away and was suddenly very, very cold. He crossed his arms over his chest. His upper arms bulged under his shirt.

He looked powerful and fit, but not bulky like bodybuilders. His body reminded her of boys on the swim team at her old school. Jana looked him over from top to bottom without being obvious about it. His death had left no telling mark or sign that she could see.

Standing this close to Mars, Jana's usually keen sense of self disappeared. It was a new feeling for Jana. Michael never made her feel this way.

When she looked into Michael's eyes, she saw herself. Jana saw herself as someone stronger. Someone bigger. When she looked at Mars, Jana got lost in his eyes. His gaze drew her inside and held her captive. Jana wanted to know what he was thinking. She was seemingly without a thought of her own.

"The second thing," Mars said. "I wanted to ask where you're from. I think we're from the same area but not the same school."

"I don't know," Jana confessed. "I've been trying to think of it all day."

"Charlotte? Knoxville?"

"Is that where we are?"

"In between," he said. "We're at the edge of Asheville, in the mountains. Black Mountain is east. Knoxville is west. And Charlotte's south. You should be from somewhere around here."

"I am," Jana said, scrunching her mouth. "I just can't think of it." Her toes were too cold for her to think.

"It happens. You forget things here. There's no pattern to it. Some things just disappear. Big things, little things. One thing you'll remember forever is your own death. That never goes."

"That's not so wonderful," Jana said.

"Tell me about it. Some kids . . . well, they don't want to remember."

"What else?" Jana didn't want to forget anything.

"You'll remember people your own age best and people you've known a long time, like your family. And things you paid a lot of attention to over the years, hobbies and stuff. But other things will just disappear. Over time, a lot of it is gone if you don't work at remembering."

Not Michael, she decided. Jana wouldn't forget Michael. Not for a minute. He was a part of her. "Webster and Haynes," Jana said out loud to keep it fresh, to keep the two of them alive in her heart.

"Webster and Haynes," Mars said. "What's that, a law firm?"

"My boyfriend," Jana stammered. She was too cold to talk. How could she tell him everything about Michael when she was going to freeze to death any minute now?

"Oh yeah, I saw his ring," Mars said absently. "Hey, wait. His ring, it has your school on it."

Jana lifted her hand close to her face to see the ring better in the dim light. It was the hand she'd been using to hold the waist of her plaid school skirt closed. The ring had a cat's face in the middle. You could see it under the blue stone. The initials CHS were molded into one side and Michael's graduation year in the other.

"Apparently I am from CHS and our mascot is either a tiger or a lion, or a fat man with whiskers."

Mars laughed. "Central High School," he said. "And you're the Panthers. One of your football players is in homeroom. He's a Stretcher. There are a couple others you'll recognize when you run across them."

"Oh." Jana meant to smile. But when she moved her mouth, her teeth chattered instead.

Mars moved closer. Jana felt his warmth like a blanket softly pressed against her. "Your hometown is Asheville, Arden Lake, or Grove Park," he said.

Jana made a face. Asheville sounded right. But so did Arden Lake. She couldn't remember.

"I'm cold," she finally blurted out. "I can't think. I'm too cold."

Mars laughed again, but it was a smaller laugh. It stayed close between them like a secret shared. Even his laughter felt warm.

"It's you," he said. "Here, give me your hand." Mars held out his hand to Jana. She placed hers inside his. He covered it with his other hand.

"Ah, nice," Jana said in spite of herself. Her hand warmed instantly. The warmth radiated up her arm to her shoulders and neck. She flushed with heat. If he put his arm around her, she thought, if she rested her face on his chest, she would be warmed to her toes.

"Didn't Davis tell you?" Mars asked. "Risers are

cold. Something happens to your body when you come here from the Planet. You're two or three degrees colder, Jana. You'll adjust."

There was a natural kindness in his voice as he spoke. She hadn't expected it. And he had used her first name for the first time.

"Do I feel cold to you?" Jana asked. She didn't like the idea that she was cold to touch. The thought made her seem more dead than ever.

"Absolutely frigid." Mars grinned. He took his hands back and let hers fall to her side. "Really, not much at all. You'll get used to it. The first few days, everything is sort of heightened, magnified. I doubt Davis even notices anymore."

Jana wondered if Michael would think she felt cold.

"I better go now," Mars said. He hoisted himself onto the railing.

"What was the third thing?" Jana asked quickly. "You said three things. One was Wyatt's knife trick. The other was you wanted to know my hometown."

"Tomorrow, you're going to a funeral."

"I am?" Jana was trying to see his face as he raised his arms over his head and teetered briefly on the railing before catching his balance.

"Take me with you," he said. "You get to take someone."

She watched his faded jeans disappear over her head.

"It doesn't have to be your roommate," Mars continued. "I'll help you talk to your boyfriend. I'll help you understand everything . . . and . . ."

He had pulled himself above the top of the second-floor fire-escape balcony and was making his way over the railing to the third floor.

"And?" Jana called after him.

"And put your skirt back on," Mars called down to her.

CHAPTER NINE

JANA SHIVERED.

Her skirt was a puddle of plaid encircling her feet.

Sometime during the conversation, she had let go of her unbuttoned school skirt and it had dropped to her ankles. Jana had been talking to the hunkiest Slider in school while standing in her school blouse, underwear, and socks. And nothing else. Without even noticing.

This balcony scene wasn't anything like Romeo and Juliet's.

Jana jerked her skirt back into place, clamped the waist closed in her fist, and rushed inside the dorm. Mars hadn't said a thing when her skirt fell. Whenever *that* was. Jana couldn't decide if Mars was the nicest guy she'd ever met. Or truly evil.

She knew, for one thing, that Wyatt's cutting himself wasn't just a trick. It was real blood that pumped from his sliced-open flesh. It looked like blood and smelled like blood.

"This is from Mars," Wyatt had said.

There was more to being a Slider than she understood just yet. And there was more to Mars than just being a Slider. He was warmer than the others. She was sure of it.

Beatrice and Christie were in her dorm room when Jana returned.

They sat on Arva's bed. Both girls wore loose cotton pajamas with small stenciled designs in light red and light blue colors. Arva stood by her desk in her cut-down prom dress.

"So?" Beatrice finally said.

She stared at Jana who looked back, puzzled.

"What happened?" Christie asked. "Did he kiss you? Did you kiss him?"

"No," Jana said. "It wasn't a date or anything."

"Close enough," Beatrice said.

"Too close," Arva chimed in, disapproving as always. She brought Jana a bottled water from an open case tucked under the computer table.

"Well, he did hold my hand," Jana confessed, accepting the water from Arva. "And it was very, very warm."

"Then what?" Christie wanted to know every last detail.

"Then my skirt fell off."

"It's too early to tell her anything," Mars said. "She's in love with this guy. She wouldn't believe a thing we said about him."

"You make everything too complicated," Wyatt said. "You think too much."

"I'm looking for clarity, Wyatt."

"*Clarity?*" Wyatt laughed. "Life's a mess. Why should death be any different? We could have shown her everything tonight. We have to do the things we have to do. And not think about it so much."

"There's a path here, Wyatt. A road. It's step by step. You just can't skip into the middle of everything or you'll get lost."

The Sliders sat on the floor of their room, their backs against the wall. Sliders almost never went to sleep. Their rooms were smaller than the four-person suites on the second floor.

"Screw the metaphors," Wyatt said. "Let's jump. For real."

"Hey, I'll still jump," Mars protested. "When it's time, you know I'll jump. But sometimes it makes sense to look before you leap. She's smart, Wyatt. She's strong."

"Well, she can handle it, then."

"We're not sure Risers can go off campus on their own."

"Sure they can," Wyatt said. "And so can we. But we aren't going to if you're going to sit here all night. It's time to get out there if we're going to jump."

"Give me a minute, will you? I've got things to think about. You cutting your arm open didn't help matters any. What if she had flipped out and screamed for help? The library Grays would have caught you. And you'd have, what, two hours before the school had you in front of the Regents Council? The Virgins had already been sent to the room to warn you once."

"Those old farts like me, Mars. I got the regents beat."

"You have them beat until you don't. You come

out on the bottom one time, Wyatt, and it's for good. It's instant."

"Instant toast," Wyatt said. "I kind of like that."

"No reason to get expelled. If you're going to be a vacancy, you may as well walk out. At least you'll have a few days that way."

"All right, already. Got it."

"Well, get this too. You can't tell any of the Risers too much their first day. And you can't show them either. They freak, then they put on their Goody Two-shoes the school gives them and never look up again. You can lose them the first day."

"She wasn't going to scream," Wyatt argued. "Besides, you said she was sent here for you or something like that. I was just getting her introduced, you know?"

"I didn't expect her to be in love with that guy. Not *that* in love. It was in her eyes when she said his name. It's deep. It complicates everything. And you were trying to scare her pants off for the hell of it. You weren't doing me any favors, that's for sure."

"I'm sorry, all right?"

Mars brushed away the apology as soon as it was offered. "I saw her die," he said quietly, almost to himself. "You saw her too. On the Planet."

"Okay, I saw her."

"She walked right through me, Wyatt."

"And then she died. So what?"

Jana had walked through Mars when she picked up her shoes at the counter. He was loitering as a ghost and he should have been more careful. But it wasn't just that she had walked through him. People on the Planet did that all the time. This girl had walked through him and softly said, "Oh." She had felt him. In some manner or another, they had touched.

"That means something," Mars said.

"It means she was going bowling, man. That's all. And *you* were the one who wanted to flip that place."

"Exactly," Mars agreed. "Don't you see? I was supposed to be there. I was supposed to save her life."

"No, you were supposed to be here tucked in bed with your teddy bear."

"I watched her die. I felt her die, Wyatt. And I was watching her when she fell. She had a wild, surprised look in her eyes."

"Watching her?" Wyatt asked. "Hell, you were on top of her the second she fell."

"I was trying to help," Mars said. "That's the ticket, Wyatt. You've got to help somebody."

It had felt like she was seeing him, Mars remembered, as she fell over backward with the stupid bowling ball in full swing over her head. She must not remember it, but he was absolutely certain she had seen him at a time when he was invisible to everyone on the Planet.

Then she was dead. By the time he materialized his body, she was dead. He couldn't do a thing about it. But he had tried.

"Ticket to nowhere, man," Wyatt said. "We're here until we aren't. Come on, it's dark. Let's go."

Mars stood up and offered his hand to Wyatt and, with a minimal tug, pulled his roommate to his feet.

"About time," Wyatt said.

"Man, what's rubbed you the wrong way?"

"A quarter mile of highway pavement," Wyatt growled.

Mars didn't laugh. Wyatt had died sliding a motorcycle on its side along a downhill run of Interstate 40. Wyatt left a lot of his skin, one side of his mouth, and one eye, along with his mortality, on the pavement behind him.

Clutching the lower metal railing with both

hands, Mars and Wyatt dangled from the second-story fire-escape balcony. When they dropped to the ground, Wyatt fell over sideways in the grass. Landing on two feet when one knee bent and the other didn't made for a clumsy getaway. But it was a getaway nonetheless and that was all that mattered.

They strode through darkness toward the hole in the chain-link fence that surrounded the closed motel. The whole world waited.

"So where are we going to jump tonight?" Mars asked, helping Wyatt through the fence.

"You tell me. You're the badass of this place. I'm the simple guy, remember? I don't plan ahead."

"I'll have to teach you how to do that, then," Mars said. "There are consequences to be afraid of here, Wyatt. It's no good not to be afraid of anything."

"*No Good* is my middle name. Always has been."

Jana had to tell it three times.

Each time she ended her performance with realizing her skirt had fallen down to her ankles. And each time Arva said, "It did not."

The last time, Jana showed her. She stood up, let

go of her skirt's waistband, and let the material drop to the floor.

"Where was he standing? How close?" Christie asked.

"Too close," Arva said. "You shouldn't have been alone with that boy, Jana."

"Hey, can I borrow your lip gloss?" Beatrice asked.

"Sure," Jana said. She stepped out of the puddle of her school skirt on the floor, found the tube of lip gloss next to her cell phone on the bed, and walked it to Beatrice. "Cute pajamas, by the way," Jana said. "Did you get those here?"

"Oh, I make them. Sometimes the Grays slip up and leave a stray bedsheet or a pillowcase in the linen room when they collect the laundry."

"What are the stencils?"

"I made those too. Mine are bluebirds and Christie's are butterflies. I found some stamp-pad ink in the school office. It's permanent ink and all, but I only have red and blue." Beatrice did her upside-down little smile. Jana noticed she wasn't wearing makeup. She saved it for school.

"After a few washings, the red looks pink, though," Beatrice added.

"They're very pretty," Jana said.

"Thank you," Beatrice said.

Christie did a quick shoulder spasm and said, "Ouch."

"Okay, I have to ask," Jana said. "Why do you do that, Christie? Do you have the hiccups? Do they hurt?"

"Love tugs," Beatrice answered for her. "Her parents won't let go. They keep trying to pull her back."

Christie made a face and shook her head slightly to let Jana know it was a subject she didn't want to talk about now.

"That's all nonsense," Arva said. "It's just the way she died. She hiccupped or something."

Jana believed Beatrice. She walked back to her bed and plopped down next to the clothes she'd been wearing when she died.

"Don't lie down," Arva barked, her croaky, whispered voice as loud as Jana had ever heard it. "You'll go right to sleep. Ten seconds, tops."

Beatrice nodded in agreement. Her yard dart bobbed along.

"I wish someone would hold my hand," Christie pouted, unable to let go of the topic of Jana and

Mars on the balcony. "The trouble is when you hold hands with another Riser, it just reminds you how cold we are."

"The right way to look at it," Arva said, "is Sliders are too warm. Risers are just right. Once you get used to it, Jana, you'll see that we're normal. We're what you're supposed to be when you die."

Jana wanted to be more than normal. Jana and Michael were better than normal. They would sparkle beyond death just as brightly as they did in life. Once he got here. They wouldn't really be dead if they were together.

She smiled warmly at the thought of holding hands with Michael.

Arva kept talking. Croakity, croakity, croak. "Sliders are just a bunch of dirty pigs in sweaty clothes. They're still touching Earth. They have one foot on Earth and the other here. Risers don't cling to Earth like Sliders do. So, yes, Jana, they're warmer than us."

"Some more than others," Beatrice added, applying a layer of Jana's peach lip gloss. She couldn't help herself. It was there and so were her lips.

Wyatt watched everything Mars did in the real world.

Because he worked at it, Mars possessed a more highly developed skill in dealing with the physical elements of the Planet. He could naturalize at will. Few Sliders could. He was able to pick up things and move objects without having to think about it. Wyatt was still learning.

The grass and weeds alongside the pavement were wet. Mars and Wyatt walked down the middle of the road in silence, looking for a car to borrow. It couldn't be too new. Those cars had alarms. They kept their eyes out for something with rust.

"You think I'm not afraid of anything? I'll tell you what I'm afraid of," Wyatt said as they walked. "Good girls. They give me the creeps."

"Nothing to be afraid of," Mars said. "Here's all you need to know. Good girls, girls like Webster, think they're bad. And bad girls think they're good. Bad girls think nobody understands them. Good girls are afraid that people do."

"Maybe that's why they give me the creeps," Wyatt said. "They're always hiding something."

A blue Toyota pickup truck turned on to the road and came toward them, its radio blasting. Wyatt stiffened and shifted his head to the side against the noise and bright headlights of the oncoming vehicle.

Mars never faltered. He walked in stride as the truck drove through the two of them. He pushed his fallen hair from his forehead once the vehicle was behind them.

"You could do real girls if you wanted to," Wyatt said, extending his limping stride to catch up to Mars. "Have you ever thought of that?"

"Have you ever thought of anything else?" Mars asked.

"Not really," Wyatt said.

CHAPTER TEN

PAULINE WAS BESIDE HERSELF.

It was the first thing Jana noticed about her roommate. Jana had come out of the bathroom to find Pauline sitting in two pieces on the bed. Her bottom half, that ended at the top of her skirt, kept its feet on the floor. Her upper half perched on the bed nearby, one hand planted on the pillow to keep from toppling.

Pauline's hair stuck out to one side. That was the second thing Jana noticed. The senior's hair was permanently swept straight out from the side of her head as if starched and lacquered into place.

"Her first day and she already had a date,"

Christie was saying.

"Okay, tell all," Pauline said, turning her hair toward Jana.

The yellow fins of the lawn dart in Beatrice's head leaned forward in anticipation of hearing Jana's skirt story one more time.

"Her skirt did *not* fall off," Arva insisted in her hoarse, raspy voice. "She's teasing us."

"It was Mars Dreamcote!" Beatrice, no longer able to contain herself, blurted out to Pauline.

The senior's expression turned stern. "Be careful, Jana. That boy's dangerous."

"That's what I've been trying to tell her," Arva croaked triumphantly.

"There are Sliders," Pauline continued, "and then there's Mars. They say he's going to walk off campus one day and live on the Planet. Just walk off. He won't last a week. If you leave campus and stay overnight, that's the same as a vacancy. You can't come back. I'm telling you, it's dangerous just to know him."

"I warned her," Arva said.

"Now, tell all," Pauline insisted.

Jana ran through the sequence of her balcony scene with Mars.

"At least your bottom didn't fall off," Pauline said. Her legs and waist got up from the bed and walked to the bathroom, hips boldly swaying just to make a point. The hem of her plaid skirt flounced. "That's how you flash a little leg. You don't just let your skirt fall off."

Jana was supposed to say something. She was thinking about tomorrow instead.

"I guess you're wondering how," Pauline said to Jana.

Jana stopped watching Pauline's legs and tried to focus on her roommate's top half. With an absentminded motion of her hand, Jana brushed one side of her hair behind her ear.

"How *what?*" she asked.

"How I died, for instance," Pauline said with a sniff.

The wind shook the pecan trees at the far side of the polo field.

A man standing next to Pauline reached into his shirt pocket for a pack of cigarettes. He put one in his mouth, replaced the pack, and held a blue plastic lighter under the tip of the cigarette. It wouldn't strike. Pauline had the odd sense that he had just done the whole thing twice, but the second time was happening at the same instant as the first.

Few people noticed the leading front of the wind shake the trees until the horses that were lined up and saddled for the match broke free. Black clouds with low, dark green edges had formed a line in the sky. The wind came through the trees and the horses whinnied, stood on their hind legs, and shook free of their tethers.

A gust of wind took Pauline's hat off her head. It was her wide-rimmed straw hat that was perfect for watching polo matches.

Pauline chased her hat.

The newborn storm surprised everyone. Pauline's father leaped from his thoroughbred as it reared wildly in the middle of the polo field. Other players tried to rein their mounts, then gave up. The horses went wild. There were forty or more of them. The horses turned sharply as the wind changed. Soon they were circling the field. Their hooves pounding the turf sounded like thunder.

Pauline almost had her hat once, then twice. But each time she reached for it, the hat flipped and rolled in the wind. She wasn't giving up. The hat was important to her. She'd worn it to the Kentucky Derby in May, when she had picked her own horse for her father to bet on and it had won.

The mounts in polo were called ponies. They weren't. Most of the mounts were thoroughbreds, large muscular horses full of run. Thoroughbreds were high-strung and spooked easily. Instinctively gathering into a close-knit herd, the horses charged in a mad all-out dash for safety.

But no place was safe. A funnel cloud formed overhead and dropped the pecans it had picked up from the trees. The hard-shelled nuts pelted the horses.

Crazed by the assault, the horses circled Pauline, who found herself in the middle of the polo field. She stopped chasing her hat. Stinging raindrops blew sideways against her legs, as if it were raining from the ground up.

The panic of the thoroughbreds frightened Pauline. She stood still in the rain, in the wind. It would be over soon. The charging mounts whinnied and screamed. Their eyes were wild with confusion and fear. The circle of horses, she believed, was protecting her. All she had to do was stand still. In a tornado.

The churning funnel of wind lifted and lowered in the dark sky, tipping from one side to the other. Pauline heard the roar above her. It sounded like a train. She heard tree limbs break. The funnel lowered. Pauline *closed her eyes. Her feet, she thought, were lifting from the ground.*

A sheet of tin from the stables roof passed through her body like a scalpel, slicing her in half. Her heart fluttered. There was no more to it than that. Pauline closed and opened her eyes.

There was nothing to see. It was the same with her eyes opened or closed. There was nothing to see and nothing left for Pauline to fear.

"A piece of tin roof blew right through me," Pauline said.

Christie said, "Ouch."

The wind explained the senior's unique hairdo, Jana thought.

"Pauline can put her ass on backwards, if she wants," Beatrice said. "You should see her at dances."

The four juniors laughed. Including Arva. It sounded like she was choking to death. Then from out of nowhere, Arva croaked and rasped, "Yeah, she's a real ass sandwich."

This was so unlike Arva, the laughter in the room became hysterical. Even Pauline couldn't help but join in.

It was the first time since she had died that Jana

was having any fun at all. Before she died, Jana would never have guessed that dead people told jokes. Or held hands. Or cared what clothes they wore. She wished Michael was there somehow to see all this.

A small black feather drifted to the floor.

The moon was out.

Mars and Wyatt rode to the cemetery in a 1997 Pontiac with a bad muffler. Mars drove. He concentrated on making his hands move the steering wheel. Materializing and interacting physically with the world required intense focus. Most of the Sliders couldn't manage it at all when they were first on the Planet. Others learned how to touch and move things, but only for short periods. Mars could go all night.

He turned the car onto a dirt road overhung with trees along one side. Mars parked in front of the cemetery entrance. The two Sliders got out of the car without opening the doors. They walked though the closed gate.

"That damn cat is around here somewhere," Wyatt said. He turned his head from shoulder to shoulder, looking for it.

"It lives here. What do you care?"

"It always follows me," Wyatt complained. "When I'm on the Planet, things are always sneaking up on me. Especially that cat."

"Cats and dogs are like that," Mars said. "They know we're here when people don't."

The things they came for sat on Mars's grave in two cardboard boxes. Mars ignored the headstone. He was tired of reading it. The big white cat was with the Sliders now and it wouldn't leave.

"Shoo," Wyatt said. "Scat!"

Mars was stronger at his gravesite than anywhere else. He could will his body back without any real effort at all. Wyatt had to work at it to pick up the lighter of the two boxes, but he got it done. Halfway back to the car, he had to set down his box. The cat was distracting him.

The cat waited for Wyatt to regain his physical strength. Materializing required practice. The more time you spent on the Planet, the better you became at interacting physically with the world. Mars and Wyatt practiced every night. Sliders had to naturalize on the Planet before they could jump. That alone made Planet practice worthwhile.

Wyatt had heard that when a Slider spends the

entire night on the Planet and doesn't return in time for class the next morning, his body naturalizes at will. Of course, you couldn't get back into Dead School. He wondered how long a Dead School dropout had before being whisked away to his chosen destiny beyond the Planet. A few days of being more real than dead might be worth it.

The cat stopped at the graveyard gate. Mars and Wyatt put the boxes Nora Headley had left for them in the backseat and drove to the house where the psychic was waiting with her clients.

"I don't think that cat's real," Wyatt said. "I think it's a ghost."

"Takes one to know one," Mars said. "And don't forget, Nora's sensitive. She can see and hear us when others can't. You can't make fun of her clothes out loud."

"Remind me to whisper," Wyatt said.

Jana lay in bed, clutching her cell phone.

Pauline had said whatever she held in her hands would be there when she was on the bus in the morning. Beatrice had suggested makeup or a hairbrush.

Jana dropped her head to her pillow and

instantly fell asleep. Sleep for the dead was like falling backwards into a hole as black as midnight. You never hit bottom. And you never dreamed.

Arva undressed for bed. She checked on Darcee. Nothing had changed. Even kids in comas had to miss home, Arva thought. She kissed Darcee lightly on the forehead and whispered as softly as a feather, "Good night, dear one." It seemed normal to do that. It was the one thing Arva could remember about her own mother.

Jana had dropped off on top of the covers. Arva took the blanket from her own bed and draped it over her new roommate. She didn't want Jana to be cold her first night in the dorm.

Arva silently counted to one hundred before resting her head on her pillow. She didn't want the day to be over. They were only in school for a certain amount of time and Arva never wanted any of their days to end. She wanted school to last forever.

Mars and Wyatt walked through Nora's kitchen.

She was set up in another room, waiting for Mars to come in and blow out one of the candles and answer questions in ghost voice.

Mars opened the fridge door and found his bottle

of soda pop cradled in a bowl of ice on the top shelf. Drinking soda pop was an addiction for Mars, one of the things that made him feel normal when he was on the Planet.

"Is someone there?" Nora called from the outer room.

She spoke in her high, trilling séance voice. Nora's clients for the evening sat around her dining table. A candle burned in a silver holder in front of each of them.

It was Wyatt's turn. He walked into the room, leaned over the table on his good leg, and blew out the candle in front of a large curly-haired woman. He touched her shoulder lightly, then stepped back. The woman gasped and shuddered.

Wyatt was improving. When Mars had first brought him to the séances, he couldn't do anything but watch. Now he could earn his share of the barter items the local fortune-teller placed on Mars's grave as payment for a few scheduled words from the other side.

"Hey, Nora," Mars said from the doorway. "What's up?"

CHAPTER ELEVEN

JANA STEAMED.

She was mad at herself for being dead. When Jana woke up she was already on the bus. She had fresh clothes, clean hair, and evil thoughts.

Jana wanted Michael here. She was incomplete without him. She hated being dead and incomplete at the same time. Without Michael, Jana was on a bus to nowhere.

She stared out the window, mad at everything she saw. Mad at her school uniform skirt. And blouse. And shoes. Mad that her cell phone was as dead as she was. Mars sitting at the back of the bus staring at her pissed her off. Henry looking straight ahead in his seat pissed her off. The smell of Ivory soap really pissed her off.

Jana opened her cell phone and snapped it shut so hard it almost broke. She plunged it back into her skirt pocket and cursed.

"It's going to be today," Arva said with a touch of excitement in her frogged-out voice. She was talking about Jana's field trip. "It's usually your second day."

"Mars already told me," Jana spewed. "I get to go to a funeral. Oh boy."

"You don't go alone, Jana. You get to take one of us with you. Most people choose their orientation roommate."

"And that would be you."

"Yes," Arva chirped.

"Whose funeral is it anyway? Doesn't someone around here die every day?"

"Yours, Jana."

Jana was amazed that she hadn't realized this sooner. Of course it was her funeral. She began to grin. She'd get to see Michael.

She wouldn't need her cell phone. Jana would sit in Michael's lap and tell him everything that was new. She would hold on to Michael with both arms and stay that way. Once she had Michael, there was nothing anyone could do to pull them apart.

Whatever happened next, it would be the two of them seeing it through to the end.

"I'm sorry," Jana finally said.

"About what?"

"My attitude. I didn't mean to take it out on you. It isn't your fault that I'm here."

"It's okay," Arva said. "A lot of us are angry at the beginning." Arva patted Jana's knee. "It gets better," she added. "I promise."

It didn't happen first hour.

Jana glanced at Mars when she could, avoiding eye contact with everyone else, including Arva. Mr. Fitzgerald assigned another in-class essay by writing the topic on the chalkboard. She wrote her essay in seconds, it seemed.

She was too excited to think about anything but Michael. She barely noticed the taste of strawberries in her mouth. Or Christie saying "ouch" over and over. Or Beatrice's yellow dart fins pointing forward as she leaned over her notebook.

When the Virgins sang the bell, the Sliders were out of class like a shot. Jana was right behind them.

As she hurried to second period, Arva had to

skip along beside her to keep up. Mars lingered in the hall, staring at her as she passed. A girl had her arm on him. She was a Slider. She wore a tiny tee and her navel was pierced. Mars was ignoring the girl as best he could.

It didn't matter, anyway. Obviously Mars liked her, but Jana wasn't available. Jana was leaving Dead School today and she was never coming back. Michael would keep her warm from here on out.

Second period, Mr. Skinner drew more boxes on the blackboard. The chalk squeaked. Despite her desire to be out of class, and out of Dead School, Jana stared at the boxes and tried to figure out what Skinner was up to. Maybe he had died drawing boxes and kept doing it for eternity.

Jana was careful not to look around. She didn't want to make eye contact with anyone. Not with Arva. Not with Mars. Not with Beatrice and her upside-down smile. Not with Christie. If Henry turned around in his seat to pass her a note, Jana wanted him to see the top of her head. She wasn't going to be one of them for much longer, not once she and Michael were together.

The first box was complicated. There were two gaps in the lines that formed the box, one at the top and one at the bottom. Mr. Skinner put an X at the bottom opening. He had filled in the rest of the box with short horizontal and vertical lines, sometimes connected to one another, sometimes not.

To kill time, Jana sealed her lips into a straight line and copied the first box Skinner had drawn into her notebook. She placed an X at the bottom of the box and left an opening at the top. She drew in the short horizontal and vertical lines. The box, she finally realized, was a puzzle. It was a maze. Just like the kind they have on the back of paper place mats at IHOP.

It was a puzzle she could solve quickly, without error, but she was well behind Mr. Skinner's progress with the chalk. Jana copied the second box from the blackboard. Like the first, it had an X at a gap in the bottom. It was the entry into the maze. The other gap was high on the left side of the box instead of at the top. It was the way out.

Jana flipped the page in her notebook and started copying the third box. She looked at Mars once. But she did it with her head ducked, peering carefully from behind the edges of her hair that fell forward over her work.

He was watching her. Jana wondered if he was

staring at her every second. Maybe he was trying to drill a hole in the back of her head with his piercing blue eyes. Tough luck. She already had one of those.

She had drawn the sixth box of Skinner's when two Virgins entered the classroom. They sang one soprano note together lightly and everyone in class looked up. Then the shimmering Virgins did something absolutely beautiful. They sang Jana's name in alternating high and low notes in delayed harmony. Jana had never heard her name sound so pretty.

Jan-ah Web-ster. It sounded like a lullaby.

In their ephemeral white gowns, with arms that seemed to float on the air, the Virgins motioned Jana forward. Their hair lifted softly on a breeze that wasn't there. Jana stood from her desk and walked to the front of class. She felt clunky.

The Virgins were at the classroom door, Jana eager to follow them. They turned and held up the palms of their hands in unison. Jana stopped. The Virgins moved their outstretched arms to encompass the classroom, their fingers undulating.

Jana was supposed to choose a student from her homeroom to accompany her to the Planet.

She looked over the class. Arva grinned at her.

Jana's roommate had closed her notebook on her desk and was ready to go. Christie, knowing she wouldn't be selected, smiled at Jana, wishing her well on Jana's visit to her real life.

Henry Sixkiller looked hopeful. Beatrice did not. Yellow fins sticking out of the top of your head really wasn't the sort of thing you wore to anyone's funeral. Mr. Skinner tapped the blackboard with his chalk, waiting to do another box.

Jana pointed to the back of the room and said, "Mars Dreamcote."

A murmur passed through the classroom. Students leaned toward each other to speak in whispers. Christie's and Beatrice's mouths fell open. Arva dropped her hands on her desk in disgust.

Wyatt, leaning sideways from his seat on his good leg, gave Mars a little shove. The dreadfully handsome blue-eyed Slider, who had seen Jana in her underwear and socks on her first day in Dead School, made his way to the front of the room. Jana tugged her hair behind her ear and followed the Virgins out the classroom door. Mars quickly caught up.

CHAPTER TWELVE

MARS SURPRISED JANA.

He didn't get on the bus when she did. Jana found a seat in the middle and watched him out the window. Mars circled the side of the bus and darted through an opening in the chain-link fence that surrounded Dead School. With her thumb, Jana played Michael's ring back and forth on the third finger of her left hand.

Mars bent over to retrieve something in the grass at the base of a tree across the road. He tucked it inside his shirt and hurried back.

Jana watched him carefully. There was restrained power in his movements. It was there when he stood still too, when he leaned against something in the hall or against the rail of the fire-escape balcony.

Like the sky, she thought. It was always about to move, about to act. Jana wished she could copy the unreleased power that was in his every moment. If she could move like that, stand still like that onstage or in front of a camera, no one would be able to take their eyes away from her when she performed.

Jana was old enough to be honest with herself. She was attracted to Mars. And he was attracted to her.

She wasn't pretty enough to attract every boy she met. And she rarely sought to sparkle in person. She'd just come up short. Jana kept her brown hair in a simple cut so she could hide, when she needed to, by ducking her head. She almost never wore earrings or a necklace. She never tied her hair back to show off the long clean line of her arching neck.

When she was acting, it was different. Jana held her face upright, her shoulders back, her entire self on display until what beauty she possessed sparkled like a star. She didn't mind being plain. Or ugly. As an actress, Jana could be either one. That's why she liked acting. She didn't have to be as beautiful as her mother.

Mars wasn't attracted to Jana the way men were attracted to her mother. Yet something drew him to her. Jana could feel it, but she couldn't put her finger on it. It was deeper than some boy thinking she was cute. It was more like she was food and he was hungry. It was as if Mars needed her to survive.

This was why she had selected him to come with her today. He needed to see Jana with Michael. With Michael, she was more than Jana Webster. She was bigger. Bigger than life. Bigger than death. Jana and Michael were forever.

Mars needed to know, to see it for himself.

"Got your cell?" he asked, sitting next to her on the bus.

Jana fished her phone from her skirt pocket and handed it to Mars. She didn't need it as urgently as before. She would be seeing Michael soon. She could say everything she wanted to say in person.

As the bus began to move, Mars pried the cover off one side of her phone and flicked out the flat square battery. He reached inside his shirt and removed a fresh battery from a plastic Baggie. He slipped it into place and snapped the cover back on to her phone.

"Now, don't open it and don't turn it on," Mars said, handing the phone back to her. His fingers touched hers and a river of warmth surged through her arm.

"It won't work on the bus," he added. "You'll just drain the battery. Once we're off the bus, I'll show you how we can make it work."

Jana fumbled the phone down into her skirt pocket and leaned back against the seat. Being next to Mars reminded her how cold she felt. Jana wanted Mars to drape his arm over her shoulders. But only for the warmth of it.

She tried to think of something else. Her funeral was on the horizon. Michael was waiting for her. Michael would be warm too.

They stood in front of the funeral chapel.

The street was lined with cars. Classmates stood in the small groups along the sidewalk. There were people Jana thought she recognized but didn't really know. Someone was dressed in a cheerleading uniform.

"It's like that when you die in high school," Mars said. "Everyone goes to your funeral."

"Look at her," Jana said, pointing at the

cheerleader. "How stupid is that?"

Mars walked beside her as she climbed the steps to the ornate double doors.

"You don't even know their names," Mars said. "It's like that."

"Some of them," she said. "I know some of them. I've seen them all before."

Jana reached for the handle on one of the doors but couldn't get her fingers around it. She tried the other one.

Her grasp wouldn't work.

"What's wrong with me?" Jana mumbled to herself.

Mars opened the door for her. She could have walked through the door without opening it at all, but life-conditioned habits died hard.

Jana rushed in. The hallway was filled with flowers. And people. Boys in shirts and neckties, and girls in dresses and heels. A few adults were among them. They spoke in whispers. Someone laughed at something that was said. Some of the girls were crying.

Music played in another room. Jana moved toward it. These doors were open. Inside, she stopped short. Mars stood behind her. Jana felt his hand on her shoulder. She spiked with heat.

Folding chairs were in rows in front of her casket. Not one seat was empty. Kids stood at the back, between the flower arrangements. Flowers also lined the walls to both sides of the rows of chairs. The front of the room, where her casket sat on a raised pedestal draped with white cloth, was also filled with flower arrangements.

Jana's funeral was like a theater. Her open casket centered the stage. Lights shone on the ornate box that held her body. Jana was the star attraction. From the back of the room, she could see her own face.

But it wasn't herself that she had come to see.

There were too many people in the room. Too many kids. It looked like a high school assembly and all the girls had been told to cry. It wasn't like *The Big Chill* at all. Glenn Close, William Hurt. And Kevin Kline.

With Kevin Costner as the dead guy. Now Jana had something in common with a famous actor. They both played dead people. Her memory was back in full stride. Jana could see the movie poster in her mind. Below the title it read, *"In a cold world you need your friends to keep you warm."*

"This way," Mars said.

He took Jana by the hand and led her to the front of the small auditorium. Mars knew what she wanted. He'd been to his own funeral and he understood what mattered once life was over. People think you're going to want to look at yourself and listen to the eulogy. Once you're dead, a eulogy is just a bunch of bull. You don't believe a word of it.

Mars led her to the seats reserved for family.

Jana stood in front of Michael, who sat next to her mother. Her mother had collapsed against him. She sobbed as steadily as most people breathed. She never looked up. Michael stared straight ahead. He was staring at nothing. He was looking right at Jana, but he acted like he didn't see her.

Look what I'm wearing, she wanted to say. *Is this dumb or what?*

"Why doesn't he see me?" she asked Mars.

Her mother's hand gripped Michael's thigh as she sobbed.

"Stop that!" Jana said. No one heard her, except Mars.

Michael's arm was around her mother. Her mother's face pressed against his chest.

"Don't fall for it, Michael," Jana said. "She's

always stricken. She always curls up like that."

The entire room of people was behind or to the side of Michael and Jana's mother. No one else could see. As she watched in horror, Michael placed his hand on top of her mother's.

"No, no, no," Jana said, tears streaking her face. "She's a drug addict, Michael! Don't do that! Stop touching her!"

Jana sobbed loudly. Her throat burned. Her heart was on fire and it hurt like hell.

Michael wrapped his fingers over her mother's. He was holding her hand.

"Stop it right now," she said weakly. Jana's words were cloth stripped into shreds. "Stop it . . . right this . . . minute."

Struggling to find her strength, Jana pushed herself forward. She leaned into Michael's knees and Jana Webster, all alone, slapped his face as hard as she could. Then, without taking a breath, she did it again. Wildly and with all her might, she battered him.

CHAPTER THIRTEEN

MICHAEL DIDN'T FEEL IT.

He didn't feel a thing. Jana swung her hand repeatedly through the air and touched nothing. It was so horrible she couldn't breathe.

Then she was falling. Jana tumbled forward, passing through Michael into the people sitting behind him and her mother. She felt Mars reach for her from behind. He wrapped Jana in his arms and pulled her backwards.

Jana flushed with heat and despair. She slumped into his arms as if she had fainted.

"Stand up," Mars said.

He tightened his arms around Jana like a safety

belt and pulled her upright until her clunky school shoes planted themselves on the carpeted floor. With his face over her shoulder, Jana could feel his breath on her neck. Jana was wrapped in a combined fever of his heat and her own grief. She tasted strawberries in her mouth all over again.

"It's all right," Mars whispered. "You're all right, Jana. It's just the way it is."

Jana couldn't bear to look at Michael or her mother. She didn't want to see and remember Nathan sitting next to Michael. Or Sherry sitting at the end with her round face done up in rainbow eye shadow and lurid lipstick.

"Get me out of here," Jana said weakly, choking on her own tears. "Please."

Mars turned Jana sideways in his arms. He took one arm away, propping her up in the other one. He kept himself between Jana and the people in the chairs. She leaned on Mars. Inside the muscular arm he kept around her waist, Jana walked slowly away from Michael. Her legs barely functioned.

As they passed in front of Nathan, Mars reached out with his free hand and tapped the senior on the head.

"Hey," Nathan said too loudly. He looked quickly left then right.

"Shhh," Sherry said.

"What was that?" Nathan said much more quietly.

"I know what you did," Mars said from the side of his mouth to Nathan.

Mars paused and looked him over. Nathan's face reddened like a light turned on. Sherry heard it too. Her mouth fell open and her head cocked sideways. She stared at the casket.

Jana gathered her strength as best she could. She wondered what it was that Nathan had done, then realized that Mars had spoken to someone on the Planet and they had heard him. She pulled away from Mars and turned to look at Michael.

"Michael!" Jana shouted. "Michael, it's me!"

No one heard a thing. Certainly not Michael. Certainly not her mother. Jana's eyes widened in confused anguish. Michael was there. She was there. Why couldn't he hear her? He was *right there*.

Mars turned her away in his comforting arm.

"It's like I'm a ghost," Jana said.

She leaned against Mars as they made their way toward the wide hallway full of flowers and people Jana barely knew.

"More like a spirit," Mars said, using his Dead School voice that no one on the Planet could hear.

In the hall, someone's little sister noticed Mars. She reached out to touch him. Mars smiled at the girl. She was one of the sensitive ones. Some people could see him no matter what he did. But not many.

Her little hand passed through his arm.

Soon Jana and Mars were outside. The same people who were standing around before were standing around now. Off to the left, the cheerleader gabbed to her friend, gesturing with her hands, tossing her hair. It looked to Jana like the girl was making a salad.

The bus was parked in the street in front of the funeral home. People on the Planet could walk right through it and never know it was there. But it was real somehow, Jana knew. It carried her weight. She could feel the seats when she sat in them. It had to be real. And so did she.

She turned a button on her school blouse between her fingers. It was real. Everything was real. Her love and her pain, which seemed like the same thing now, were real.

"Tell me I'm real," she said to Mars. "Tell me all this is really happening."

Jana held her hand to her mouth and bit down on her own flesh just above the forefinger. It hurt. How could she not be real?

"Tell me I'm real," she said again. When Jana breathed in, she swallowed tears. They burned like peppers.

Mars had tried not to look when she bit her hand, but he understood. It was like jumping. Jumping was a more extreme way of being real, but it was just like biting your hand to prove you were there. That you were real somehow.

"I'm not going back," Jana told him. "I don't have to."

Jana ran down the steps to the sidewalk.

She wasn't much of a runner. She had never been athletic that way. Jana couldn't catch a ball. She couldn't run in a straight line unless it was by accident. But she ran. As fast as her legs would let her, she ran. She ran past the idling bus, past the kids on the sidewalk, the kids standing under trees.

Her chest heaved. Her heart pounded. She ran like she could not stop. Like a little kid down a steep hill.

Jana turned at the end of the block on to a

treelined side street of large houses set far back from the road. Her legs kept going, her arms pumping at her sides. She was surprised she was still running, still able to run. A bird flew in front of her, from one side of the street to the other. Like the bird, Jana was a thing of motion, her skirt flying.

She was also a thing of muscle and blood and urgent breath. Her body worked. Jana was real. Her chest ached. Sweat appeared on her forehead. Veins throbbed in her neck. A sharp pain stabbed her side.

Jana slowed. Her clothes felt heavy. She trotted two steps, then walked with her hand pressed against the probing pain in her side. Her heartbeat sounded like drums inside her head. Her face was red with heat, but at the same time she felt cold again. The cold was always there.

She stumbled into someone's yard and collapsed in the grass. Jana sprawled on her stomach and stretched out her arms. With her chest and belly and legs pressed against the earth, her breathing finally caught up. Jana hugged the earth, trying to hold on to it.

"Hey, are you okay?" Mars asked, catching his breath. He stood at her feet.

"Dunno," she said without opening her eyes.

Jana's head was spinning.

"I guess we have a few minutes to make sure. The bus won't leave till the service is over. Most people stay at their own funeral. They give you enough time to stay."

"Did you stay at yours?"

Jana rolled over on her back. She drew up her knees. Her face was stained from being pressed against the grass.

Mars didn't answer. Jana studied him through half-closed eyes. Unlike the other students she'd met, he wouldn't talk about his own death.

"You can do things here that I can't," she said. "I don't understand. We're both dead, but you're not as dead as I am."

"Sliders have one foot still touching Earth," he said in a serious tone. "We don't get to leave Earth entirely."

"Not ever?"

"Pull your skirt down, Webster," he said without looking at her. "I can see your underwear."

"I don't care. I'm not really here."

"Yes, you are. When you're with me you are."

Jana tugged her skirt hem down over her legs. "Promise?"

"Cross my heart . . ." Mars said, then paused. They looked at each other. Their eyes locked. A hint of what Mars was about to say danced at the edges of the perfect blue gaze of his eyes looking into hers.

"And hope to die?" Jana finished for him.

His cheek dimpled, then his mouth broke into a wide smile. Soon he was laughing. And so was she. Mars laughed so hard he had to sit down to catch his breath. Jana laughed until she felt like crying. Her tears were always close by.

Jana sat up in the grass and smoothed the front of her blouse.

"It's like this," Mars eventually told her. "Here on the Planet you're like a spirit and I'm more like a ghost. A spirit, you know? People can't see you, except in their dreams. A ghost, though, can interact and talk to people one on one while they're wide awake and walking around. Sometimes they can see me. If I want them to, they can see me."

"Like you did with Nathan? He didn't see you, though."

"No. But he felt me and he heard me when I talked to him."

"How can you do that?" Jana asked. She wished she could.

"I work at it," Mars confessed. He pushed his dark hair from his forehead. "It's what I do. The kids in school don't work at anything. They just do their classwork and think they are getting something done. They think that's it. They accept things the way they are. I don't know how to say it, really, but I have ambitions that have nothing to do with school."

She understood perfectly.

"I want to do something out of the ordinary, Webster. Going to school on the Planet really is doing nothing. You just sit in the classes someone else tells you to sit in. You learn things you didn't choose to learn from people you didn't choose to teach you. Then one day they tell you it's over and you have to go out there and learn the world for real.

"And that's if you're lucky. That's if you don't die in school."

Jana snickered. She was with him every word. She was working to be an actor. Besides taking speech and drama and being in a play now and then, she worked at it mostly on her own. She studied old movies, for one thing. She practiced acting all the time. When other people were just having conversations, Jana was working. She was watching reactions closely to see what clicked and what didn't.

"I've had real jobs since I was thirteen," Mars told her. "I had to if I wanted anything. I worked when I was on the Planet and I work now that I'm in Dead School."

"Why?" Jana asked. "We're dead. Work's over."

"No, that's the thing. Dead School is different. You have to figure things out on your own. There are rules, but it's not the way Arva says it is. She wants it to be like regular school and so do most of the others. But in Dead School, you have to do it on your own. And you have to figure it out for yourself. Nothing's the way it was and there's nobody to explain it to you."

"Figure what out?"

Mars grinned. "That's it exactly. You have to figure out what you have to figure out. It's going to be different for everybody."

"What's going to be different?" As far as Jana was concerned, being dead was different enough.

"Our destinies. That's what happens when you graduate, Jana, or get expelled. You go to your destiny. I go to mine."

"So why not just go now? Why Dead School at all?"

"That's the right question," Mars said. He stared into her eyes as if looking for something there. "It's our chance to learn to change our destinies. We died while we were still in school, with almost none of our future determined. There are still things to learn in Dead School, Webster. There's still time."

Jana let out a sigh. Despite his misstep with her mother at the funeral, Michael was Jana's destiny. She didn't need more time to learn that.

"Look," Mars continued. He spread out his hands and studied them. "Every Slider in school could do what I've done so far. But it's work and most of them don't want to work at anything. We're bad kids to begin with, you know? And almost nobody wants to improve. They don't even realize they have the chance."

"What about Risers?" Jana asked. "Can't we learn to do what you do?"

"You're not as close to Earth as we are. You're not Earthbound. For most Risers that's good enough. Your eternity is going to be . . . *better* than ours."

Mars paused.

"What's your hometown, Webster?" he asked out of the blue.

"Asheville," she said. Jana smiled to remember it

so easily. Being on the Planet had its advantages and memory was one of them.

And when she smiled she was real again. Everything was real again. Dead School was real. Jana was real. Mars was real. But everything worked in a new way. She'd have to learn how it all worked to be with Michael again. He was real too.

"Michael thinks I'm dead and gone," Jana said.

"Yes, he does."

"But I'm not gone, am I?"

This time Mars smiled. "Maybe we should let him know that, Jana. Hand me your cell phone and I'll show you a few tricks."

CHAPTER FOURTEEN

IT WAS TIME TO TALK TO MICHAEL.

Jana fished her cell phone from her skirt pocket and handed it to Mars. She tried to steady her excitement, but her grin turned into a beaming smile. The Planet smelled sweet. The yard they sat in had been mown the night before and it smelled like watermelon rind and clover.

Mars flipped her phone open and turned it on with one hand. "The kid sitting next to your boyfriend, you got his number?"

"It's in there somewhere," she said. She took the cell from him. "His name's Nathan Mills. He and Michael are best friends, don't ask me why. The girl with the boobs is Nathan's new girlfriend. Sherry Simmons. But I want to talk to Michael."

Jana pushed the menu. Her list of contacts didn't come on-screen.

"Hey, my phone won't work."

"It's not the phone. It's your fingers when you're on the Planet."

"I forgot. I can still feel my body."

"There's a bit of you here," Mars confessed. "Just not as much as there is when you've had more practice."

"You mean, I can get to be like you?"

"No," Mars said. "You're a Riser. You can do better, but . . . Here, let's try it this way." He scooted closer, took the phone from her hand, and held it open in front of her. "Do the numbers. Start with Nathan."

Jana pushed the code for her contact list and found Nathan. Her fingers worked the phone as long as Mars was holding it. She pushed Send. Mars lifted the phone to his ear while the number went through. It rang six times without an answer.

"Voice mail," Mars said to Jana. He waited for the signal. "Hey, Nathan," he said into the phone. "It's me. We met at the funeral today, remember?

I'm your new best friend."

Jana giggled.

"I know what you guys did and I think you should tell someone," Mars went on. "I mean, if you don't get around to it pretty soon, I'll have to drop back by and talk to you about it in person. What's a good time for you?"

Mars winked at her while he talked into the phone. She thought he was making stuff up to get Nathan's attention.

He clicked the cell closed to end the call.

"Here, let me," Jana said.

Mars flipped the phone open and held it again for her to push the buttons. She brought up Michael's number. His picture appeared on the screen. She had taken the picture of him at a rehearsal and he had a crazed expression on his face. It was supposed to be lust, she remembered. Michael was good-looking and all that, but Jana was a much better actor.

Michael's voice mail was short. "Not here," he had recorded, followed by, "Message. Now."

Jana didn't know what to say. And she waited too long. A service voice said, "We didn't get your message, either because you were not speaking or because of a bad connection. To disconnect, press one. To record your message, press two."

Jana pressed two. It beeped.

"Michael? It's me," Jana said. Her voice quivered with excitement. "I'm still here and you can find me. Call me back and . . ."

Jana was interrupted by the recorded service voice. "Unfortunately the system cannot process your entry. Please try again later. Good-bye." There was no beep. The phone was silent.

"Your voice isn't registering," Mars said. He was close enough to hear the recording.

"You mean, it can't hear me? Michael can't hear me?"

"Take my hand," Mars said.

He leaned in. Jana huddled closer and placed her hand in his. Her left hand, the one with Michael's ring on the third finger. She blushed as his heat moved through her like a tide.

"Squeeze," he said.

Jana closed her fingers tightly around his hand and felt so much warmth move through her she wanted to shut her eyes.

"Now try it." Mars made a face like he was working on a math problem. A long black car drove by, followed by another one.

"Michael," Jana said after she got the signal. "It's me." She paused, then quickly added, "I'm still here. I'm always here. Call me." Her hand that held on to Mars tingled. Michael's ring felt large and heavy and out of place on her finger. Jana pressed harder. Even her toes were warm.

Mars watched the other Jana, being driven in her casket, roll by.

"I love you," she said into the phone. Jana's neck and chest were flushed with heat. She'd felt this way before when she and Michael were kissing, when they lay on the couch together and kissed.

She let go of Mars's hand.

Mars snapped the phone shut. Jana dropped her hands into her lap and watched an ant crawling on her wrist.

When she did talk to Michael, she knew what he would say. He would say he loved her and that he needed to be with her as much as she needed to be with him. Jana tried to flick the ant away from her wrist and realized she was crying again.

There were more cars on the street. They moved slowly, their lights turned on. A dog barked in someone's backyard.

She flipped her finger across her skin again. The ant was still there.

"All I do is cry," Jana said to Mars. "I'm not like this in real life."

Mars flicked away the ant for her. She looked at him through her tears. Jana's mouth trembled. Her tongue drew back in her throat. She tightened her lips as much as possible and tried to breathe without gasping. She wiped her eyes with the back of her hand. "Fart, fudge, and popcorn, Mars. I just want to be normal!"

Mars nodded as she spoke. He was listening without judging her. Mars understood.

Jana made herself stop crying. As an actor, it was never difficult to stop crying once you started. You just said your next line. When crying happened to you for real, it was difficult to turn it off.

"You are normal," Mars said. "You're more than normal, Webster. Not less."

A Virgin appeared.

She stood in front of Jana, seeming to float. A piece of pretty paper with eyes and lips. The dog stopped barking. The Virgin sang one word. *"Time."*

"The original singing telegram," Mars said,

standing up. The Virgin was gone as quickly as she had appeared.

A lock of dark hair had fallen onto his forehead.

"We gotta go now," Mars said. He held out his hand to her, offering Jana his strength, his warmth.

The grass under her legs felt cold.

"What if I don't? What if I just stay?"

"Can't," Mars said. "You're a Riser. In a few minutes you'll be sitting on the bus. We may as well walk. When you learn to leave campus on your own, you can stay on the Planet longer."

What if she wasn't a Riser? Jana wondered. Her hands felt like ashes as she dusted her palms across each other. Her knees, she noticed, were grass stained. The inside of her elbow was streaked with dirt where a trickle of sweat had dried.

Jana took his hand and pulled herself to her feet. She and Mars were standing too close. Embarrassed by proximity, but not wanting to step away, Jana straightened her blouse and brushed off her clothes.

"If there are bugs in my hair," she said, shaking her head, "I'll just die."

Mars tried not to laugh. But he couldn't help it.

As they walked together on the sidewalk, Mars opened her cell. He turned it off and handed it back to her. Jana wanted to try to call Michael again, but slipped the phone into her skirt pocket. She didn't need the frustration of not being able to push the numbers on her own. He'd get her message. That was enough for now.

"Remember," Mars said, "on the bus or on campus or in the dorm, don't even turn it on. You'll kill the battery."

"Might as well be dead like the rest of us," Jana said.

When Michael listened to her message, he would remember how much he loved her. When he heard her voice, Michael would need her again. The real her. The Jana who still existed. The Jana who was his whole world.

The side of her body walking next to Mars was warm. Her other side felt chilled. It was like walking in two different weather patterns at the same time. Jana imagined a TV forecaster offering the day's predicted high and low temperatures with the words "*depends on who you're with.*"

"We might be dead, Webster. But that doesn't mean there aren't things we can do with ourselves."

"So what do you want to do with yourself, Dreamcote?" Jana tried out his last name for the first time. It seemed right since he chose to call her Webster most of the time. "Cure cancer?"

"Something like that," Mars confessed.

"Really?" Jana stopped walking.

"Well, sort of," he said. "If finding a cure for cancer is saving lives, then that's what I want to do."

"Save lives?" Jana was surprised. Mad, bad, and dangerous to know Mars wanted to save lives?

"Okay then, one life. I want to save one life."

"Anyone in particular?"

"I'm looking," Mars confessed.

"You're looking for someone to save?" This didn't make any sense to her.

They were walking again.

"Okay, tell me quick, what do you want to remember?" Mars asked. "Say it out loud. You'll forget little things once we're back in school."

"I don't know . . . I . . ." Jana was confused. There was nothing she could think of she would want to remember because, really, she remembered everything.

"Your hometown," Mars suggested. "Say it again."

"Asheville."

"Address?"

"Thirty-eight Biltmore Forest Road."

"Best friend?"

"Wait," Jana complained. "This is like trying to memorize lines I already know by heart. It doesn't . . ."

"Best friend?" Mars repeated, cutting her off.

Jana was embarrassed. All she could think to say for the longest time was *Michael*. She didn't have any best friends. By not being there all those years, her mother had taught Jana to be her own best friend.

"Sherry Simmons," Jana lied. Sherry's name had simply come to mind. Michael was Jana's best friend. There was no doubt. Jana knew better than to say it to Mars. He wouldn't understand.

"What's your favorite—"

Jana cut him off. "Stop it, Mars. I don't want to do this anymore."

"Last one, I promise. Who were you with the night you died?"

"Michael Haynes, Nathan Mills, Sherry Simmons," she recited. "Okay, that's it."

"What does her dad do for a living?"

"Locksmith. Hey, you said 'last one' already."

The bus waited. Mars and Jana approached from behind.

An open jeep full of jerky-looking boys was parked across the street from the bus. Mars's gait stiffened when he saw them. He hurried his step, reaching for Jana's hand as he stepped off the curb. The bus door opened to the street. She gave him her hand and stepped along quickly to keep up. Jana tasted strawberries with every breath.

There were four of them in the jeep. And one sitting on the hood. Losers, Jana thought.

In her old school, they were called streeters. They were the kids who hung out on the street and in parking lots day and night, graduating from skateboards to cars without changing clothes. Streeters looked like they smelled of gasoline. Their graffiti were black tire marks left in streaks in the middle of the street.

The one who sat on the hood of the open-top vehicle wore a jean jacket with the sleeves ripped off. He held an aluminum softball bat in one hand. As Mars and Jana stepped into the street, he slid from the hood. The others hopped out of the jeep. The one from the driver's seat stepped quickly in front of the others.

"Get on the bus," Mars said.

"Who are they? What do they want?"

"Rogues," Mars told her. "I'll tell you later. Get on the bus."

With a rapid inward curling of his outstretched arm, he pulled Jana to him, then urged her on, letting go of her hand and stepping away from her.

"Now!" Mars said loudly over his shoulder to Jana.

Without hesitation, Mars strode into the middle of the pavement to cut off the group of advancing streeters from Jana and the bus. The driver of the jeep was carrying the bat now. He wore a light blue policeman's uniform shirt with a yellow-and-black shoulder patch. The shirt was without buttons, open entirely from top to bottom.

Jana did as she was told. She caught a glimpse of the streeter with the bat as she rushed to the bus. He had a tattoo of a skull and crossbones on his chest.

The bus door was open. Jana clambered up the three steps. Her school shoes clattered down the aisle as she flew to a window near the back. Jana fidgeted with the latches and managed to pull the top glass down six inches.

"Kiss the ground," she heard the one in front shout at Mars. "You know the drill, you Slider piece of puke. Kiss the ground!"

Mars kept standing. His arms lifted out slightly from his sides. He bent forward at the waist. Jana could see his shoulders rise and fall with his breathing.

"I ain't going nowhere," Mars said calmly, loudly. The actor in Jana instantly recognized the change in his voice. He was being street tough in a stage voice. Mars was acting. And he was good. But he should have been running away, she thought. There were five of them.

There was motion off to the side. Jana looked to her right in time to see that one of the gang had drifted down the street and was flanking Mars. The others closed ranks to Mars's left. Mars had turned toward them. He was blind to the rushing movement from the right. The kid was running hard, straight at Mars.

Jana screamed.

It was too late. The running streeter slammed into Mars in a headfirst dive. The two of them fell sideways onto the pavement. She heard their bodies hit the street.

Jana screamed again.

CHAPTER FIFTEEN

MARS'S SHOULDER CRACKED.

Fully materialized to fight off the Rogues, Mars suffered a blinding pain that bolted through his arm and neck as he hit the pavement. By reflex alone, he managed to keep his head from slamming against the street. He drew up his knees and struggled to catch his breath.

The kid on top of him spread out like a fat spider working quickly to hold a captured moth in its place. The other Dead School dropouts rushed to join the assault. They pulled his arms and legs, and roughly turned Mars facedown on the street. His mouth and chin were scraped in the process. His lip bled.

The lead Rogue poked the end of the aluminum bat into the middle of their victim's back. They had him pinned. The one who had blindsided him took Mars's wallet out of his back pocket.

The bat lifted while they rolled him over on his back. They wanted his pants.

It was tradition for Rogues to pants a Slider when they were lucky enough to catch one on the Planet.

Jana rushed to the front of the bus.

She had to help him. She didn't know how, but she had to do something. Her head spun. She'd tell the streeters that her father was a cop. They'd leave.

The bus door was closed.

"Open the door!" she shouted. "They're killing him!"

"Can't," the driver said, without so much as looking away from the windshield. "The door doesn't work like that."

"I don't care how it works," she said. "Open it!"

Jana backed up a step. With both hands, she pulled the chrome handle next to the driver, the handle that opened the folding door. It wouldn't budge. Bending her knees, she put her whole weight into pulling the handle. Jana pulled so hard she ended up sitting on the floor of the bus. Her arms trembled from exertion.

She got to her feet somehow and flung herself at the thick glass of the door. Jana pounded on it with both hands. It was no use.

His jeans were down over his shoes and off by the time Mars could catch his breath. The pain slowly subsided. He sucked air into his chest, tightening his belly.

There weren't enough of them to hold him still. Rogues didn't have the courage to get the best of him. His body slowly mended. Mars focused. He arched his shoulder against the pavement for leverage.

With a single thrust, Mars twisted sideways. His limbs flexed on solid muscle and in one instant he freed both arms from their clutches and managed to kick a standing Rogue a direct hit just below his knee.

The Rogues scattered instantly. Except for the leader, who lunged toward Mars. Sunlight flashed from the blade of a small knife he held in his hand. Mars spun over on all fours, scraping his bare knee on the rough pavement of the street. His other knee was flying in a roundhouse backward kick, which caught the Rogue with the knife squarely across his legs. The Rogue fell.

Somehow, before Mars could drop him, the Rogue had managed to cut Mars's leg across the flesh of his thigh. The knife blade was razor sharp. It left a deep slash that burned like a hot wire had been drawn across the meat of his upper leg.

Mars never stopped moving and was on his feet in a flash. The lead Rogue scooted backwards on his bottom as quickly as he could to keep from being kicked in the face. Mars picked up his jeans in one hand, flung them over his shoulder, then quickly snatched up the bat.

The Rogues backed off in a wave.

Mars had the moment.

He pointed the bat at each Rogue in turn until he found the one holding his wallet. Mars held out his free hand, palm up, and flipped his fingers twice. The Rogue stepped forward and placed the wallet on the street in front of Mars. He wore a large steel safety pin in one ear. Mars picked up his wallet and flung the bat away. It clattered to the street.

Mars was in jockey shorts and shoes. Blood ran down one leg from the cut.

The Rogues were through. He turned his back on them, stuck his wallet in the back pocket of his jeans, and pulled on his pants. One of the Rogues picked up the bat and walked away. The others followed him to the jeep.

Jana was saying something out one of the bus windows. As he watched, she left the window and moved frantically to the front of the bus. Mars latched his pants.

He limped on his cut leg to the door of the bus, and couldn't help but smile. He'd won. His mouth tasted like blood. His torn lip hurt. And so did his shoulder and leg. It was a really good day on the Planet. He swore he heard a bird singing.

Mars was back to the bus on time. Jana had feared it would leave without him. She stood at the front of the bus. Mars easily pushed open the door from the outside.

"You're hurt," she said, holding out her hands to him, her arms.

"It's nothing."

"Here," she said, and Mars took one of her hands. She tugged him up the steps of the bus. "You're bleeding. Are you sure you're okay?"

"I'm fine," Mars said. "Just glad I wore underwear today."

"It's not funny. They could have killed you!"

"Aren't you forgetting something, Webster? I'm already dead."

Jana dropped her gaze and stared at the oval of blood that had soaked through the upper leg of his jeans. He felt awfully warm to be dead, she thought. Even when he was beaten up and bleeding, his body was warmer than hers. He could open the bus door and she couldn't. Mars wasn't as dead as she was. At least on the Planet, the planet where Michael lived.

"Well, they could have cut off your ears," Jana said. "Or something."

The bus was moving. She let go of his hand.

Mars motioned Jana toward the back of the bus. They sat there together so Mars could stretch out his leg.

Jana couldn't help herself. She wiped blood from his lower lip with her fingers. It was sticky and cold. She wiped her hand on the front of her blouse. His soft lower lip looked as inviting as ever.

"Who were those guys?" Jana asked, still breathless from the horror of being trapped on the bus while Mars was being attacked.

"Rogues," Mars said. "Dead School dropouts. Rogues are Sliders who leave campus and don't come back. They're rebels, I guess. They don't have long out there. You almost never see the same one twice."

"Someone comes by and picks them up?" Jana asked.

"You might say that." Mars pushed his hand through his hair. "But everybody gets a chance to change, Webster, even Rogues. Even if it's only for a day or two."

"They don't look to me like they want to change."

"True," Mars agreed. "Rogues go to all the high school funerals, looking for tagalongs. I should have remembered that."

Jana watched people's houses slide by outside the bus window. She was thinking of Michael and how they were supposed to have a house in Ireland someday and maybe one in southern France. And an apartment in New York.

She was suddenly ashamed of herself. Mars was hurt and she wasn't even considering that. She should do something to help him.

"Take off your pants," Jana said. "We need to do something with your leg."

"It's okay," Mars said.

"They cut you," she insisted. "You're bleeding. It's deep. We need to make a bandage or you'll bleed to death."

"It stopped bleeding," Mars told her. "It wasn't that bad at all."

Jana stared at the blood-soaked faded jeans stretched over his thigh. The stain looked like it was drying. It wasn't glistening like before. She wanted to touch it to see for sure, but thought it would hurt him if she did.

"You're going to figure this out sooner or later, so you may as well know," Mars said. "It goes away."

"What goes away?"

"Whatever you do to your body, it doesn't stick. Sliders and Risers are a little different, but it's about the same. You can cut your hair, Webster, but that's about all. It's not part of your body. I mean, it's not alive or anything."

"We're not alive," Jana said.

"Okay. But we have our bodies for now."

"So if I were a Slider, instead of being a spirit who can't open doors, I could get into fistfights on the Planet and thump people on the head at funerals and . . ."

"And use a cell phone. And be seen when you want to be seen and heard when you want to be heard. You might be able to do some of this stuff with practice already. Risers don't usually leave campus on their own, so we don't know for sure."

"Either way, though, I could do more on the Planet as a Slider than a Riser," she said. "That's right, isn't it?"

"Yes."

"And if I can do more the way I am now, I want to do it now. I want to leave campus with you tonight. Will you show me how?"

Mars didn't answer.

"Look, I'm not stupid, Mars. I can leave campus on my own if I can leave at all. How does campus work, anyway? I don't get it."

"We're not supposed to understand everything," he said. "I don't understand everything. That's the whole point of Dead School, Webster. And for some reason that's where they want us."

"You mean the Regents Council?"

"Davis is telling you more than I realized," Mars said. "No one in school knows much about them. But they're in charge."

"They're angels," Jana suggested. A tiny smile at

the edge of her mouth said at least she hoped so.

"More like old librarians than angels. Everything's not going to make sense in the beginning, Webster. Trust me, I've been trying to figure out all this for several months now."

Jana looked at the tear in his lip. It was healing.

"Okay, your body feels pain when you're in Dead School. You can walk around with it and poke it with sharp objects. I got all that. But if I cut off my hand, it reattaches itself?"

"Yes, your body fixes itself. It returns to the way it was when you died."

"That's what Wyatt was showing me in the library," Jana said.

"He was being stupid, but that's what he was doing. And he wanted to gross you out to, you know, get a rush from your reaction," Mars said. "It's against the rules to damage your body on purpose to have an effect on someone else. See, that's the most important rule—you can't impede other students. It's best to go off campus if you want to experiment."

Mars spoke softly and watched Jana's eyes to make sure she was understanding what he said. His eyes gave off warmth just like the rest of his body did. Jana secretly wanted to touch his eyebrows with her fingers to see if they sparked. Thinking such a thing about another boy made her think of Michael. Fast.

"I want to go to the Planet tonight," Jana reminded Mars. "I want to be with Michael."

"You'll get demerits."

"You sound like Arva. How do demerits work?"

"Nobody but Arva *sounds* like Arva," Mars said in an imitation of her croaky voice.

Jana laughed. It was the day of her funeral and it felt good to laugh. The warmth from sitting next to Mars had soaked through her skin and she felt warm inside.

"Look, I can't answer all your questions. Risers and Sliders are different. I've been trying to figure out my end of things since I've been here. So I don't really know how demerits work for Risers. I've heard of one or two Risers getting into enough trouble here that they become Sliders. But I don't know how it works exactly. I'm not sure anyone does."

When someone tells you he doesn't know something, it makes you believe everything else he said. Jana believed everything Mars told her.

"Can I tell you a secret?" she asked. "I never had,

you know, just a friend I could tell secrets to."

Mars nodded. His eyes found hers.

"I want to kill Michael," Jana said.

Mars's dimple disappeared. He looked away.

"I was going to ask you to help," Jana confessed. "But I really think I should do it myself."

She loved him that much, Mars thought.

Mars knew that love wasn't all red-paper valentines and candy hearts. Love wasn't always joy. Love could be hot-blooded pain down to the bone. Sometimes love was despair. And sometimes love was wrong. Jana loved Michael enough to kill him for it. Jana loved Michael to death.

CHAPTER SIXTEEN

"OH GOD, HE RAPED YOU!"

Arva's face, when she first saw Jana at their table in the cafeteria, was a mixture of wild-eyed shock, anguish, and triumph. Arva had been right, after all. Rules had been broken and this was what it led to. Wanton savagery.

"No," Jana said. "Not at all." She shook her head and drew her lips together, admonishing Arva for such a wicked flight of fantasy.

Jana arrived late to lunch and had rushed in without going by the girls' room. Her appearance was the last thing on her mind. She set her bottles of water on the table being shared by Arva, Beatrice, and Christie. Everything was just like yesterday, only Jana's clothes were a wreck.

She tucked the back of her wrinkled blouse into her skirt waist as best she could. Her face was smeared with dirt from having wiped away her tears with the back of her hand. She tugged her hair behind her ear.

Jana breathed in. At least her clothes didn't smell like Ivory soap so much. She smelled like grass and dirt and sweat. She smelled like Earth. Like life.

Beatrice stared at Jana's face. The yellow dart fins leaned left and right, then left again.

"A quick roll in the hay with Dreamboat?" Christie asked Jana pleasantly, getting his name wrong on purpose. "Your eyes look greener than before. They say your eyes are brighter after, you know, you've been doing it."

Jana grinned and shook her head no. In the world as viewed by Christie, a roll in the hay with Mars Dreamcote was the best thing that could happen to a junior at Dead School. Jana glanced around the room as she sat down.

Everyone had blue-tinted faces, those who didn't have their faces bashed in or their heads sitting next to them on chairs. A third of the students looked like refugees from train wrecks. Another third looked worse. It didn't seem fair to Jana that when she showed up with her blouse untucked and a little dirt on her face, it caused a riot.

"There's blood on your blouse!" Arva pointed her finger at the place where Jana had wiped her fingers after touching Mars's wounded mouth.

"It's chocolate," Beatrice said. She looked excited. "You had chocolate on the Planet. When I was there, I couldn't eat anything. Now that I'm here, I don't want to."

"No," Jana told her. "It's blood."

"I'd forgotten about chocolate," Beatrice said quietly.

"See," Arva creaked out. "I knew something awful would happen."

"Leave her alone," Christie said. "Funerals are hard." She jerked her shoulders and quietly said, "Ouch."

"Are you okay, Jana?" Beatrice asked. "How do you feel? Was it okay?"

"I feel like I've been dead a long time," Jana answered honestly.

Jana screwed the cap off a bottle of water and finished half of it in one long drink. She felt like she'd been dead a long time, but she also felt like something new was alive inside her. She had a plan to come up with and to put into action.

Arva kept talking. "I knew it," she rasped. "I knew something awful would happen when you chose a Slider to go with you."

"Maybe a Slider chose her," Mars said.

He was standing behind Jana's chair. He'd walked up to the table of girls without their noticing his approach. All eyes had been on Jana.

Arva stuck her current bottle of water in her mouth and looked away. If she could have sniffed and sucked water at the same time, she would have. Beatrice and Christie beamed their best sunshiney faces and smiled at Mars.

Jana closed her eyes momentarily when Mars lightly touched her on the shoulder. She accepted his warmth now without surprise. It came inside her like an invited guest. Instead of speaking, or doing anything at all to greet Mars, she let the warmth of the moment have its way.

"I hope you don't mind, ladies. There's someone I'd like to introduce to you."

The kid in glasses from the library stepped forward. He'd been standing behind Mars.

"This is Jameson. He's just agreed to be Jana's personal tutor. She's having a little trouble concentrating in class these days."

Jameson pushed his glasses up on his nose and turned red. He wasn't used to talking to girls. After securing his glasses in place, he didn't know what to do with his hands. So he pushed his glasses against his face again.

"Hi," Beatrice said.

"Hi," Christie echoed, then added a shoulder bounce and one "ouch."

"Davis," Mars said, waiting.

Arva took the bottle of water from her mouth. "Hello," she squeaked, only glancing in the general direction of the two boys standing at the table.

Mars took his hand away and stepped back. A trail of warmth lifted from Jana. She scooted her chair sideways to look at him. His face was clean and his hair was combed. There wasn't a bit of blood or even a slight bruise on his face.

But the blood had been there. The dark stain was still on his faded jeans. Like he'd cut out his own heart and stuffed it in his pocket.

"Things to do," Mars said. He threw one hand open and tilted his head, as if to say there was no getting around it. His blue eyes slid over Jana before he turned and walked away, leaving Jameson behind.

Without the slightest limp from having had his leg sliced, Mars left the cafeteria. He'd never sat down. He hadn't gone through the line. Mars got his water from the fountain in the hall and used his cafeteria time for other things.

Jana watched Wyatt rise awkwardly from a table of Sliders by the windows. He glanced at her with a flash of his one good eye, but wouldn't catch her gaze. He seemed to be frowning. It was hard to tell for sure, because half his face was shaped into a permanent frown. Leaning to one side on his damaged leg with every step, Wyatt followed Mars out the cafeteria doors.

Jameson sat in the empty chair at the table.

"Haven't we run into each other before?" Jana asked. She looked at his straight brown hair and cowlick. It was a small distraction compared to Beatrice's yellow dart fins.

Jameson did not reply.

"In the library," she tried.

Jameson nodded. He started to say something, then changed his mind.

"I'm Jana Webster," she continued, knowing how

shy boys like Jameson could be around girls. She didn't add "of Webster and Haynes." It was just her for now. Jana intended to see that it didn't stay that way for long.

Jameson walked Jana to fourth period.

Arva approved. You could see it on her face.

Jana stopped off at the girls' restroom while Jameson waited outside. They had a few minutes between classes. No one knew how many, because the clocks were screwy. And cell phones didn't work, so you couldn't check the time. Maybe they started class when everyone got there. There wasn't anyplace else to go.

She checked the stall doors. There were no toilets in the stalls. Each stall was outfitted with a simple oak chair you could sit on. It was a place to sit and think, if you were in the habit. Or a place to be alone, when you needed to cry.

Thank heaven they had paper towels. Jana ran water on two towels and washed her face in the mirror. She ran her hands over her hair. With careful fingers, she felt the uplifted lock of hair on the back of her head, the small crack of skull underneath.

She folded a corner of the wet paper towel and washed carefully around the corners of her eyes.

Jana saw her mother in her own face. Just like that and for only a second, her mother appeared then vanished. Had her mother known love when she was sixteen or had she been too beautiful?

Jana knew love. You couldn't love without being able to forgive. It sounded like one of Arva's rules, but it was true. She forgave Michael the minute she left the funeral. He was weak without her. He was devastated by the loss.

Her mother was a different story. If she knew love, she knew the love you take, not the love you give. Jana wished her mother had been someone she could talk to. But she wasn't a listener. She made regular pronouncements and requests and took it for conversation. She used people to talk to. Jana's mother never talked *with* anyone.

Marilyn Webster was a born user. Using alcohol and drugs, and people, was all she knew how to do. She used her beauty to take the things she wanted. She was good at it. Jana had to get Michael away from her mother.

"What's with the teachers?"

"They're dead," Jameson said. "Is that what you mean?"

"Got that," Jana said. "But do they have to be so

boring? It's like they hate what they're doing."

"Best in their fields. They rotate through for a year and then they're gone. Some are rather fascinating, but you're right, most of them don't know how to teach. I guess they provide examples of people who have done things well. Maybe they've done things we were planning on doing."

"How would we ever know?"

"You can ask them questions if you like," Jameson said. "Most students just sit through class, though. We're all trying to deal with being dead, I suppose."

Jameson only looked at her when he was certain she wasn't looking at him.

Jana asked him about the original guidebook in the library. "So, you understand what it says, then? And there *are* rules for Dead School?"

"Bits and pieces," Jameson said in an apologetic voice. "Different people wrote different parts at different times. They all used the language differently. Or the language changed. Some of it is Aramaic. Some of the languages we don't even have names for now. It's all very ancient. But yes, there are rules. Some are stated plainly. Others are parables."

Jana stopped walking and grabbed his arm. "Can I leave campus on my own at night? Can Risers do that?"

"Oh, it doesn't actually say that." Jameson's face reddened when she touched him. Jana took her hand away.

"The main rule in the book is free will," he continued. "You have free will to make your own choices here. If you make the right choices, it can be like atonement, you know? And if you make wrong choices . . . well, you can go backwards. Most Risers just try to ride it out the way things are. The status quo is in your favor, so to speak."

They continued walking. Jana's thoughts tumbled quickly into some sort of understanding. "So, you can *rise* to the occasion or *slide* backwards. Is that it?"

"Yes," Jameson said. "Mostly that's it. There are earlier rules too. I keep finding one more here and one more there."

"Okay," Jana said. "How do I become a Slider?"

This time Jameson stopped walking. He looked at Jana for the first time while she was looking at him. He pushed his glasses up on his nose.

"That would be going backwards," he stammered.

"Let's think of it as a place to start," Jana said.

She smiled. If going backwards meant she would be in Michael's arms again, then backwards was the only way to go. Sliders could physically interact on the Planet and Jana needed to interact with Michael. Right away. Besides, she thought, it wouldn't hurt to feel a little warmer while she figured out a way to kill him.

Michael's car was parked out front.

Sherry and Nathan sat on the porch swing at Jana's house. Nathan was worried about the voice mail he'd received on his cell.

"At first I thought it was God," he said. "You know, the voice at the funeral home. And when he asked what time was good for me, I thought he meant what time was good for me to meet my Maker."

Nathan did his lawn mower laugh, but it was all worry and nerves. Nothing was funny right now.

"It's not God," Sherry said. "Will you shut up about that already?"

"I know that now. I think it's the guy from the bowling alley. The one who showed up out of nowhere and was giving her CPR. He must have taken her cell phone. We have to find out who that guy is."

"Why is Michael taking so long?" Sherry asked.

"Her mom's a wreck. You know how it is. She's totally out of it. He's putting her to bed or something."

"He just better *not* get in there with her," Sherry said. "That's all I've got to say. Why did they have to bury her with Michael's ring, anyway? He's not with her anymore."

"And you are," Nathan said. "Everybody knows that already."

CHAPTER SEVENTEEN

JANA WAS EARLY.

Her drama elective was taught onstage in the auditorium. A semicircle of student desks was arranged at the back of the stage. Only a few of the acting students were already in their places, standing near their desks. Jana recognized Henry Sixkiller instantly. Nobody but Henry had hair like that. His head was three inches of black brush that stuck straight up and straight out from neck to crown.

Jana smiled at him. He smiled back, his Cherokee cheeks tightening into shiny apples, and walked over.

"Hey," he said. "I'm Henry." He thrust out his

hand to Jana. Actors can have courage onstage even when they're not acting. It was interesting to see that the shy, note-passing kid in homeroom found his charm on the stage.

"Hi," she said. "Jana Webster."

She shook his hand. There was no heat in the touch. A ragged scar inside his grip pressed against her palm.

"I know, I know," he said. "Of Webster and Haynes. I sit in front of you in homeroom."

"Second and third hour too."

"Hey, you went to your funeral today," Henry said. "Are you doing okay?"

"I'm fine."

"No one can believe you took a Slider." Henry made an actor's face, opening his eyes wide and tossing his pupils from side to side. He feigned shock by dropping his mouth open and bringing up one hand to cover it.

Jana grinned. She loved being around other actors.

"I thought it was cool," he said.

"Not stupid?"

"Not stupid," Henry said. "It was brave."

"Thank you," Jana said.

"It's Mars Dreamcote, then? Second day in school and you're already hooked up. Guess I wasn't fast enough."

"You never know," Jana said. "The next new student may be the one. I love your hair, by the way. How do you get it like that?"

"Toaster," Henry replied.

Jana lifted her eyebrows.

"I stuck a fork in one."

Mars stood in front of her desk.

"Let's go, Webster," he said. He handed a slip of paper to Henry, who sat in the desk next to Jana's. "Give that to the teacher for me, Sixkiller, when she gets here. I'll owe you one."

Henry nodded.

Jana stood from her desk, once again enveloped in the warmth of being close to Mars. She hated to miss her first drama class, but Mars was going to help her find her way to Michael. And that was more important than school. Any school.

Mars walked Jana to the basement swimming pool. They were alone now. The Risers who dove from the high board only used the pool two days a week.

Small lights over the locker-room doors barely lit one end of the room. The remainder was dark. Jana stood alone in the edge of the dim light and waited. She felt cold surrounded by the darkness. She ducked her head slightly and let her hair fall forward in an effort to keep her face warmer.

Except for two feet at one end of the pool that caught and reflected the dim light on its surface, the water was black.

Mars came out of the boys' locker room in red swimming trunks. He turned on the underwater lights. He left the overhead lights turned off. Lit up from underneath, the water was deep and pretty. Jana stared at it. The pool looked like a three-dimensional movie screen, waiting for her to move across it, inside it.

He stood next to her. Standing near his body was like standing in sunlight for Jana. She wanted to run her hand along his bare shoulder, down his muscled arm, until their hands met. Jana shook her head. If she touched Mars that way, it would only make her want Michael more. If she kissed him to swallow his warmth, it would only make her desperate to kiss Michael again.

"Aren't you getting in?" she asked.

Mars nodded. "We need to talk," he said. "This is our only chance at school."

"Okay. It's kind of spooky here."

"Do you swim?"

"I'm clumsy at it," Jana admitted. "But I float real well. I'm buoyant."

"You're not afraid, are you?"

Jana waited. "Yes," she finally said. "I'm afraid all the time."

Mars let it soak in.

"What are you afraid of, Webster? Me?"

"No, not you. It's everything." Jana bit her lip. "I'm afraid of everything. Aren't you scared to be here?"

"Maybe," Mars said. "Sometimes."

"I guess I'm afraid of being alone."

"Being dead is like that."

"That's it," she said. "Exactly that. I'm afraid of being dead."

Jana turned to look at him. She'd said too much and wondered if he noticed. When Mars looked back at her, his blue eyes sparkled in the reflected light of the pool. Like lenses that magnified existing light and color, his eyes were small blue mirrors. Jana saw her face in his eyes. There was one of her in each blue eye.

They were both afraid, she realized.

Mars looked away and Jana felt a chill.

"Jameson told me you want to be a Slider," Mars said. "That's not the way to go, Webster. You don't want to go in that direction."

"Don't tell me what I want," she warned him.

"I know what you want," Mars told her. "You want Michael."

"I'm in love with him. He's in love with me. Michael wants to be with me, Mars. And I need him here. Does that bother you?"

"Some of it does," he admitted. "I don't think you should kill him."

"Why not?" she asked. "You're the one who is all about *murder*, aren't you?"

"Okay, okay," he said. "I wrote those messages in your notebooks. I wanted you to know . . . to remember. You didn't just fall, Webster. I was there. I saw everything."

"Yes, I did just fall," Jana insisted. Her words echoed off the tiled walls.

"I'll show you later."

"What were you doing there, anyway?"

"Just walking through," Mars said, "remembering what it was like to go bowling."

"It hurts. That's what it's like to go bowling," Jana said.

"You saw me, Webster. You don't remember, but you saw me. As you were falling, you looked right at me. Your eyes looked like green traffic lights. It was like you were asking for help."

"No," Jana said quietly.

"I watched you die."

Mars turned away. He dove into the pool.

Her eyes were greenish at best, not as bright green as traffic lights like Mars had said. The color was plain. Not like her mother's eyes. Her mother's eyes were rich with pure, photographic color. Jana's were dull in comparison.

His legs scissor-kicked just under the surface of the underlit water. Waves of eerie light and shadows, reflected through the movement and color of the water, moved around the walls of the room. It looked like she was dreaming.

Jana was dreaming of Michael being with her again. As soon as she was a Slider, she'd find a way to save Michael from his empty life without her. Jana would find a way that didn't hurt him. Or if it did, it would be fast, like pulling a tooth.

Sitting down beside the pool, Jana tested the

water with her fingers. The water wasn't as cold as she feared. She tugged her skirt under her bottom and, sitting sideways, took off her school shoes and kneesocks.

Jana wanted to be in the water. She wanted the weight of the water wrapped around her like a blanket. She put her feet in and wiggled her toes.

Soon Mars was next to her, his elbows over the edge of the pool. His dark hair was soaked through, and water ran down his face in tiny rivers.

"I wanted you to know this is here," Mars said. "That it's an option. Aren't you coming in?"

"Don't know." Jana pushed her feet out into the water until her toes appeared above the surface. "Looks wet."

"There are swimsuits in the girls' locker room."

"I don't think so. The last time I wore someone else's clothes . . . well, shoes, anyway . . . I mean, I might drown."

"I'll save you if you do."

"Are there towels in the locker room?"

"Yes," Mars said.

"Are they plaid and pleated?"

"Normal, regular dead people towels," Mars assured her. "Swim in your underwear, Webster. I won't watch, I promise. I'll wait at the bottom of the pool."

"But you have to come up for air," she said.

"Turn the lights off, then. The pool's the best thing they've got in this place."

The water was warmer now than when she'd first put her feet in. It was Mars, she decided. His body temperature had warmed the pool while he swam, while he loitered next to her, kicking aimlessly behind him to keep the weight off his elbows on the pool's edge. The water was definitely warmer. And it was deep. Jana wanted it that way. She wanted to be covered up entirely in water.

"I guess I'd better hurry," Jana said.

CHAPTER EIGHTEEN

MICHAEL SHUDDERED.

A chill climbed up his spine every time he listened to the voice mail. It was Jana's voice. There was no mistaking it. And the call was from her cell phone.

"Michael. It's me."

Marilyn Webster was his concern now and that gave him the creeps, as well. She smelled strongly of stale wine and had breathed with her mouth open through the entire funeral. She'd practically ruined his best dress shirt with makeup and tears.

"I can't be alone," Jana's mother said. She had one elbow stuck in the air with her hand bent behind her neck, trying to start the zipper on the back of her black dress.

"Turn around," he said.

She nearly fell onto the bed when she did. Michael unzipped her dress. Somehow she managed to pull her dress over her head without falling down. The material lifted her hair and it didn't quite fall back into place.

Jana's mother sat on the edge of the bed and kicked away her shoes.

"Stay with me, Michael."

No. She would be asleep in two seconds. She'd taken a handful of pills on their way to the bedroom. Michael had seen it all before. Jana's mother reached for pills as often as a smoker reached for cigarettes. She was a walking pharmacy, when she could walk at all. And that was on top of the wine.

"Be a good girl," Michael said. "Go to bed."

"Good girl," Marilyn said, mimicking him.

"That's right, go to sleep now."

She lay back on the bed, her eyes closed. Michael opened the drawer of her bedside stand, took something from the back that Jana had never known was there, and slipped it into the side pocket of his suit jacket.

He looked at Marilyn carefully before leaving the room. She had been a model when she was young. A supermodel. At sixteen, she'd made the covers of magazines. She'd dated NFL football players and movie stars. She did TV commercials for shampoo. Michael didn't see it when he looked at her. She just looked thin.

Jana was twice as pretty as her mother. Everyone knew that but Jana. She'd been the perfect girl for him to be seen with.

"I'm still here. I'm always here."

But, he thought, pretty didn't matter anymore.

Standing on the porch, holding up his hand for Nathan and Sherry to wait to say anything, Michael called the lady next door. She took care of Jana's mother when Jana wasn't there.

"Fine," he said when she asked how he was. "But Marilyn isn't. Can you come over after a while and check on things? Spend the night if you want to. There's plenty of food in the fridge. And the money is where it usually is if you need to buy anything."

"Call me."

Did he dare?

• • •

Jana considered her options. She didn't have all day.

She left her shoes and socks on the wooden bench in the girls' locker room and looked through the swimsuits that were stacked in rows on an open shelf. They were bright red one-piece suits with wide shoulder straps. She held one up. The bottom half was huge compared to the top. When the whole thing got wet, the bottom would bag to her knees.

Jana struggled to work the buttons on her skirt through the double-sewn buttonholes. She took off her skirt and blouse.

She couldn't wear her bra into the pool. It wouldn't be dry in time for fifth period. Same thing if she put her blouse on without her bra and got into the pool. And she couldn't wear the school's famous granny panties into the pool either. They'd weigh five pounds wet and be around her ankles in no time.

Jana ran out of options.

She took off everything, bra and panties too. She placed Michael's class ring inside her shoe on the bench. Jana wrapped herself in one of the towels from the rack by the door and slipped out of the locker room. She'd seen where Mars had turned on the pool lights. She walked quickly to the switches and flipped them, one after the other, until the lights inside the pool went out.

Jana heard a motor whir. She'd accidentally turned on the pumps that sucked water from the drain at the bottom of the pool and sent it through jet sprays to agitate the surface of the water for the high dives. Jana wasn't sure what it was, but she could hear the water moving. It sounded something like a whirlpool.

The spill of light from the locker rooms was enough to get into the pool by. Three or four feet from this end of the pool, she would be in darkness. She'd be safe.

Jana couldn't see Mars, but he was in there somewhere. She used the exit ladder to climb backwards into the pool, removing the towel as her knees submerged. She tossed the towel on the concrete, and with a quick push backwards, Jana was in the water altogether.

It was wonderful. The water was as warm as a bath. If they'd let her sleep here, she would.

Jana dog-paddled with her head above water to the edge of the light, then she dropped under the surface with her legs stretched tight, her feet together. Chlorine stung her eyes. Jana held her breath until her toes gently touched bottom, then she came back up to the surface by waving her hands like wings.

With her head above the water, she pushed her hands through her wet hair. Even her hair felt warm. She swam back to the edge of the pool. Jana made circles with her feet, lazily keeping her chin just above the surface of the pool.

"I thought you couldn't swim." Mars's voice reached out to her from the darkness.

"I'm not as bad as I thought," Jana said. "Where are you?"

She turned around. Jana placed one hand back over her shoulder to grip the edge of the pool. She kicked slowly to stay in place.

"Here," he said, splashing her.

Mars appeared from the darkness. Moving toward her. He stopped where she could see the outline of his face. But his warmth didn't stop. It moved toward her and touched her. An underwater wave of heat bathed her body. It was impossible, she thought, that he was only one or two degrees warmer than she was.

Jana was surprised how comfortable she felt being naked in the water and so close to Mars. He wasn't the flirty, pushy type. Other than flipping Jana the bird her first day on the bus, he'd never misbehaved. Jana wasn't afraid of Mars. She was afraid of herself.

"I was sitting on the bottom," he said. "I felt the water surge when you turned on the pumps. It causes a current toward the drain. You're not supposed to go near the drain when the pumps are on. If you put your hand on the drain, and you aren't strong enough, it can hold you there."

"Oh, I never go to the bottom, except my toes," Jana said. "Too buoyant to sink, remember? I think it's my ears. They're like water wings."

"It's your lungs," Mars said. "It's because you hold your breath. If you let all the air out of your lungs as you slip underwater, you'll drift down. It's like being suspended in air."

He moved a little closer, then his shoulders lifted from the water. Mars raised his hand in front of his face and pointed downward.

"Come on," he said. "Drop down. When your head is under, Webster, let all the air out of your chest."

Air bubbles rose above her as Jana submerged into darkness. Mars was right. She sank.

It felt like she was floating in air, a fallen leaf caught on the breeze. With the slightest motion of her hands she could rise a little, or drop farther. It was pitch black. When her feet touched bottom, she let her knees bend. Soon her fingers touched the bottom of the pool.

Then she stretched out backwards and stayed still, an inch from the bottom, maybe two. Jana felt the current created by the pumps slide under her. The drain was in the dark end of the pool. When she needed to breathe, Jana folded her arms over her chest and leaned forward and up until her legs where under her again. She pushed her feet hard against the bottom and shot to the surface like a rocket.

Michael drove.

Sherry was in the passenger seat, her feet on the dashboard. In the backseat, Nathan played the mystery voice mail message over and over again.

Nathan couldn't shut up about it. "It's the guy from the bowling alley, the one who tried to save her life. We have to find him before he finds us. We have to protect ourselves."

"Give it a rest," Michael said. "It was an accident.

Nobody killed her on purpose or anything."

"I don't care," Sherry said. "I don't care at all. You wanted to be rid of her, Michael, and you are. So what if she died? People do, you know. It's the same as breaking up with her. She just did it for you."

"With a little help," Nathan said. He punched the code to play the voice mail again.

Michael worried that it would keep him out of college if anyone found out. He didn't know whether or not what they had done was a crime. Technically it probably was, he thought. And he'd done it to her. If it was against the law, he was the one the cops would come for.

"You ever watch old movies?" Jana asked.

"Not really."

"I watch them all the time. Some of them over and over again. However old you are in a movie is how old you'll be forever. For actors, that's how old you are when someone watches the movie—even if it's a hundred years from now."

"Guess it's the same with characters in books," Mars said. "Tom Sawyer is the same age every time you read it."

They were in the water, near the edge of light, dog paddling.

"Here's one," Jana said. "All these actors were just kids. Jeff Bridges, Timothy Bottoms, Ellen Burstyn, Randy Quaid. They're all in high school and they go skinny-dipping in a swimming pool."

Jana waited. It was one of her all-time favorites. "And Cybill Shepherd. It was her first movie. Got it?"

"Not yet."

"*The Last Picture Show*," Jana finally said. "I'm sure you've seen it."

"I don't think so."

Jana bobbed below the surface and came up with her mouth full of water. She spit it out like a fountain. It left the taste of strawberries in her mouth.

"Okay, how many demerits do I have to get to become a Slider?"

"Don't joke about that, Webster."

"I'm not joking. How many? Ten, fifteen, twenty-five?"

"Probably a couple hundred. It's a major change of status here. And Risers are the good kids. You could do all sorts of stuff wrong and it wouldn't hurt you in the end. And since you're Risers to begin with, you don't do much rule breaking anyway."

"Maybe it's time to start," Jana said. "How many? No kidding. I need to know."

"Well," Mars said, "I think killing someone on the Planet would just about take care of it."

"Now you're joking," Jana said spitefully. "You know I can't do anything on the Planet without becoming a Slider first. I want to be like you. I want one foot on Earth, Mars. Is that so much to ask?"

"Give it a day, Webster. To think it through."

"I want Michael to see me! Can't you understand that? Before it's too late. Before . . . you know, things change."

"I understand," Mars said softly. "You're in love with him."

"Let's go back," Jana urged. "If you hold my hand like you did before, he'll be able to hear me. Let's go back."

"Maybe," Mars said. "You'll definitely get a few demerits for going off campus."

"Okay, then. That's settled. We'll do it tonight. What time?"

He didn't say anything. Jana felt alone despite the increasing warmth of the water when Mars was near.

"What's wrong?" she asked.

"I want to save a life, Webster. And you want to kill someone. You might say we have a conflict of interests."

"I'll help you if you help me," Jana said. "Conflict resolved."

Mars didn't say anything again.

"Well," Jana said loudly, "that's why you brought me here, isn't it? To ask me to do something."

"Maybe," Mars said.

"Listen." Jana spoke more softly. "I'm not stupid, Mars. I know you want or need something and it's important to you. And I know it has something to do with me. With where I died or how I died or something. You've been staring at me since the minute I was on the bus the first day. So just tell me. What are you afraid of telling me?"

Jana waited.

"Have you done the mazes yet?" he eventually asked.

"What?"

"The mazes in second hour. I saw you copying them down. Mr. Skinner's sharp, Webster. Try those mazes, do them all in order, and then we'll talk."

She might be on the plain side compared to her

mother, but Jana's body was just what most boys wanted. She was naked. She was only two feet away from him. And he was telling her to do her homework. Unbelievable.

"Are you kidding me?"

"No," Mars said pleasantly.

Jana wanted to call him a name. Mars was the most frustrating guy she'd ever met, the most frustrating guy on or off the Planet. Jana didn't have time for mazes. She wasn't Arva, afraid to do anything. And she wasn't her mother, who let everyone else do things for her, including raising Jana, because she was beautiful.

If there was something to do about the situation, Jana wanted to get it done. Now. Lights, camera, *action*!

"Look," she finally said. "Whatever you want me to do, I'll do it. So, let's go save a life and let's go kill Michael."

CHAPTER NINETEEN

JANA EARNED THREE DEMERITS.

Her hair was wet from the pool as she rushed to fifth period. The Virgins appeared side by side in their diaphanous gowns outside the open door to the classroom, blocking her path. Jana skidded to a halt.

She faced the shimmering Virgins and waited. They sang her name in four quick notes. *Jan-ah Web-ster.* Just like the warning Virgin in the library, the demerit Virgins sang alto. Each one beautifully intoned a number in a descending scale. *One. Two. Three.* They held out their hands and wagged their index fingers in front of her.

Yes! She had three demerits for skinny-dipping. Arva would just die.

"Shut up about your voice mail," Michael barked at Nathan, "and listen to mine."

He and Nathan were alone, parked behind the Waffle House in the west end of town. Michael held his cell between them and played the message Jana had left him.

"It's her," Nathan said in a whisper. It couldn't be, but it was.

"It was during the funeral."

"So was mine," Nathan said. He flipped his phone open and punched up his voice mail list. "Look, they were only a minute apart. He had her with him."

Michael snapped his cell shut. "We saw her body. It wasn't her on the phone. We saw her body in the casket. We were looking right at it when the calls came in. Her lips weren't moving, Nathan. Jana wasn't talking to anyone."

"How'd he do it?"

"He recorded her voice or something like that. She knew beforehand."

"No way," Nathan insisted.

"She must have known that guy, then. She'd

been going out with him or something behind my back."

Nathan shook his head. "I don't think so. She was totally devoted to you. I mean, that was the problem, wasn't it?"

"Yeah," Michael said. "It was like being smothered. She had our future all mapped out. We were supposed to spend every minute with each other until we got old and died."

"I got it," Nathan said. "He has her cell phone, right? So she has her own voice on there. She recorded voice memos and stuff. School notes or lines from a play. He lifted some of her words, rearranged them, recorded them that way, and played it back."

"Maybe," Michael said. There were all sorts of pauses in the message, like she was having trouble talking.

"Yeah, that's it. It's just that guy, then. In my message, he told us we have to tell someone what we did. Her message wasn't anything like that. She wasn't dead when she said those things."

"I guess not," Michael said. "Do you think she knows how she fell?"

Michael had the creeps again.

• • •

Arva didn't say a word on the bus after school. Jana didn't care.

In the dorm, they both said hello to Darcee and changed out of their school clothes. Jana agreed with Arva that their comatose roommate, even though she wasn't officially dead, was likely listening to the things they said. Jana thought maybe they should prop open Darcee's eyes once in a while so she could see things too.

Arva put on her blue cut-down prom dress skirt while Jana slipped into her capri pants. Jana could still smell the pool in her hair, on her skin.

"That boy has ruined you!" Arva finally announced. "You're going to end up just like them. You're going to be a Slider before you're through."

That was the idea, Jana thought, trying not to smile.

"Relax a little, Arva. I just went swimming. No big deal."

"Oh, I know what you did. Everyone is talking about it. You went swimming *naked*. Why didn't you just walk off campus and flag down a trucker on the highway?"

"Can't," Jana said. "They wouldn't see me."

Arva sputtered frog words and turned away

from Jana. "I'm leaving," she said. "I'm going across the hall."

"Wait," Jana said. *"Please."* Jana needed to do what she wanted to do, but she didn't want Arva hating her for it.

"What?"

"Sit down and talk to me a minute, then you can go."

The door opened and Pauline came in. She turned her top half around on her waist to pick up something from the bed.

"You still in love with that boy, what's-his-name?" Pauline asked Jana casually on her way back to the door. "Did he cry at the funeral?"

It took Jana a moment to realize that her senior roommate was talking to her.

"Michael," Jana said.

"Yeah," Pauline said. "You're wearing his ring and all. Well, he isn't going to love you forever. You're dead, he isn't. You do the math."

With that less than cheerful note, Pauline was out the door. Both halves.

"I knew I didn't like her," Jana said. "Now I know why."

"PMS," Arva told her. "Don't take it to heart. She

died like that and now she has PMS every day."

"Aren't we the lucky ones?"

"Yes, we are when you think about it," Arva said, barely whispering. There was a feather at the corner of her mouth. She plucked it away.

"Aren't you ever going to run out of those things?" Jana asked.

Arva shook her head. "I think it's the same one every time. Either that or I get a new batch when I wake up on the bus every morning. What did you want to talk about?"

"You and me. I want to get along, Arva. And I just keep upsetting you."

"I can't help it. You just . . . I don't know . . . You just seem to want to break every rule there is."

"It's tempting," Jana admitted. "But I don't think you realize that everything you say to me either begins or ends with 'better not.' I've started thinking of you as the Better Not Girl. I was going to have a bumper sticker printed with the words *Better Not* and stick it on your butt."

Arva grinned. There was a sense of humor in there somewhere, Jana was pleased to note.

"I'm sorry," Arva said, coughing up the words. "It must seem that way to you. But I'm your orientation counselor. It's my job to tell you what you can't do."

"Maybe we should think about what we can do. You can't follow every single rule there is even if you tried. I'm not trying to hurt anyone, Arva. I'm really not."

"Yourself. You might hurt yourself. When you break the rules, bad things happen. Like Beatrice. She let that guy touch her breast and . . . well, you know."

Jana didn't think it had anything to do with Beatrice. It was something else.

Arva paused to pluck the small black feather from the corner of her mouth again.

Jana had seen enough feathers in Arva's mouth to last an eternity.

"So, tell me," Jana said. "How did you die?"

Arva took a deep breath. It sounded like someone swallowing fuzz.

"Well, you already know it was prom, since I showed up here in this dress and all. So, it was prom. Only I never got there."

Alan was on time.

Arva had the most beautiful blue dress for prom. She wore a necklace that had been her grandmother's.

214

It was silver with a topaz teardrop dangle. Her grandmother called it a blue diamond. She wore her mother's expensive perfume. She dabbed it behind her ears so Alan would be intoxicated by scent when they danced.

When Alan had asked her to prom, he was just another guy in school. She hadn't really noticed him. In the two weeks leading up to prom, Arva began to like him better and better. He turned out to be almost dreamy, in fact. He had an older brother in medical school. He had his college picked out.

He was a quiet achiever, Arva decided, one of those people in school you would hear about later and not even remember. Except she would remember Alan. He asked her to prom before she even had time to worry about having a date. His family paid for a limo. Arva was thrilled.

The weather was perfect. Alan's mother and father had followed the limousine to Arva's house. They took pictures of the prom couple in the front yard. The driver held open the limo door for both of them. Alan adjusted his cuff links as he stepped in. For a moment, Arva was confused. She thought she'd seen him do that already—lift his foot, adjust his cuff links.

Alan sneaked champagne into the limo and Arva sipped some from a silver flask he carried inside his *tuxedo. They weren't old enough to drink legally and that made it exciting. Though the champagne had gone flat and it tasted awful, Arva loved sipping it anyway. She felt sophisticated.*

When Alan got the moonroof open, Arva stood on the leather seat and stuck her head and shoulders through the opening. He soon joined her, and the two of them rode through a small portion of her very special evening stuck out the top of a limousine. It was going to be the best night of her life. Until a small bird interrupted it.

A sparrow flew into Arva's face. She must have been talking, because her mouth was open. The little bird folded up like a feathered fist and slammed into and inside Arva's mouth. She felt like she'd been hit on the lip.

She had no choice. Arva swallowed it. Almost.

Arva choked. The bird was stuck in her throat. She couldn't cough. She couldn't breathe. With wild eyes, she looked down and saw blood on her dress. It was the sparrow's.

Her throat hurt. Arva tried to swallow. Then she tried to heave. She could do neither.

Arva made no sound at all.

She started bobbing her head up and down. She didn't know why, but she thought it would help. Bright lights showed up behind her eyes. Brilliant, stabbing shards of silver light, like fireworks going off. Her grandmother's necklace came free of its clasp. The topaz teardrop fell silently on its silver chain to the carpet of the limousine.

"I must have blacked out then," Arva said. "That's all I remember."

Bowling was an easier way to die, Jana thought. At least it was faster. It had to have been horrible for Arva. Jana pictured herself enacting the scene. She would bring both hands to her throat, then slowly let her hands fall, keeping her startled eyes open as she died. Her body would drop inside the limo, moments behind the fall of the shimmering topaz necklace.

"It was my own fault, though."

"Oh, I don't think so," Jana said. "I don't think so at all."

"No, it was. Sticking your head out of a moonroof in a limousine is against the rules. They tell you not to do it when you ride in one. I broke the rules and I died."

Jana considered it. The only thing Arva had done wrong was be happy.

"But look," Jana said, "I wasn't breaking any rules when I died. I guess I could have stayed at home and never gone bowling in my entire life." She laughed. "I could have lived with that."

Arva left.

Holding her cell phone, Jana sat on her bed with her back against the wall. When she called Michael again, he would answer. And he would say he couldn't wait to be with her.

Jana would tell him almost everything. She would tell him she was becoming a Slider to help them be together. She would tell him she was altering her destiny so they could be together forever. The way Jana and Michael would have been if she hadn't died first.

"I do bad things," Jana said out loud. "Arva says so." She bounded off the bed and marched across the room. She hit an imaginary mark, stopped, turned around dramatically, and completed her soliloquy.

"I'm Jana Webster, dead girl. When there is something bad to be done, I do it."

She was doing something that night, in fact. Mars had warned her not to go to sleep. That it would be late. When things outside were really dark.

She glanced at Darcee and said, "You're supposed to clap."

Jana's notebooks were stacked neatly on the desk in her dorm room, as they had been the day before, as they would be every day after school. She picked up her second-period notebook from the desk. And a pencil.

One by one, Jana worked the mazes. They were easy. She did them quickly. But when she got to the last one, she goofed it up. She had to erase her line twice. She spent as much time on the last maze as she had on the first five.

Turning to a clean page, Jana used her pencil to draw a big heart. I love Michael this much, she thought. No, bigger than that. Then it came to her and she wrote on the page, *I love Michael with all my heart.*

Jana said Michael's name, first and last, ten times fast. So he would know she was thinking about him.

Pauline was right. Michael would go on with his life without her. She needed to kill him as soon as possible. She couldn't be a Slider quickly enough unless she could be one that very night. If not, Jana wondered whether she could earn a couple hundred demerits in one day at Dead School and kill Michael tomorrow night.

It wouldn't be easy. She'd have to find a way to kill him that wasn't prolonged or painful. And she wanted Michael to see her when she did it, so the permanent memory of his death would also be of Jana. When he told people at Dead School how he died, she and Michael would hold hands like old couples on the Planet do when they tell a stranger how they met.

"Sometimes being in love means you have to kill somebody," she told Darcee.

You have to love someone a lot to kill them, Jana decided. And she loved Michael at least that much.

Jana returned to the mazes. She looked at each one in order and traced her lines. When she got to the last one, she saw the difference. She'd worked the first five mazes by taking three left turns at the beginning. The last one, though, started with three right turns and that's where she had messed up.

Skinner's boxes had conditioned Jana to turn left to begin the puzzles, even though she didn't realize she was making left or right turns. To solve the last puzzle, she had to turn the other direction and she wasn't used to it.

• • •

When Arva came back to the room, she was in a much better mood. She and Jana chatted merrily about this and that. Jana even mentioned Rogues to her in passing.

Arva finished her last bottle of water for the evening. "What are Rogues?" she asked.

Jana thought she was kidding. "Rogues, you know. They came to my funeral today. Rogues. The bad guys?"

Arva still wasn't getting it.

"Rogues, Rogues, Rogues," Jana said. "Dead School dropouts."

"There are no Dead School dropouts. You can't just quit. It's not in our guidebook. You're here or you're a vacancy. There's nothing in between."

"What about the vacancy in homeroom, Arva? You said she walked away and stayed overnight. And she was a Riser."

"It's just a rumor she did that. And if she did, then she's a vacancy." Arva coughed and sputtered. She spit out her final croaky words like they were poison. "Not an outlaw dropout monkey snatcher . . . *whatever*!"

"Trust me, there *are* Rogues," Jana insisted. "I

saw them. And they saw me."

"No. It's just not so."

"Arva, the guidebook the students put together isn't everything there is to know about Dead School."

"It's good enough for me," Arva said. She poked her tongue at a small feather stuck on her lower lip. "It's good enough for Risers," she added in a huff. "So it's good enough for me. And it's good enough for you."

Jana answered a knock at the door.

It was Mars. She felt his familiar warmth wash over her.

"Close your eyes, Davis," he said, peering over Jana's shoulder. "I'm coming in."

Jana waited. Arva sat on the bed with her legs crossed, her eyes squeezed tightly shut. She was frowning.

"Webster," Mars said, "you have to ask me."

"Ask you what?"

"To come in. I have to be invited."

Arva was shaking her head, but didn't say a word.

"Oh, please come in," Jana said.

Mars walked to the foot of Jana's bed. "I have to

show you something, Webster." He picked up her bowling shoes.

"Come here," he said. He held a shoe in each hand. As Jana approached, he flipped the right shoe over and held it out to her.

"Touch the sole. Rub your fingers across the bottom."

Jana didn't really want to, but she did. Her fingers slipped along the bottom of the bowling shoe like they were greased. She cocked her head, her hair falling over her cheek.

"Now, try this one." He held the left shoe upside down for her. When Jana rubbed her fingertips across the sole, they found resistance. Her fingers didn't slide easily and she had to push them along the surface.

Mars carried the shoes to the bathroom. Jana followed. He set the right one down on the tile floor and gave it nudge. It slid across the bathroom. He did the same with the left shoe and it didn't move. The left shoe would move across the floor only as long as he kept his hand on it, pushing it. The right one had taken off on its own.

"Silicone spray," Mars told her.

"The bowling alley sprayed my shoe? Do they

charge extra for making people fall down?"

Mars's cheek dimpled. "Not the bowling alley, Webster. It's the kind of spray you use to loosen old locks so the key turns smoothly through the tumblers."

"So that's your murder plot?"

"Silicone spray," Mars repeated. "Locksmiths use it all the time."

"Oh." It clicked. "Sherry's dad is a locksmith. That's what you meant when you told Nathan you knew what he'd done. Sherry and Nathan did it. He was laughing. I remember that. He was laughing at me."

She wouldn't believe him if he told her the truth, Mars decided. Not yet.

CHAPTER TWENTY

MARS WAS READY TO GO.

"Let me pack," Jana said. She wedged her cell phone into the pocket of her striped capri pants. "Okay, then."

"You can open your eyes now," Mars called to Arva as he and Jana left the dorm room.

The hallway was anything but empty. Doors were open and lights were on. Girls stood in their doorways and chatted, two or three at a time. They were watching Mars, who had just made his rounds. A Gray stood at the far end, at the door to the stairway, watching nothing.

Wyatt stood in a doorway across the hall from

Jana's room. He had handed Beatrice a small package of makeup and now leaned against the wall with his head ducked, speaking quietly to Christie.

Christie looked up and smiled at Jana and Mars. Wyatt pulled away and lumbered toward them on his bad leg. Christie caught Jana's eye and silently mouthed the words *thank you*. Jana was taken by surprise. She pointed to herself and turned her face into a question mark. Christie nodded vigorously.

Jana was warm standing next to Mars. As Wyatt reached them, she noticed the warmth increase. When she was a Slider, Jana thought, she would be warm all the time.

"I got the directions," Wyatt said to Mars out the side of his mouth that was still there. "It's way up in Madison County, though. You better find one with lots of gas."

Wyatt's one working eye locked on Jana. "Are you sure she has to come with us?" he asked Mars.

Mars nodded. Wyatt turned and walked away, his tall form listing from side to side with every step, like the mast of a ship on a tossing sea.

"Where's he going?" Jana asked Mars. "You said he was coming with us."

"To the fire escape. It's easier for him than the stairs."

The Gray monitor never looked up as Mars and Jana walked past him and into the stairwell.

"So, these are your contraband operations in action?" Jana asked once the door closed behind them. "You and Wyatt steal things from the Planet and make a killing selling them to Risers?"

"It's not as simple as that, Webster." He talked while she followed him down the stairs. "I don't steal. I can't take anything from the Planet and bring it here unless it is given to me."

"Your rule or theirs?" Jana asked.

Mars stopped his descent. "Mine," he said. "And theirs. If you steal something, it won't go through the fence."

They were going downstairs again.

"But you and Wyatt make money finding what students want and bringing it to them."

"Money?" Mars said. "What's money here, Webster?"

He stopped on the landing between floors and turned to look at her. Jana was on the last stair. She and Mars were the same height now. His blue eyes held hers.

Jana was slightly unnerved. There was heat in his eyes and she'd never been this close to them before. His face was closer to hers now than when they'd been in the pool together. Jana feared he could feel her breath when she spoke.

"So you just give them contraband for the heck of it?"

"No, Jana, I don't."

He used her first name. He felt the closeness too, she thought.

"I'm not stupid," he continued. "I know the difference between what people want and what people need. You said I bring them things they want. It's not like that. They want everything, Webster. I bring them things they need."

"People need makeup?"

"Yes. Most girls do, if you haven't noticed. They need it to feel normal. You said it yourself when you were sitting on the lawn after your funeral. You said you just wanted to be normal. And almost everyone's a little blue. Makeup helps them take the edge off being dead."

First impressions can be so wrong, Jana thought. And so could Arva.

Jana hadn't given Mars enough credit. As her eyes moved back and forth, watching each of his watch her, she wondered again how he had died. She wondered what bad thing he had been doing at the time of his death to have become a Slider.

"That's your cure for cancer, then, Dr. Dreamcote." Jana tried to smile, but her mouth opened only slightly instead. She drew in a shallow breath of air. "You take the edge off being dead." Her voice was soft and low.

Before he could turn away from her, Jana placed her hand on his shoulder and brought her face to his. She kissed him. It was meant to be a little thank-you to Mars for liking her, for putting up with all her questions, for helping her. And for helping others.

Mars blushed. It was a small kiss with her lips closed. She'd taken it away almost as soon as either one of them had felt it. It was just a quick kiss, but it melted her lips. Jana's heart raced. Her toes tingled.

In a world without Michael, Mars was a possibility. Jana wasn't ready to go to that world yet. It would mean giving up on Michael. It would mean giving up on endless love.

Mars was away before either of them could say anything.

At the bottom of the stairs, he led her outside. The night was cool. Jana was too excited to notice. There was a bench beside the door. A Gray stood next to it. Mars and Jana walked quickly through the squares of yellow light that fell from the dorm windows across the concrete sidewalk at their feet.

Wyatt waited around the corner of the building.

"Okay," Mars said to Jana. "Watch us leave. There's a hole in the chain-link fence back this way. Watch where we go, and when it's time, you'll come out the same way. Go back to the bench out front and wait. We'll be in a car, that way." Mars pointed. "I'll blink the headlights."

"Can a Riser do that? Just go through a hole in the fence?" Jana asked.

"Until you're off campus, you have a body, Webster. The front gate is locked. Unless you want to climb over the fence . . ."

"But can a Riser do that? Just walk away and be on the Planet?"

Mars stared at her, then looked at Wyatt.

"We'll see," Wyatt answered for him.

"It's been done," Mars said.

"We think it has, anyway," Wyatt added.

"Don't get up," Jana said.

The Gray was sitting on the bench when she got back. She wondered if he would be there all night. She sat down next to him. At night, he was almost invisible. A shadow.

Jana stared at her clunky shoes. She had time to kill. She thought about Sherry Simmons. Her father was a locksmith. Jana remembered seeing the can of silicone spray in Sherry's purse when they had been in the restroom together. The sophomore had lied to Jana and told her it was pepper spray. Wasn't it just a joke, something to make Jana look stupid when she started to bowl and couldn't stand up?

Jana thought about the messages Mars had written in her notebooks. She wondered whether it was murder when someone did something that kills you when they didn't think it would.

It was over now. A prank gone wrong. Jana had other things to think about. Brave things. Bold things.

Once she was off campus, Jana could use her phone. With Mars's help, she could talk to Michael. Tell him to be somewhere in the next day or two where she could kill him quickly. Webster and Haynes were destined to be together again. And it had to be soon. As soon as she became a Slider.

Jana stared into the darkness. She fought silently to remember Michael's voice. It wasn't there.

"What's your name?" she asked the Gray without

looking at him. They seemed to prefer it.

"Barry," he said.

"Cool name," Jana lied to be nice. "There are actors named Barry, you know. Barry Bostwick, for one. He was in *The Rocky Horror Picture Show*. My name is Jana Webster. I'm an actor. That's why I remember old movies when no one else does." But she couldn't remember Michael's voice.

The Gray kept his chin on his chest.

"Will you try to stop me when I leave?" Jana asked.

"No," he replied softly. "But I'll tell. I have to." His voice sounded like leaves.

"That's okay. I need demerits. Loads of them and in a hurry too."

Jana wished someone knew how many demerits it took for a Riser to become a Slider. If she had to do five hundred things against the rules, she would do them all tonight if she could. Since she had earned only three demerits for skinny-dipping, she knew she needed to do something much more extreme.

"Do you know what jumping is?" Jana asked. She looked at him this time.

Barry shook his head no.

"Me neither." She sighed. "But I'm going to do it

tonight if I can. Maybe six or seven times."

The Gray got up and slowly walked away.

While she waited, Jana reconsidered Mr. Skinner's mazes.

The first five mazes conditioned you to turn left. Then you had to turn right to move correctly into the final maze. You were reluctant to do it and it messed you up. You had to turn the wrong way to go the right way.

Life had conditioned Jana, she realized. And everything life had conditioned her to do didn't necessarily work any longer. She had to turn the other way. Now that she was dead, life was different. Jana was in the sixth maze. Here, the bad boy needed to save a life. The good girl was going to take one.

About the time her teeth were starting to chatter, Jana saw the headlights blink on and off. And on and off again. She jumped up and nearly ran around the corner of the building, crossed the grass to the back fence, and found the hole in the chain-link. The night seemed darker here at the edge of the Planet. The trees rising behind the dorm emerged from impenetrable black shadows.

She thought of the Rogues as shadows in the

night, shadows at the base of the trees, shadows with eyeballs and teeth. The thoughts chased her all the way to the car. Mars was in the driver's seat. Jana rushed to the passenger side. The window was down. She reached for the door handle, but her hand wouldn't work it.

"Just get in," Mars said. He patted the empty passenger seat. Mars sat with a bottle of flavored pop between his legs. It was from the six-pack they'd hidden in the weeds just off campus.

Jana stepped through the closed car door and sat in the seat. She was warm again.

"I watched you walk here," Mars said. "What you do naturally still applies. You just can't move anything with your hands. Just like when you left the funeral. Your feet touch the ground and you can walk. You can sit on things. You can touch things when you don't think about it. Eventually you'll be able to do more."

"When I'm like you," Jana said.

Wyatt sat sideways in the backseat, chewing a piece of gum. He even smacked the halves of his lips that would smack. Jana ignored him. Wyatt returned the favor.

"Hold my hand, Mars. I want to call Michael,"

Jana said. She leaned back and to one side to remove her cell from her pants pocket.

"Not yet," he told her. "We have to get away from here." The car moved along the street.

"Why? Are they watching us?"

Wyatt snickered in the backseat. "Someone might recognize the car," he said.

"Drive with one hand," Jana said. "Hold mine with the other."

"Can't, Webster. I have to focus on one thing at a time or we'll go off the road."

They'd found the car just a few blocks away. When Mars concentrated, he could start and turn the engine off without a key by partially materializing and by keeping part of himself a ghost. His fingers slipped through the steering column. Once there, his touch naturalized just enough to push the wires together until the engine started. Then he took his hand away and focused on gripping the wheel and pressing his foot on the gas and brake pedals.

Jana held her cell phone and stared at it.

"Wyatt," she said loudly. "Give me your hand."

CHAPTER TWENTY-ONE

JANA SQUEEZED WYATT'S HAND.

The heat from pressing her palm against his was similar to holding hands with Mars. It moved through Jana in a wave, like drinking hot chocolate.

But it was different too. Jana's heart didn't race. Her toes didn't tingle. Wyatt was warm like an electric blanket. Mars was warm like the real thing. His was the heat of a large breathing animal about to leap.

Jana flipped open her cell phone and turned it on with her thumb. Soon Michael was staring at her from the lighted viewing screen. She punched Send.

He answered. A new warmth came to Jana's neck and face.

"Michael," she nearly sang. "It's me. Michael . . ."

"Who are you?" he said. He could hear her. Jana flushed with excitement and relief.

He disconnected.

She squeezed Wyatt's hand as hard as she could. Jana's other hand was shaking when she pushed Send again. Six rings and it switched to voice mail.

She pushed Send again. Voice mail. She pushed Send again. Voice mail. Then dead silence.

Jana slumped. She let go of Wyatt's hand. Her lips trembled.

"He won't answer," she said. The back of her throat clinched. Tears burned her eyes.

"He's scared," Mars told her.

"So!"

"We'll go see him tonight. I promise. We'll find him for you."

Jana tried to stop crying.

"Not right now, okay? We have to do something first."

"Okay," she said quietly.

"I've been thinking about what you want to do, Webster. I don't think you should become a Slider to get it done."

"I think I should." She sniffed. "I want to be a

Slider. Tonight. I want to jump. Will you show me how?"

Wyatt swallowed his gum.

Michael didn't want to touch the thing. He stared at his cell phone for the longest time.

"Who was that?" Sherry asked.

"That's what I'd like to know," Michael said. "I'm calling Nathan. Hey, get dressed. Let's go get a pizza or something."

Jana recognized the road.

They were driving into the mountains. A fine mist appeared on the windshield as the elevation increased.

"What do you do when you jump?" she asked.

Mars didn't answer.

"We jump," Wyatt eventually said from the backseat.

"I know it's not like jumping jacks in third-grade gym," Jana said. "And I'm guessing it has nothing to do with hurdles. Do you jump over things? Do you jump on the backs of cars and go for rides? Do you jump on girls?"

"No," Wyatt snarled. "We jump *off* things. You

can't feel things on the Planet like we do. You wouldn't understand."

"What sort of things?"

"Bridges, waterfalls, cliffs," Wyatt recited for her. "You name it, we jump off it. As long as it's high enough."

Jana thought he was joking.

"It's like flying," Mars told her. He turned on the windshield wipers.

"Sure," Wyatt said, "just like flying. Until you land."

They *didn't* jump off cliffs, Jana decided. Or bridges or waterfalls. That would be suicide.

Mars turned on to a winding, climbing two-lane road. "Where's the ridge turnoff?" he asked.

"Two and a half miles on the right. Watch the odometer," Wyatt said. "There's a sign, but she said you wouldn't see it."

They'd risen above the fog. Jana could see glimpses of stars between the trees. They looked like shooting stars, flashing on then disappearing as the mountain trees slid by the window. Everyone came to Asheville to see the mountains. Jana didn't like them much. There were snakes. And spiders.

"Where are we going?" she finally asked.

"To a meet and greet," Wyatt said. "With witches."

Mars didn't talk much while he was driving, Jana noticed. He almost never looked at her.

"No way," Jana said.

"It's for Christie," Wyatt said. "You know, 'Ouch, ouch'? These witches, they're picking on her. We're going to ask them to stop."

"Witches, real witches?"

"Worse, actually," Wyatt said. "Conjure men."

He told her all about it. Up in the high hills, there were male witches. Most were called cunning men. Cunning men were healers and herbalists, like granny women but men. They could remove the heat, and sometimes the scar, of a burn by rubbing it with their hands. Cunning men could cure a sore throat by blowing in your mouth. They could make chickens lay eggs and cows give milk. They helped you find lost things.

"Do they make potions?" Jana said.

"Ointments mostly," Wyatt said. "There are no doctors up here. People don't have money, anyway, or health insurance. They go to cunning men for everything. They can find wild honey by following a bee, and tell you where to dig your well to hit water."

"What are they doing to Christie?" Jana asked.

Mars found the turnoff to the ridge road. It was gravel. And it was a climb. He switched the headlights to bright. They seemed to point up at the sky as often as they did the winding road in front of them.

"They aren't," Wyatt said. "Cunning men are good witches. But the ones we're going to see tonight, these are conjure men."

"They're evil," Mars said, as if it was a normal thing to call someone.

Conjure men practice the black arts, they told Jana. They were the witches that put curses on people. They could make something catch fire. Or make a fire go out. People were deathly afraid of them.

"Sometimes people need them for one thing or another," Wyatt said. "Christie's parents went to them when she died." Wyatt pulled himself forward with his hand on the front seat. "For the right price, Webster, conjure men resurrect the dead."

"At least they try," Mars said without looking at Jana. He was leaning over the steering wheel, watching the road. It turned every which way now.

Wyatt laughed. He dropped back sideways in the seat.

"Really?" Jana asked. "Can they do that?"

"No," Mars told her.

"Well, if they could . . ."

"They can't," Wyatt said. "They're not very good at resurrection. But they try. Right now, they're bringing tiny little bits of Christie back to life for just a second or so when they cast their spells. She said it's like being pinched in different places or pricked with a pin. And for some reason, the conjure men are keeping at it."

"What are we going to do?" Jana wanted to know. "Ask them to stop it?"

"They want resurrection. I'm going to give them a sample of the real thing. They ain't seen nothing till they get a look at me. They might stop conjuring altogether."

"I would," Mars said.

Jana smiled despite her fear of visiting conjure men. They probably had a house full of snakes and spiders.

"How did Christie die, anyway?" she asked.

"You don't tell that on other people," Mars said.

"Your death is your last real story," Wyatt

added. "It's the one thing everybody gets to tell for themselves."

She hadn't liked Wyatt in the beginning. He was always mean and snarly to Jana. That thing he did in the library didn't help any. Now, she realized, there was another way of looking at him. Wyatt had held her hand when she told him to. And he was the one who had talked to Christie in the hall. This errand belonged to Wyatt, not to Mars.

Mars pulled over to the side of the road and parked.

He and Wyatt got out of the car. Mars stood by Jana's window.

"We walk from here," he said.

"Okay," Jana said.

"Wait here."

"No way!" Jana didn't want to be alone.

"Please?"

"They won't see me anyway."

"They're conjure men, Webster. They'll see all three of us."

"I'm coming with you," she said. "And that's all there is to it." Jana got out of the car with her door still closed. The Sliders had no choice.

Wyatt was already on his way. It didn't take Mars

and Jana long to catch up.

"What are you going to do when we get there?"

"Shhh," Mars said. "They'll hear you."

"Really?" Jana liked the idea that somebody on the Planet could hear her, even if it was nasty old conjure men.

There was a light on.

"Keep her here," Wyatt said. "I'll go in alone."

Mars and Jana waited at the picket gate in front of the little house in the woods. A dog howled and wouldn't stop. The air smelled like pines. Jana looked up at the stars. There were a million of them.

She believed stars held wishes. Stars were tiny threads of light that reached to the earth. Like beads, dreams and wishes slid back and forth on each thread. One of the silver threads was tied to her, Jana thought. But which one?

Michael showed Nathan the gun that he'd taken from Marilyn Webster's bedside stand.

"What's this for?" Nathan asked.

"We have to protect ourselves," Michael said. "Twenty-five caliber semiautomatic. The clip is fully loaded."

"Do you even know how to use that thing?"

"It's fairly simple, Nathan. You turn the safety off."

"Who cares?" Sherry said. "We didn't do anything wrong."

Michael stared at her. Yes they did, he thought. And somebody had seen them doing it.

"So what are you going to do?" Nathan asked. "Shoot your phone the next time it rings?"

Wyatt was satisfied.

He was laughing as he left the house. "If they weren't crazy when I got there, they are now," he told Mars and Jana when he reached the gate.

"Maybe you could do this for a living," Mars suggested as the three of them walked back to the car. "Show up at kiddie birthday parties, things like that."

"Good idea. And on Christmas Eve I could visit the houses of kids who were naughty."

"Yeah," Mars said, "Santa Burger."

Wyatt chuckled. "Half burger, half man," he said. "I think I should get my own comic book series."

Jana had had enough. "You're good-looking, Wyatt. You really are," she said. He was too. At least half of him was. Maybe more.

"Well, sugar," he drawled, "I only have one eye that looks at all."

Jana had her eye on an idea of her own. An idea that would change things. Mars didn't want her to become a Slider. That was the start of her new idea. She'd thought of it while looking at the swirling stars when she and Mars waited for Wyatt to come out of the witches' house. On the ride along the dirt and gravel ridge road, she thought it through again. When they reached the pavement, she decided to try it out on Mars.

"I was thinking I might not have to become a Slider, after all," she said.

Mars looked at her with interest.

"Listen to this," Jana continued. "If you hold my hand, Michael can hear me. I can talk to him, right? What if you and Wyatt both hold my hands, or Mars, you put your arms around me, something like that? I think he would be able to see me."

"So?" Wyatt said from the backseat.

"You have to understand love, Wyatt," Jana said. "When he sees me, he'll want to be with me. I'll be standing there. I'll be real. I'll ask him to join me and he will."

"We can't bring him back with us, if that's what

you mean," Wyatt said.

"Not that. It's true love. Real love. Like in *Romeo and Juliet*. You know how that ends, don't you? If he sees me dead, Michael will kill himself to be with me. You don't understand what Michael and I are together. It's bigger than the world. It just is."

No one said anything.

"So I don't have to be a Slider and we can do it tonight," Jana finished.

"Won't work, Webster," Mars said.

"But we can try. Maybe if he just hears my voice in person."

"*Romeo and Juliet* is bullshit," Wyatt said from the backseat.

"Is not!" Jana told him. "It's perfect. They're perfect. It's perfect love. And perfect love doesn't end."

"Maybe they didn't have Dead School back then," Wyatt suggested. "But it won't work now."

"Yes, it will," Jana insisted.

"If he kills himself, he'll be a Gray. What good is that?"

"He'll be with me, Wyatt. . . ." Jana said, then his words sank in. "He'll be here with me. . . ." she tried again, trying to not think about it.

"It wouldn't be him," Mars told her. "Grays have no will."

They were right.

"Fart, fudge, and popcorn," Jana said. "I'll have to be a Slider, then. I don't want Michael to be a Gray. I'll have to be a Slider so I can kill him."

Wyatt started to say something. Mars turned in the driver's seat and stared him out of it. Mars finished his soda pop and Wyatt smacked another piece of gum on the drive down from the mountains.

Jana believed Mars was being too quiet. Even if he had to concentrate to drive, he could still talk to her now and then and not hit a tree or turn the car over in a ditch. Maybe it was because she had kissed him. He hadn't tried to kiss her back. He should have, she thought.

Mars wanted to be with her, but he didn't seem to want more than that. He should at least want to talk to her while the three of them drove around on the Planet all night. He kept letting Wyatt do it for him.

The fog was on the windshield again. They were almost back in town.

"You don't talk much, do you?"

Mars glanced at her, but didn't answer.

"The smart ones never do," Wyatt answered for him from the backseat. As always, she thought. Jana realized that Mars was holding something back. She didn't know the real Mars at all.

Wyatt laid out their plans. It was late now and everyone would be home, even seniors with cars. They'd start with Sherry, he decided. She was a sophomore and would definitely be home before the others.

"Hey, Mars, let me do the girl," Wyatt said. "I'm on a roll. Then you can do the other one before we catch up with this Romeo guy."

Jana wanted to see Sherry's face when she saw Wyatt, when he talked to her with half a mouth. Then Jana wanted somebody to punch the girl's lights out. She let the Romeo comment slide.

"I'm coming with you," she insisted.

"Why not?" Wyatt said. "They're your people."

CHAPTER TWENTY-TWO

THEY WERE ALMOST THERE.

The fog lay on the streets in west Asheville. It wrapped the trees and bumped against the houses. Porch lights and the streetlights all wore halos. The stars had gone away. It was a perfect night for ghosts.

"Man, I love flipping people's houses," Wyatt said as they searched for the right house numbers.

"Flipping? What's that?" Jana asked. "Do you do cartwheels?"

"You know, flip. Show up, walk through, leave. When you flip something, you're getting it done, like flipping a page in a book."

"You don't turn over the furniture or things like that?"

"I just like people's houses," Wyatt said. "They're different inside than what you expect. They're not like your own, you know what I mean? I like thinking I live there when I walk through, or that I might have grown up there. My house, we just had junk all over the place. These other houses, it's like everything has been arranged. I like seeing how different people do that."

Jana smiled. Listening to Wyatt, she felt less dead than usual. Being around him was almost like being alive again.

When they found it, the Simmons house was like the others: shrouded in fog. Wyatt, Mars, and Jana walked inside without opening the door. A golden retriever was on the couch. It raised its head and stared in their direction. Mars had forgotten to tell her that although most animals couldn't see them, dogs always knew when dead people showed up. This one didn't seem to care. It put its face back down on the cushion and stayed where it was.

The room was dark. Jana walked through one corner of the coffee table before she noticed it was there.

Sherry's bedroom was at the front, they discovered. They stepped inside. Mars, focusing only slightly, pushed her bedroom door closed and leaned against it with his arms crossed. Jana stood near him, just in front, staring at the bed where Sherry slept. A night-light glowed in a nearby outlet.

"Look at this," Wyatt said.

He pointed at the dresser top. In the middle of all the things on Sherry's dresser sat the aerosol can of silicone spray lubricant. Someone had tied a two-inch black ribbon around it. The bow wasn't done right, Jana noticed.

Wyatt approached the bed. He leaned over Sherry, concentrating. He placed his hand on her mouth. Sherry felt the weight of his flesh. Her eyes shot open. At the same time her feet kicked wildly, like they were on fire and she was just noticing it. Wyatt pressed down.

"Stop it," he said. "I'm not going to hurt you unless you scream. This is a friendly visit. I just want to talk."

The red and yellow streaks in her hair quit moving. He took some pressure off his hand, studying her reaction with his one eye.

"Okay?" he asked.

She seemed to agree. A little less pressure, then.

"I mean it!" Wyatt said, lifting his hand entirely from her face.

Sherry gasped for air. She whimpered. Tears came to her eyes.

Jana didn't care. She hated Sherry for having tied that black ribbon around the can of silicone spray.

Wyatt's conversation was brief. Sherry had to tell someone about Jana's accident, he said. She had to tell or he would come back.

"Who?" Sherry managed to ask. "Who do I tell?"

"You know who," he growled at her.

"My parents?"

"Shit no," he said. "Parents don't matter. They'll just say it was all right. You know who you have to tell."

Wyatt turned around to look at Mars. Wyatt flung his hand in the air. He'd forgotten her name.

"Sherry," Mars told him.

"Sherry," Wyatt said solemnly. "You have to tell the cops. I'm a monster from beyond the grave. I will be here every night until you tell."

He backed up. He walked to the dresser, leaning down hard on his bad leg and back up straight again. "Say okay, Sherry."

"Okay," the sophomore said quickly.

Wyatt picked up the can of silicone spray. "One more thing. I want you to give me this. You have to give it to me or I can't take it."

She didn't want to. Her face was wet with fear, but she didn't want to.

"Sherry," Wyatt said, "if you don't give it to me, I'll have to come back and ask again."

"Okay," she said.

Wyatt slacked off. She could see only his outline now.

Jana reached behind her to take Mars's hand. She touched his jeans instead. Mars put his hand on her shoulder. His warmth tumbled through her. She was filled with the heat of the earth. She materialized. Sherry screamed when she saw Jana standing in her room. Mars took his hand away and Jana disappeared.

The scream woke up the house. Sherry's father rushed from the master bedroom into the hall.

The three of them left. The dog watched the can of silicone spray float through the living room and out the door. Mars backed the car up the street with the headlights off.

• • •

It was Mars's turn to go to work.

The television was on at Nathan's house. They saw him through the window. Nathan sat in a chair bathed in the light of the TV. He was still dressed, but his shoes were off.

Mars stuck his head through the door and said, "Nathan, come here a sec."

Nathan looked at the door. He climbed out of the chair and opened it. Wyatt stood off to the side to watch. Jana kept near him for warmth. Nathan stepped outside in his socks.

"Over here," Mars said from the edge of a rhododendron bush. He moved quickly away.

Nathan stepped into the grass. "Michael? Where are you? Come on, my feet are wet."

He took one more step. Mars tackled him from behind.

Nathan hit the ground and went limp. Mars, fully naturalized to the Planet now, rolled him over for their little talk. Nathan recognized Mars as the guy from the bowling alley. Nathan's hair was coated with droplets of fog that looked to Jana like spiderwebs. Nathan licked the corners of his mouth while Mars talked to him. There were webs there too.

● ● ●

Michael was next.

"His dad works the graveyard shift," Jana told Mars. "His mom's married to someone else. He'll be home alone."

Wyatt traipsed through the house with his peculiar gait. With each step, it looked like he was leaning in to peer at something on the wall, then leaning out again. Jana took Mars to the bedroom. Michael was asleep. Mars turned on the lights. Michael didn't wake up. He was sprawled on his back in bed.

Jana had been in his house often enough. She knew the books on his desk, the posters on the wall. The brand of cereal he kept on top of the refrigerator in the kitchen. His toothpaste and his shampoo.

She sat on the edge of Michael's bed and watched him sleep. He was beautiful. His breathing was so soft, so quiet. Did she really want him dead?

Yes.

And he wanted to be dead too. Once they were together, Michael would never be alone again. The sooner the better, for both of them.

"I want him to hear me," Jana said. "I want him to see me."

"To see you he'll have to see me too," Mars said.

"If I talk to him, will he think he's dreaming?"

"Maybe."

"Okay, I want him to see me first. Stand behind me, Mars. Put your hands on my shoulders."

Mars pressed both his hands on Jana. She kept her eyes on Michael as wave upon wave of smoldering warmth entered her, held her.

"Wake him," Mars whispered in her ear, his breath as warm as his hands.

Jana opened her mouth slightly to take in more air. She pulled the covers away from Michael. He slept bare-chested. She placed her hand there, her breathing trying to catch up to the heat lowering itself into her body, over and over like the tide. She massaged his chest with short gentle strokes.

"Michael, wake up," Jana said softly. "Wake up, Michael. It's me."

His eyes came slowly open.

Michael jerked away from her, bolting himself against the headboard. He screamed like a little girl. The crazed look in his eyes could have knocked down bowling pins.

Mars took his hands away.

Jana flung herself on top of Michael.

"Shhh," she said. "It's okay. It's me. I'm here."

Jana faded before Mars did. She faded quickly. Michael could barely hear her, could barely feel her weight on top of him.

Wild-eyed and panting, Michael stared at Mars. He'd left the automatic locked in the glove compartment of his car. He wouldn't do that again. Mars slowly disappeared.

Wyatt came into the room. He walked to Michael's computer and touched the mouse. The screen saver popped off. There was a Google search on the browser: *How to fire a pistol.*

Half of Wyatt's face found humor in Michael's current research project.

Jana rode in silence for the longest time.

Michael had screamed when he saw her. He was supposed to have smiled warmly, to have reached for her. Jana had tried to hold on to him, to hug Michael's body with all of hers. It was no use. Once Mars let go of her, Michael didn't know she was still there. Jana had felt Michael's heartbeat, but he couldn't feel hers.

Jana could touch, but she couldn't hold. She might as well have been the fog.

The Sliders decided not to jump. It would be light in an hour and the guy whose car they drove might be up soon. Besides, everyone was exhausted. Jana's thoughts were drowsy. She couldn't concentrate.

"I just have to be a Slider," Jana finally said.

Wyatt was tired of hearing it. "She doesn't even know what she's asking," he said to Mars.

"I'm right here, Wyatt," Jana said curtly. "And I can hear you."

"But can you listen, that's the question," he barked at her. "Look, let's get this over with. You do *not* want to be a Slider. It's going backwards. It's going the wrong way."

"Yes, I do," Jana said. "I want to be a Slider just like you."

"No, you don't. You just think you do. Look, it's Chutes and Ladders once you're dead. And Sliders aren't sliding up. What do you think happens to us when we graduate or get kicked out, whichever comes first?"

Jana was silent. There was nothing he could say that would change her mind. She didn't just want to be a Slider, she needed to be one.

"It's not all angel cake and ice cream, I can tell you that much," Wyatt continued. "They don't have

Twinkies where we're going. They just bake them there."

Wyatt was angry for some reason. Mars wasn't saying anything to help. It was the end of the argument. And it was the end of their night on the town.

The Sliders dropped her off out front.

"Just walk through the gate and don't stop," Mars told her. "You can walk through it while it's closed from this side. You'll be good as new once you're on campus."

As good as dead, Jana thought. "Okay," she said.

"Drink some water before you go to bed."

The dorm looked different from outside the fence. There were weeds everywhere; there wasn't concrete. Windows were broken, some with boards nailed across them. No lights were on. To the real world, the Dead School dorm was a vacant building. A yellow school bus, spotted with rust, sat on flat tires inside the fence. A metal No Trespassing sign at the front gate had been tagged with black spray paint. A heavy chain and a heavier lock held the gate closed.

Fog shadowed her feet as Jana left the Planet.

She walked through the gate as if it wasn't there. When she did, lights came on in the building and over the lobby doors. The windows were repaired. The bus looked new. She felt her body's physical presence return.

The Gray named Barry wasn't waiting for her on the bench. Instead, a trio of Virgins greeted her at the entry to the dorm. They sang a song to twenty, then floated away. It was probably a Riser record for demerits earned in one night, but it wasn't enough to satisfy Jana. She'd have to jump, or something worse. She'd have to do a lot of things.

As she climbed the stairs, Jana considered how she would kill Michael once she was a Slider. She couldn't cut his throat or he'd look like that in Dead School. She could shoot him while he slept. It would leave just a little hole in the back of his head if she did it right. But if she didn't do it right, it would blast a ragged hole in his face when the bullet came out the other side.

She thought of Beatrice. Jana might be strong enough to push an ice pick through his skull. Or, with practice, she could use a hammer and give the handle of an ice pick one solid hit. Would he jump around until he died? Would he struggle if she strangled him? Probably, she decided.

If she plunged the ice pick into his chest until it pierced his heart while he slept, he might wake up and pull it out. She'd have to hide his cell phone so he couldn't call 911 for help. What if he struck out at her before he died? She didn't want Michael hitting her to be the last thing he remembered from real life.

Jana would drug him. She'd tie his hands and feet to the bed. Then smother him in his sleep. Michael would be a little blue in Dead School. That didn't matter anyway. Everyone was. Poison, of course. Drugs and poison were the same thing. Everything about *Romeo and Juliet* was just right.

CHAPTER TWENTY-THREE

ARVA FROWNED AT THE WORLD.

"I don't want to know where you went last night," she said.

Jana sat between her roommate and the window on the bus to Dead School. Jana smelled like Ivory soap again. Everyone did. The scent of soap reminded Jana of a song from grade school. *"We're all in our places with bright, shining faces."* The ones that had faces.

"And I don't want to know what you did." Arva's usual hoarse whisper turned into a creaking sound when she tried to be adamant.

Jana knew Arva was mad because Jana didn't

depend on her for information any longer. Risers thought they had all the answers, but they weren't the only kids who had tried to figure out what they were supposed to do and not supposed to do at Dead School. And, frankly, Mars and Wyatt had done a better job of it.

Climbing up on her knees, Jana turned around and placed her arms on the back of the seat. The student behind her had incredibly pink puffy cheeks. His entire face was puffed out like a marshmallow. Or a balloon. His eyes were swollen shut. Bee sting, she thought. Or poison ivy. Jana looked beyond him and saw Mars. She ate Mars for breakfast with her eyes.

Then she laughed. Jana couldn't help it. Her natural smile took over and stayed there. She batted her eyelashes. Mars stared at her as if she wore clown makeup and a red rubber nose. She wasn't good at being naughty yet. She'd get better at it before the day was through, Jana decided. Twenty-three demerits weren't nearly enough.

"You went walking through the dead of night with those two Sliders," Arva said without looking at Jana. "I know you did." Creak, creak, croak.

Mars shook his head at Jana, then looked out the window.

Jana turned around in her seat as the bus began to move. "Arva, we *were* the dead of night," she said.

Christie caught up to Jana before homeroom.

"Thank you," she said. "They're through. I can tell they are." Christie smiled. It made her hair glow. The slightly diagonal red line across her forehead was barely there when she smiled like that.

"It wasn't me. It was Wyatt," Jana said. "He did it by himself."

"Isn't he a dream?" Christie asked.

"Just that," Jana said. She smiled at the thought of a guy who looked like a refugee from a nightmare being Christie's idea of a dream. Jana realized she was smiling more now that she had decided to be a bad girl. She smiled naturally without thinking about it first. It just happened.

There was a flyer printed on blue paper on every student's desk. Jana sat in her seat and read hers. *SOCK HOP!* was centered in large block letters. *Third period. In the Gym.* In much smaller type near the bottom it read *Arva Davis, Publicity Committee.*

Jana turned to ask Arva about it, but her roommate wouldn't look at her. She turned around and asked Beatrice instead. It was a come-as-you-are school dance. You had to take off your shoes to dance on the gym floor.

"But we don't have to hop, do we?"

Beatrice tilted the yellow yard dart fins to one side. "Can if you want," she said brightly. She wore a lighter color of blush on her cheeks today. There was a brush of glitter under her eyes. Beatrice sparkled.

Jana was sure twenty-three demerits were far short of her goal. And she didn't know what that goal was. Maybe two hundred. Maybe two hundred and fifty. She would have to do better. She opened her homeroom notebook and tore out a page from the back. She wrote a short note and passed it to Henry.

She couldn't stop looking at Mars. He seemed brand-new to her. He'd taken her to the world with him and brought her safely back. Now that she was a bad girl, they had something in common.

Jana knew everything about Michael. It was different with Mars. She had no idea what dreams and sorrows lived behind his darting eyes and perfectly arched eyebrows.

It was time to act. Second period, Jana waited until Mr. Skinner had drawn his first box on the blackboard. Jana stood from her desk. A few students looked at her.

She straightened her hair with her hands, tugged up her kneesocks to get them even, then bounced to the front of the class. She lifted the chalk eraser from the tray and, standing next to Mr. Skinner, erased the first maze he'd drawn while he worked on the second.

Jana turned to the class and bowed from the waist. Two of the Sliders clapped. Others laughed. Mars looked down and massaged the center of his forehead with the thumb and fingers of one hand. Arva buried her head inside her arms crossed in front of her on her desk.

A Virgin appeared inside the classroom door. She was a little wider and taller than the others and she sang in as low a voice as Jana had ever heard a girl sing. Then she motioned Jana to the door. Outside, a Gray escorted her to the library. Jana had earned detention for the remainder of the hour.

She was surprised to see Jameson sitting at the table where she'd first met him. He was alone this time. Jana asked if she could sit down. Books were spread out in front of him. He glanced up at her, then returned to his work. His straight brown bangs touched the tops of his glasses. His cowlick looked like a little hand of hair waving hello.

"You aren't in class," Jana said.

"This is my class," Jameson told her. "I'm a full-time student librarian. I'm good at languages."

"That must be fun," Jana said politely. "Do you graduate and everything?"

"Well, no. Not really," he mumbled.

"What, then?" Jana asked. "If you don't graduate, what happens to you?"

"I shouldn't tell you."

"Go ahead," Jana said. "I won't rat you out."

"I'm a regent," he whispered.

"A what?"

"A regent. Right now I'm the student represent-ative on the Regents Council. I died too young, I guess."

Jana's mouth dropped open. "You run the place?"

"No," Jameson said. He looked up from his books, pushed his glasses against the bridge of his nose, and looked back down. "Not yet," he added.

She asked about demerits. Jana told him everything she had done and that she had earned three for skinny-dipping and twenty for leaving campus.

"Then I got detention," she said. "That's why I'm here."

"I see," Jameson said absently.

"I need more demerits," Jana told him. "A lot more."

He leaned back in his chair. "For starters, don't disrupt class," he said. "You'll just end up here. Detention is meant to keep you from bothering other students. You can't do that in Dead School. Every student gets equal opportunity to learn, to achieve."

"To change?" Jana suggested.

"That's what you really want, isn't it?" This time Jameson looked into her eyes, his stare magnified by the lenses in his glasses.

"I want to be a Slider."

"That's going to take some doing. Demerits are meant to warn Risers. Not much more to it than that. The easiest way to get more is to do the same things again. Since they're a warning, it won't be too much the first time you do anything. When you do it again, it is taken much more seriously because you have already been warned."

"I got three demerits for skinny-dipping," she said. "If I do it again, I'll get a bunch more?"

"First of all, you earned three demerits for taking your underwear off at school. They don't care that you went swimming, and you didn't know you were skipping class, so they didn't see that as a choice you made. If you do it again, you'll get nine demerits or maybe ten. It's rather subjective."

"How many demerits until I go before the Council? Will they make me a Slider?"

"It's unclear," he confessed. "Look, you're a Riser. You're one of the good kids. They allow for you to mess up and joke around. That's why they have demerits in the first place. If you were a Slider, your actions would have more dire consequences. Sliders don't get demerits. They just get expelled. And that's an instant vacancy. But as long as Sliders don't disrupt other students here, they let them do about anything until they finally do something that is . . . bad enough."

"How much do I have to do to get the regents to make me a Slider?" Michael had better appreciate this, Jana thought.

"Risers don't go before the Regents Council. So you have to become a Slider on your own. Then . . . well, then you don't want ever to be called before the regents."

"I'll be a good Slider, I promise," Jana said. "I won't bother anyone on campus. Just tell me what to do, Jameson. You know it can happen and you know how it's done."

"Yes, it's possible," he said. "I can tell you that much. But I can't tell you exactly how to do it. That would make me a collaborator. Besides, it would be different for everyone. Whatever it is, it would have to be egregious."

Having to figure out everything on your own was getting old fast, Jana decided. No wonder Arva wanted to believe in a simple set of rules other students came up with.

"Okay, but I want it to be soon," Jana said. "Do they take forever to decide?"

"Most vacancies happen instantly. Ditto for any change in student status, I would think."

"Instantly" would be good, Jana thought.

"He came to my house last night," Nathan told Michael.

"Who?"

"The guy on Jana's phone. He was saying I had to tell about the accident or . . ."

"Or what?"

"Something about a cliff and what it felt like to fall to your death from real high up. He said you fall so fast, you can't breathe. That you almost black out. Then he said you wished you had. Look, the guy's a lunatic. I had to fight him off. It was a real tumble, but I got him out of the yard finally."

"Was he alone?" Michael wanted to know.

"Yeah, the guy from the bowling alley. The guy who saw it happen. So listen, I've been thinking about it and—"

"He's just trying to scare you," Michael interrupted. "You ran him off. It's over."

"I don't think it's over. Maybe it's time we tell someone the truth."

Michael closed his eyes and took a deep breath. It would ruin him. There would be an investigation of some kind. There would be a record. It would be in the paper, show up online, and Michael would be an Ivy League leper.

He wasn't guilty of anything, and it would ruin him. His scholarship to Dartmouth would fly out the window. That would mean he would have to stay local for college. Local college was a joke when it came to the goals he had set for himself.

Why didn't she just fall down like anyone else would have and get back up again? It was her fault, really. Not his. It was supposed to be a comedy and she'd made a tragedy out of it.

"You won't do that," Michael said. "You won't tell anyone anything at all. Because where are you going to go when they fight again? Where are you going to go when your parents start tearing the house apart at three in the morning?"

"Have you known of any Risers who became Sliders?" Jana asked Jameson.

He looked at her for almost a minute without answering. He pushed his glasses on up his nose, although they were already there to begin with.

"Yes," he finally said.

That was the easier of the two questions she might have asked. Jameson had been researching the other one for Mars. A Slider becoming a Riser was much more difficult and exacting. It involved free-will atonement for a previous act with absolutely no regard for possible reward or advancement. It had to be an accomplishment by the Slider in a moment that was pure of heart. Perfectly pure of heart. Given too much time to consider the outcome almost nixed the deal for anyone. If you even thought you were doing good on purpose, it didn't count.

"How many?" Jana wanted to know.

"How many what?"

"How many Risers have become Sliders? That you know of."

"One or two."

"How did they do it?" Jana could use some pointers.

"One of them slept around. She was a Slider for part of her last semester here. She's gone now."

Jameson bent back over his work.

"And the other one?"

"She committed suicide and it failed," he said. "She completed the act that would end her existence. It just didn't work."

"How, exactly?" Jana asked.

"I don't remember the details," Jameson said without looking up.

Jana thought about failed suicide. You carried it through, but it didn't kill you, for some reason.

"Like firing a gun into your chest and missing your heart?"

"Yes, that's the idea," Jameson agreed. "You commit the act that would normally kill you and you're convinced that it will kill you. You take a huge overdose that puts you in a coma, for example. That's another way. Of course, a coma induced in

Dead School only lasts a little while."

"And if she had succeeded, she would be a vacancy, right?"

"Oh yes, successful suicide here is instant vacancy. Your status doesn't matter on suicide. You're expelled for good. Grays committed suicide in real life. Once you're here, it's simply not tolerated."

This path to becoming a Slider wouldn't work at all. She'd have to kill herself for real and then by some quirk have it fail to take. That left her original plan in place: as many demerits in as short a time as possible.

Jameson's talk reminded Jana of an old movie she liked. It was a Julia Roberts one. Kiefer Sutherland, Kevin Bacon. And, dang it, she forgot which, one of the Baldwins.

"There is a window when you die," Jana said. "Sometimes there is. Your body dies but you don't totally leave, or something. Like in the movie *Flatliners*? Have you seen that one? They die and everything, but they can come back from death because that window hasn't closed."

"Yes," Jameson said. There seemed to be a bit of joy in his voice because Jana had managed to advance the conversation. "People experience death on the Planet. Then they're resuscitated. It happens all the time. They hit them with the defibrillators and they come back. It would be the same here. The window, I mean. But I don't think anyone in Dead School has ever had a heart attack."

"I guess not," Jana said. She thought of Darcee. "Maybe people in comas are the ones that get stuck in the window."

Jameson looked at her more closely. He touched his glasses with two fingers.

Their conversation was stolen by a sudden rolling clatter of noise in the hall. It sounded at first like someone was bowling.

Jana scooted her seat back and stared at the windows that lined the library wall facing the hallway. The noise changed and intensified as it approached the windows. It sounded like tiny bowling balls, several of them rolling in unison on the hardwood floor of the hallway. The sound came nearer and nearer. Then she saw him.

It was a skateboarder loose in the halls.

Jana rushed to a window. Jameson followed.

The kid wore his hair to his shoulders, parted in the middle so the sides closed over his face when he leaned in. He wore a dark tan tee that reached to his knees, where the lateral rips in his jeans began. Sliders came out of the classroom doorways to watch the boarder work the halls on a platform that looked like it had seen several jumps that had gone askew. Its sides were nicked and the front curve was pocked with scars.

The skateboarder managed a quick turnaround at the end of the hall by stepping back hard on the plat, lifting the front wheels. He touched the front curve of the board with two fingers and spun in place. The plat came down hard and, with two or three powerful kicks, the boarder sped back toward the library, weaving a mad pattern of S-curves from one side of the hall to the other.

Mars stepped into the hall from Mr. Skinner's class.

"Nice work!" he called to the hall surfer.

The kid in the oversize tee nearly capsized. He stepped sideways off the board, flipping it while it was still rolling and catching it in his hand. The kid stood perfectly still. But only for a second. He turned a circle, breathing hard, his mouth open. Then he took off running with his board under one arm and never looked back. His long hair bounced along as he passed the library windows.

"It's a kid from the Planet," Jameson told her. "They break in through the basement. They come through here sometimes, but once the Sliders start talking to them, they never come back."

"Can they see us?" Jana asked, but she knew the answer.

"One or two of the Sliders, the ones that practice contact on the Planet, can make themselves heard on campus," he said. "But not seen. Planet people can't see any of us here."

It should be more fun than it was to be invisible, she thought. Then Jana had another thought. She could kill Michael with a poisonous spider. She could put it on his big toe while he slept.

When second period was over, she stepped behind a bookshelf and managed some tricky arm gymnastics. Without taking her blouse off, Jana was able to hang her school bra by one of its straps on the push-bar of the library door as she walked into the hall.

The two Grays behind the library counter tilted their head in unison to one side, then the other, as they watched her leave. Soon they stared at their shoes again.

•••

It wasn't difficult to find the gym.

All the Dead Schoolers were making their way to the Sock Hop. Jana walked with the others. You just had to get more demerits when the whole school was your audience, she thought. Henry showed up at her side.

"Did you mean it?" he asked her.

The note she'd handed him in class said *Wanna dance?*

"Yes." Jana stopped walking. "But listen, it's an act, okay? Everything will be an act. I'm rehearsing a role." Henry was in drama. He would understand. Besides, she wanted to touch his hair. Just once.

"Got it," Henry said.

He was looking at the front of her blouse.

"And don't be rude," Jana snipped. "Now go ahead. I'll find you there when I'm ready. And remember, it's not a date or anything like that." She held up her left hand and wiggled Michael's class ring for Henry in case he had forgotten.

CHAPTER TWENTY-FOUR

SHERRY SKIPPED SCHOOL.

Once her mother had left, she'd phoned Michael and Nathan. They were at her house now, on their lunch break. Michael paced. Nathan sat on the couch and played with the golden retriever's ears.

"Visited?" she said. "He almost raped me!"

"But what did he say?" Michael asked. He wore a dress shirt with a black armband around one sleeve. He could have missed school entirely today. But he thought it was important to be there, to show his courage under such dreadful circumstances, to carry on in spite of personal challenges and, in general, to be morose in front of everyone.

"He told me not to scream and he wouldn't kill me."

"What else?"

Sherry looked at Nathan. He wasn't much help. "He told me I had to tell the police what you did."

"What I did?" Michael stopped pacing. "No. Listen to me, it's what *we* did. You brought the spray, remember? And it was your idea in the first place."

"Hey, it was a joke," Nathan broke in. "It was just a joke that went wrong. We didn't do anything that bad. She fell wrong. It was an accident. Like falling in the bathtub."

"We tried to save her," Michael said, creating a list of good deeds the three had accomplished that night. They'd followed the ambulance to the hospital.

"No, that was the other guy," Nathan corrected him. "The other guy tried to save her."

"We did everything we could," Michael insisted. "I called 911, didn't I?"

"I think that's what pissed him off, that he couldn't save her," Nathan continued. "And that's why he's coming to our houses."

"I saw her too," Sherry interrupted. "Jana was

with him last night. She was hiding, but I saw her."

"You dreamed that part," Michael said.

He hadn't told either one about his bedroom visit from Jana. He wasn't going to. Michael was president of the district student council. The whole district, not just his school. District presidents did not see ghosts. Not if they wanted to keep their scholarships to Dartmouth, they didn't.

"The guy from the bowling alley isn't the one who tried to rape me," Sherry continued. "It was another guy. He was tall and ugly. He was all messed up." Her voice softened to a whisper. "He had only half a face."

Nathan and Michael looked at each other. Then Nathan giggled, like a motorcycle trying to start.

"Are you making this up?" Michael asked.

"No!" Sherry said. "My dad's taking me to the police station to look at mug shots when he gets home from work today. He's really shook up because none of his fancy locks kept the rapist out. The house alarm never even went off."

Michael's thoughts tumbled, then locked into place. Sherry was unreliable.

"You can't say a word to the police about the other thing, I'm warning you," he said. "Or your father. I have pictures of you on my cell phone. I'll send them to everyone in school if you cross me."

"I won't," Sherry promised. "I won't say anything. Look, my dad is making me. I have to go."

"Pictures of what?" Nathan asked, looking from one to the other.

Michael ignored him. He pointed his finger at Sherry. "If you tell, I will destroy you," he vowed. "I'll ruin your entire life."

The gym smelled like Pine-Sol and socks.

The bleachers on one side of the gym were folded against the wall. On the other side, the seats filled up quickly. Girls sat with girls for the most part. Boys sat with boys. Sliders stood in small groups at one end of the gym.

The Stretchers were tied in gurneys that were arranged in a long row on the side of the floor where the bleachers were left against the wall. Their feet pointed to the middle of the gym. Grays had cranked the top half of the gurneys partially upright so the Stretchers could watch. Two microphones were bent over an antique record player on a table.

The setting was just right for her all-school performance debut, Jana thought.

The overhead lights blinked, then dimmed. The speakers crackled and a song began to play. It was "Hawaii Five-O" by The Ventures. The sound of rolling guitars crashed into the gym walls. Students, milling around, bumped into one another trying to stay off the dance floor.

"It's like 1975 around here," Jana said to a Riser standing nearby.

"More like 1969. My dad's uncle had all these records. They didn't have CDs and downloads then. They had to stay home to listen to anything. Or drive around in their cars and play eight-tracks. He said you could play one of those about ten times and then it started messing up, so he bought the records."

Jana saw Beatrice across the gym. She was easy to spot in a crowd. It was like someone had drawn an arrow pointing to her head. Beatrice sat on the second row of bleachers with Arva and Christie. Henry Sixkiller was sitting just below them. He saw Jana at about the same time she spotted his hair. He got up, carrying his shoes, and made his way around the gym floor. Soon he was standing next to her.

"Wait till they do a slow one," Jana told him. "Then let me do the work. You just stand there."

"Okay."

"And don't touch anything."

The Ventures ended. "Get Back," a Beatles song, came on next. Students slid in their socks into the middle of the dance floor. Some of the girls danced with each other.

Pauline was the center of attention. The senior danced with two boys at once, one in front of her, and one behind. She turned her top half to face one while her bottom half faced with the other. At one point, the boy dancing with Pauline's top half took her hand and twirled her around from the waist up. Both boys had to duck in turn when her hair, permanently swept straight out to one side, came around.

Risers danced with Risers and Sliders with Sliders, Jana noticed. Most of the boys just shuffled their feet. She watched Wyatt at the Sliders' end of the gym. He was taller than most of the other students in Dead School. No one had a name for the dance he did. He stood in place and rocked from side to side, using his good arm to roll imaginary toilet paper around his wrist.

Mars was dancing too. It surprised her, for some reason. The girl he danced with was the one with the pierced belly button who Jana had seen standing next to him in the hall. She wasn't right for him. They didn't dance alike at all. Jana's mouth tasted like strawberries as she watched him dance.

She thought of the times she'd danced with Michael. When they danced, they became one person. They gave themselves to each other. Just like when they kissed. His lips were hers. Her lips were his. When she and Michael kissed, they owned each other, but not themselves. Two people becoming one person was the way Jana had always imagined true love.

Mars wanted to save a life. So did she, Jana thought, but more than a single life. She was trying to save an entire relationship. Two people. She just had to kill somebody to do it.

The slow number came next. "Easy to Be Hard" by Three Dog Night. Most of the kids left the center of the gym and regrouped along the sides. The Risers who had been dancing stood in front of the bleachers. Jana tugged her blouse out of her skirt. She opened all but one button. She nudged Henry, who took her hand and walked them to the middle of the floor.

When he stopped, Jana bent her head forward

then flipped her hair back. Jana the actor pushed herself against him. She ran her hand over his hair. It felt like a sable brush. She pushed herself away, stood six inches in front of Henry. She opened her mouth and ran her tongue over her lips, then danced as dirty as she knew how. Students on the gym floor stopped dancing and turned to watch her.

Murmurs ran through the crowd.

Henry took it all in stride and managed somehow not to burst out laughing while he pretended to be seduced. In the midst of it all, Jana's last button came open. The circle of students on the dance floor thickened as other students from the outer edges rushed in to try to catch an eyeful.

Jana blushed, but kept on dancing. Michael was worth the embarrassment. Anyone who had ever been in love would understand.

In the end it was only twenty demerits. The same number she'd earned for leaving campus. Jana had hoped for more.

Dancing topless was something of a bust. Apparently it wasn't egregious even a little bit. For all she knew, the majority of her demerits were for having hung her bra on the library door on her way to the dance. Her dance was sufficiently daring enough, however, to offend the publicity committee, and Arva left the cafeteria as Jana arrived at lunch break.

"She took her bottles of water with her," Beatrice told Jana. "She said she wasn't coming back until you put on a bra."

"She'll have to wait until tomorrow, then," Jana said. "I lost it somewhere."

"Don't worry," Christie assured her. "You'll wake up in the morning wearing one. I threw my shoes out the window once. They walked back in while I was sleeping and climbed on my feet."

Jana told Beatrice her makeup was pretty, that it had been just right for the dance.

"And you." Jana looked at Christie. "How did you get your skirt like that? Your legs looked so long and sleek."

"Beatrice did it for me in the restroom. She cut out three pleats and folded the waistband under. It took about three seconds. She went to sleep with scissors and needle and thread in her hands. It was just like *Project Runway*."

"Christie was wearing shorts when she died," Beatrice said. "There's not much you can do with that, so I thought it would be fun to see what we could do with the uniform for the dance."

"And all we really needed to do was cut the buttons off my blouse," Christie said, smiling at Jana. "Why didn't I think of that?"

Jana grimaced, but just a little. She deserved the joke.

"So it was summer when you died," Jana said. "Do you mind if I ask?"

"Shoot no. That and a bunch of TV shows are about the only things I remember anymore. And honestly, it was kind of fun. I almost didn't feel a thing, except the speed of it all."

"It was fast?" Jana wanted it to be fast for Christie's sake.

Christie dreamed she left her body.

She dreamed it all the time. She would lift out of herself and see her body asleep in bed. In her dreams, she traveled to other places, other rooms. She watched things happen to people. Once she watched a man walk a dog on a mountain road. He didn't know it, but a butterfly was following him. That was a good dream.

Another time she watched a hole open in the

ground and she had to fly away to keep from being sucked into it.

When she woke, she thought the hole was death. Christie believed she'd dreamed her grave. A grave, she decided, was just another place to sleep. And she thought that when she was finally dead she would leave her body and travel to other places too. She'd have all the time in the world.

It was a hot weekend when her uncle showed up at the house. He was out having fun on his four-wheeler. He asked Christie if she wanted to go for a ride.

Her mother had told her she wasn't allowed to do anything with her uncle on the weekends because he was always drunk. He worked hard all week and drank hard all weekend.

"Where?"

"Around," he told her. "It's too hot to sit still."

She was hearing it for the first time, but Christie thought she heard him say that twice. Her uncle removed his ball cap and turned it around backwards.

"Where do you know that's cool?" she asked.

"Lordy, girl, if we go fast enough in big circles we can make it rain. Don't you know anything?"

Christie climbed on the back and he took off across a field where the family down the road used to keep horses. There was no second seat on the four-wheeler. Her uncle sat lower than Christie. She sat on the rack on back and grabbed his shoulders with both hands.

They raced to the end of the field, the four-wheeler bouncing on its fat tires. Christie held on tight. Riding the four-wheeler was a rush. The wind lifted her hair. Birds lifted from the field. Her uncle slowed down just enough to circle the telephone pole at the edge of the field to come back.

The four-wheeler tilted up on two wheels. Her uncle leaned far to one side to bring the other wheels down in mid-circle.

Christie should have ducked, but neither one of them saw it in time. A steel cable, used as a guide wire on the telephone pole, was anchored in the ground two yards off.

The two of them rode under the angled cable. Well, mostly. The cable caught Christie across her forehead and snapped her neck. She lifted out of herself, just like she did in her dreams. She watched the four-wheeler scoot on along without her, her uncle scrunched down in the seat.

Christie's body sat on the ground beside the telephone pole. She didn't stick around to see the hole

they placed her body in. Christie traveled to far-off
places instead.

"I ended up here," Christie said, cringing. "I was hoping for Paris."

She told Jana that she hadn't felt a thing. That it was like a sudden stop and that she didn't remember hitting the ground. "I can push my head all the way back if I want to, but I don't like doing it in front of other people. I think it's rude. A lot of us are like that. When this room relaxes, body parts hit the floor."

Jana would have laughed, but it was likely true.

"Mars Dreamcote can lay his head over to the side anytime he wants," Beatrice told Jana. "Either side. He can rest his head on his own shoulder." She smiled upside down.

"Really?" Jana asked.

"He used to sit like that in class when I first got here," Christie said. "Anyway, don't cry for me. There are lots of worse ways to die. Just look around the room."

"And it did wonders for your hair," Beatrice said.

"I know," Christie said happily. "It really did. Plenty of bounce."

Jana saw how Christie's death fit in with Arva's view of things. Christie's uncle had been drinking. If Arva had been there when the uncle showed up, Jana was certain she would have said, "Better not." And Arva would have been right, Jana had to admit. Still, you weren't going to get anywhere if you never did anything.

"Speaking of bounce," Beatrice said, "you're lucky one of these didn't fall on you at the dance today." She pointed to the yellow yard dart fins at the top of her head.

"Or two!" Christie added quickly. Both girls burst out laughing and Jana had to smile.

"Maybe if I'd been dancing with Brad, one would have," Jana said.

Beatrice stopped laughing. Her face softened and she smiled warmly at Jana, her little upside-down smile stretching into a real one.

"Thank you," she said. "I'd almost forgotten his name, and I never want to forget that. What we did may not be a lot for some people, but it was special to me. It was the first time I'd ever felt like an adult. You know what I mean? When he touched my breast, when he closed his hand over it, I felt like a woman instead of a girl."

• • •

Jana didn't even consider going to drama class.

Students she didn't know said hi to her in the halls, especially the boys. Jana was popular now. Neither Wyatt nor Mars had been in the cafeteria for lunch. She feared she might be unpopular with both of them for the time being. No, she thought, Wyatt would have gotten a kick out of her performance. It was Mars she worried about.

She found her way to the basement swimming pool on her own. This time the overhead lights were on. Two Risers stood near the diving board. Jana walked to the edge of the pool. The surface of the water looked like light blue satin.

Jana pulled off her shoes and socks. Mars sat on the bottom of the pool. She felt cold and didn't want to be. She took off her skirt, practically bruising her fingertips on the ridiculously tight buttons that held the waist closed. She left her skirt where it fell. She carefully removed Michael's ring and placed it inside one of her shoes. Leaving on her blouse and school uniform granny panties, Jana jumped into the pool feet first.

CHAPTER TWENTY-FIVE

JANA JUMPED IN AND WENT UNDER.

Water covered her in warmth. She came back up and quickly took a breath of air. She swam to the middle, where Mars was waiting below. Jana pointed her toes straight down and, with a push of her arms upward, dropped beneath the surface.

She released air in a series of rising bubbles and swam toward Mars. He was watching her. He waved one arm, then the other, rising into a crouch, his knees folded under him. He brought his hands to his sides, and in one powerful push he shot straight up toward the surface, passing Jana in her slower descent.

Jana rowed her arms through the water, bringing her legs under her. Her feet touched bottom. She pushed gently away, upward, and rose to the surface.

Water ran from their hair and faces. Mars gasped for air.

"Are you trying to set some kind of record?" Jana asked. She wondered how long he could stay down there before he was forced to surface.

Dark eyelashes batted away droplets of water from Mars's blue eyes.

"I thought you were the one trying to set a record, Webster." Mars tried to look like he was angry with her, but one corner of his smile wouldn't quite disappear. "Most demerits per minute in the history of the world."

Jana grinned. Mars understood. She didn't have to explain anything. She didn't even care if her ears stuck out of her wet hair.

"I think you should know," he continued, "demeriting is not an Olympic event."

"Not yet," Jana said. The warmth from his body broadcast through the water in a widening circle that included Jana. It was like swimming in heated milk.

"You're trying to think of a movie, aren't you?"

"No," she said. It surprised her that she wasn't, in fact, doing just that. She was thinking, instead, of an electric blow-dryer dropped into Michael's bathtub. "They haven't made this one yet."

Nathan decided not to go back to school after lunch. Anyone who knew Jana at all had an excuse.

"We have to get this behind us," Michael said. "It was a joke, a stupid joke. And now it's over."

Nathan didn't want to say the wrong thing. He recognized a bad mood when Michael was having one. They were parked in Nathan's driveway. He couldn't get out of the car until Michael was through talking.

"You know, she thought it was all about her," Michael went on. "When I talked about my plans, she thought I was talking about us, the two of us. Every waking hour, I swear, she was right there next to me. It was humiliating the way she stuck to me like that. She was into this *Romeo and Juliet* thing to the core. There was no end to it. It's like her hands were superglued to my belt. She was really holding me back."

"I can see that," Nathan said.

"So it was a little joke. That's all. Listen, there

were words I wanted to say that would have hurt her more than falling down at a bowling alley."

"You were going to have to break up with her sometime," Nathan said. Michael had told him that a hundred times or more, so it was safe to say.

"Exactly. You know, it's probably better this way. She died happy. She didn't know about Sherry and me doing it behind her back. And I swear, it was going to break her into pieces when we split up. Her dying spared her that."

"You didn't do it on purpose. It just happened."

Michael stared bullets at Nathan. "*We* didn't do it on purpose," he said slowly, firing each word from between his teeth.

The Risers were waiting to dive. Mars and Jana climbed out of the pool. Mars turned on the pumps while Jana retrieved her skirt. She needed to get out of her wet blouse and dry off.

"Come with me," she said. "I want to talk."

Mars followed her into the girls' locker room. They both grabbed towels. While he rubbed his chest and legs with his towel, Jana turned her back and slipped off her blouse. She wrapped herself in her towel.

"I thought of one," she said.

"One what?" Mars stopped rubbing his hair with his towel. It looked terrific half wet and tousled like that, Jana thought.

"Movie," Jana said. "Wring this for me." She handed Mars the soaking, dripping lump of cloth and buttons that previously had been her blouse. Jana took another towel for her hair. She'd have to comb it with her hands.

She watched Mars twist her blouse into a snake, water pouring out of it. He folded it over and twisted it tighter. His stomach tightened as he worked, his biceps flexed. She put on her skirt, keeping the towel draped over her shoulders.

Jana spread a fresh towel on the locker room bench. She sat on one end of the towel. Mars unwound her blouse, shook it loose, and draped it over a towel bar by the sinks.

"Come here and sit down," Jana said. "I'm cold with my hair wet."

Mars sat next to her.

"So, what's the movie?"

"It's silly," she said. "I bet you saw it when you were a little kid. Johnny Weissmuller and Maureen O'Sullivan."

"Got it, Webster. *Tarzan of the Apes.*"

"Close. The first one was *Tarzan the Ape Man.* This was the second one, Tarzan *and* Jane. It's *Tarzan and His Mate.*"

"Me Tarzan. You Jana?" Mars asked. "Is it the way I talk or something?"

"No, you doof. They go swimming. Jane skinny-dips. They show it underwater. They cut the scene out of the movie for years and years. Then they put it back."

They listened to a diver hit the water from the high board. He messed up, Mars thought. It was too big of a splash.

"So, what do you want to talk about, Webster?"

"I don't. I want you to talk. I don't know how to be nice about this, but I want to know how you died and why you want to save a life. I also want to know why you chose me. My first day here, you chose me, Mars, like you pick out something at the store to wear. Why me?"

"It wasn't your first day here," Mars said. "It was before that."

Like most guys, he looked straight ahead while he talked. Jana watched his face, the way his eyes moved when he was remembering things. He told her everything, beginning with when she walked through him at the bowling alley shoe counter and ending with when he frantically blew air into her throat by sealing his lips over hers.

"I almost had you back," he said. "Your eyelids fluttered. I almost made you breathe again."

Jana moved the tip of her tongue between her lips and swallowed. Strawberries.

"And you'd been drinking strawberry pop," she said. "I can still taste it. I guess I brought it with me when I died." Mars had been trying to breathe air into her mouth, she realized. But it was the same as if he'd been kissing her.

"Listen to me," Jana continued. "You couldn't have saved me. It was the little crack at the back of my head. That's what killed me."

"But I saw it happen, start to finish. You don't know how it feels to fail at that. To have someone dying and no matter what you do, they just keep dying . . . until they're gone. It tore me up."

Jana touched his leg as a gesture of understanding. The heat from Mars's body leaped through her hand, up her arm, across her shoulders. It moved down inside her like she was drinking it. Her neck and face reddened. She took her hand away.

"You tried to give me my life back, Mars. Thank you."

He didn't say anything. Jana listened to him breathe. She had said enough. He would answer her other request if he wanted to.

"You know, it's funny," he finally said. "On the Planet, you meet people and they tell you the story of their life. Here, we tell each other how we died."

Mars combed his fingers through his wet hair.

"I was drunk," he said. "Wasted. In the middle of the day. I was drunk and I was angry. I wanted to get away from something and there was nowhere to go, really. So I just drove. I got on the interstate. I drove past three exits, got off at the fourth, and turned around and drove back."

"Get away from what?" she asked.

"My father," he said quietly. "He was a drunk. He hated himself and he saw himself in me, I think. And maybe he should have. I was becoming just like him. I hated him and I was becoming just like him. Stupid, huh?"

Jana didn't answer.

She thought about her mother's addictions. Alcohol, cocaine, heroin, pharmaceuticals. Mostly her mother was addicted to her own beauty, addicted to being adored. Her mother became dependent on drinking and drugs because not enough people loved and admired her. Her mother was the only star in her own sky, and no matter how strikingly beautiful she was, she could never shine brightly enough. Jana might have loved and admired her too. If her mother had ever been there.

"What happened?" Jana asked.

Mars and his car were just alike. Motors roaring, nowhere to go.

The speed of it all, the scream of engine and tires, was under his right foot. His car fishtailed on the interstate ramp. The sound in his head was louder than the engine.

He raced past a semi in the slow lane by driving ninety on the shoulder.

Windows down, the wind rushed through. The sound of the truck was deafening. But not loud enough.

It had to be louder. And faster.

Mars raced through traffic and sunlight, drove past three exits, hit the exit ramp at the fourth. He hit the brakes to hold the curve. He spun the steering wheel to the left, running the stop sign at the end of the ramp.

His hands were meaningless. The car knew where

he wanted to go. Motion and direction were thoughts in the pulse of his blood. The car zipped under the highway, cut off traffic as it turned left again, and slid up the reverse direction on the ramp like a bullet in the barrel of a gun.

If he drove fast enough, long enough . . . loud enough, the rage inside would lessen, would become a heartbeat again, would eventually go away.

But not yet.

There was no comfort now in anything but speed. The trees along the highway slammed by. They challenged him to go faster. Speed could make them disappear. And Mars could disappear along with them.

He changed lanes constantly, passing cars, passing trucks, weaving, letting available space among the traffic reveal itself once he was upon it.

It was easy until he topped a long incline, right foot to the floor. His mouth open, dry, his eyes mere slits, Mars was behind traffic just like that. He was moments from plowing into somebody. In that instant before he could touch the brakes, there was nothing to do but swerve.

The swerve, his last chance to avoid an accident, cost him control. Mars was pushed against the inside of the driver's door. He stomped the brakes. It was too *late. His world jolted, turned, lurched, and the brakes merely barked once as the car left the pavement.*

The car flew. It was an airplane, with four wheels and no wings. There was no gear for landing. Mars tried to think of a prayer. He didn't have one. His car flew over the ditch alongside the interstate, nose down into the base of a tree.

It might have saved him if he had a car with air bags. At least Mars was belted in. His harness held. That might have saved him too. But it didn't. Hitting the tree was like hitting the wall at the Indy 500 straight on. Dead stop.

"That's what killed me, Webster."

Mars closed his eyes.

"Coming to a stop killed me. My brain threw itself forward inside my skull. Like you throw a fist against the wall."

His voice was thick with pain. Mars turned around and stood in front of her.

Jana watched the rise and fall of his flat belly as he breathed. She looked at his bare chest. She could almost see his heart beating. She wanted to place her hand lightly there, to keep it from hurting him so much.

"Look at me, Webster." Mars tapped a finger against his cheekbone.

His blue eyes glistened with tears. "Look at me," he said again. She hadn't stopped. His eyes held hers to the finish. "I wasn't the only person who died when I wrecked."

CHAPTER TWENTY-SIX

MARS CHANGED.

He came out of the boys' locker room looking like he'd never been wet. Except his hair was a little more tousled than usual.

Jana looked like she'd been in over her head. Her blouse was badly wrinkled and damp. Her hair was in semi-corded tangles. She looked like a Slider, she thought.

"You saw me the night you died," Mars told her.

"I don't remember that."

"That's the thing. You looked right at me as you fell. Wyatt and I were ghosting. No one could see me, but you did. Your eyes were wild and wide.

When you looked at me, your eyes pleaded for help. That's when I materialized. I decided to be there for you."

"There was a moment when things froze," Jana recalled. "Everything slowed down. For less than a second, everything stopped. But I didn't see you."

"When you were on the bus your first day here, I thought you would recognize me. I thought you knew."

"I'm sorry, Mars. I didn't know you had been there. I didn't know you tried to save me."

"You must have thought I was a total creep." He grinned and combed his damp hair back from his forehead with his hand.

"I didn't have to think anything," Jana said. "Arva told me you were as dangerous as poison."

"Am I?"

It was Jana's turn to smile. "Yes, I think you are. But not for any of the reasons you would guess. You're poison because I'm in love with Michael. He's my destiny."

Mars stopped walking. "I turn off here," he said. "I don't do classroom work in the afternoons."

"Vocational training?"

"Yes."

"I just thought of something," Jana said quickly. "You know, you don't have to go to the Planet to do good things for people here. You can save a life right here, Mars, without leaving campus."

He waited, his perfectly arched eyebrows raised as he gazed at her.

"Beatrice," Jana said. "Do something to get that dart out of her head. She has to feel like the elephant man every minute of every day. Believe me, you would be saving her life. You guys have metal shop or something, don't you? You can take pliers and yank it out of her head."

"It would be there the next day, Webster."

"There must be something you can do."

"I'll think about it," Mars said. "You better go now and pick up your demerits. The Virgins will be waiting for you."

"Let me ask you something first? Real quick, I promise."

He nodded.

"When I kissed you last night on the stairs and we were nose to nose like that, did you want to kiss me back?"

"Maybe," Mars said, his eyes dancing with mischief.

Jana laughed. "Why didn't you?"

"You already said it, Webster. I'm not your destiny. He is." Mars turned and walked away from her. If Jana had been Pauline, she could have left with Mars and stayed with Michael both. But Jana wasn't Pauline.

Jana did fairly well.

All told, her demerits now neared a hundred. Cutting a class must be a big no-no. Leaving her panties in the locker room at the pool and coming to fifth period commando seemed to have helped.

She was tired of the game for the day. If she acted up in class, she'd get detention again. And she had run out of things she could take off and still live with herself. The only thing to do, she thought, was to jump. If she jumped, they'd have to make her a Slider. Jameson had almost said as much.

When Dead School was over for the day, Jana walked to the back of the bus and rode to the dorm with the Sliders. It didn't seem to make anyone comfortable. Sliders didn't talk to Risers on the bus, Jana learned. Not even Wyatt. And he never kept his mouth shut.

Arva left her alone in the room with Darcee.

Jana didn't blame her. Jana's recent behavior obviously alarmed and dismayed her roommate to no end.

Jana opened a bottle of water. "Is it insane to kill him?" she asked Darcee. "It's not madness if I know he will be here with me. I'll be saving both of us. For all time." Darcee, as always, reserved her comments for later.

"A lifetime isn't enough time for love," Jana said. "Not my lifetime, anyway." She changed into the clothes she'd been wearing the night she died. "A lifetime isn't enough time, period."

It was obvious from last night that Jana would have no chance to talk Michael into cooperating. He had gone crazy when he saw her sitting next to him on the bed. It almost broke her heart. Now she thought she understood it. A woman can talk to a ghost. They did it all the time in movies. A man can't handle it.

Jana considered a nail gun. There wouldn't be an exit wound and she could shoot Michael in the same spot where her own skull had a hole it in. They'd be just alike in Dead School, sort of. But a nail gun might be too heavy, she decided, and she didn't know how to work one. She'd have to rent one and take lessons or something. No go.

She returned to favoring electrocution. As a Slider, Jana could materialize long enough to pick up something plugged in and toss it into the bathtub with Michael. And then he'd have really cool spiky hair. Just like Henry's. Only it would look better on Michael.

When Arva came into the room, there were other students with her. Jana didn't know any of them, although she had seen them all in class.

"We want to talk to you," Arva said. Everyone nodded solemnly. Arva held an open notebook in her hands.

"Yearbook staff?" Jana asked, smiling.

"Sit down and listen." Arva stated it as strongly as her hoarse choking breaths would allow. Hoarse feathers, Jana thought.

"Publicity Committee?" she tried. "I won't mess up your dance again, I promise. That was a one-time thing and—"

"Intervention," Arva announced. "You need help, Jana. To stop what you're doing. You're destroying yourself and damaging those around you, the people who care about you. We're here to help you help yourself."

Suddenly Jana had somewhere else she had to be. Without saying another word, she helped herself out of her dorm room as quickly as possible.

The third floor was her only refuge.

Jana marched out of her room and walked past the lone Gray at the stairwell. As she climbed the steps, the noise grew louder. Upstairs, from one end to the other, the old motel rocked. At least three stereos played different music at the same time. The hall was filled with Sliders.

A metal door in the brick fire wall in the middle of the long hall was propped open with a table from the laundry room. Yellow stenciling on the door read *Girls Only*.

If this half of the third floor was the girls' dorm, it was hard to tell. An almost equal number of boys and girls leaned against the walls and sat on the floor. They talked and rocked in place to the music. They didn't seem to notice her. The air was filled with cigarette smoke. Everyone smelled like beer.

Jana walked to the table holding the dividing door open. Candles were burning there. They'd been arranged on a paper plate.

"It's a birthday party," a girl with a cigarette in her mouth said to Jana. "We ran out of cake." The Slider's eyes were dark red where they should have been white. They must have filled with blood as she was dying.

"Whose birthday is it?" Jana asked.

"Who knows? It's one of the things you forget. So we have a birthday party once a week just in case."

Jana searched her memory. Michael's birthday was missing. It seemed impossible that she didn't know when it was. He was a Leo, she thought. Or was she?

The Slider drew on her cigarette, watching Jana's face. "Someone can check your gravestone if it matters to you," she said. A narrow white finger of smoke rose from the back of the girl's head. She must have gone bowling, Jana thought.

"Guess not," Jana said. "Do you know where Mars Dreamcote's room is?"

"Sure. All the way to the end of the hall next to the fire escape."

"Thank you," Jana said. She stepped around the table and walked into the boys' half of the hall. Two Sliders tried to talk to her. She smiled but kept on walking. A neatly penciled sign on the door read *Knock*. Mars had said they'd leave after dark. It was after dark. Jana knocked.

Half an hour later, Jana sat on the bench out front with Barry. The Gray wasn't talking much. She was getting used to that. Grays were like potted plants. Something to look at, but lousy when it came to conversation.

Headlights blinked twice on the road out front. She hurried to the hole in the fence.

A police detective was on the phone.

"I need you to write out a statement and sign it," he said.

"Yeah, whatever," Michael said. "Do you always call people this late?"

"It's been a long day," the detective apologized. "What can I tell you? This isn't our top priority. Routine paperwork is all. I don't get it done, I get in trouble. You understand that, don't you? It's like homework. It doesn't always matter, but you have to get it done."

"The whole thing was an accident," Michael said. "She fell and hit her head on her bowling ball. I don't know what else I can tell you."

"Oh, that will do. You just write that out for me. I have to file your statement is all. You were a witness. It's entirely routine, Mr. Haynes. I have to do a chain-of-events type thing. You know, she picked up the ball. She walked over there. She fell down. Look, I can come by your school tomorrow and we can do it there."

"No," Michael said. That was the last thing he needed. "I'll drop by like you said. It's across from the courthouse?"

"Park in the municipal lot. I'll give you a voucher. What do we say, then? Ten o'clock?"

"Ten's okay."

"We're all set, then. Hey, look, I know this must be an emotional time for you, Mr. Haynes. But the sooner we do this the better. You were going to get married, right?"

"No," Michael said. "Nothing like that."

"Oh, okay. I had that wrong, then. Say, she wasn't pregnant, was she?"

"Of course not." Michael's hand started shaking. He moved his phone to the other one.

"Wait," the detective said, seemingly distracted. "I've got it right here. Her blood report. Oh, of course, you're both good kids. I can see that. Let's see, you're going to college at the end of the year, is that right? Early entry in the summer. Leadership scholarship . . ." He sounded like he was reading a list. "Dartmouth, what do you know. Ten o'clock, then, tomorrow, and I can get this paperwork out of the way."

The detective finally hung up. The investigator was lying, Michael decided. They'll say anything to get you to talk. It was more than paperwork he had on his mind. As for "chain of events," Michael was the one who was chained to events. He didn't deserve this. He couldn't believe Jana had done this to him. She fell down the wrong way and now they were going to ruin his life over it.

Mars drove into the mountains south of Asheville. The automatic transmission of the car they'd borrowed geared down for every climb on the winding state road that brought them nearer to their jumping-off place.

"Lookaway Rock," Wyatt said from the backseat. "Elevation somewhere around four thousand feet, but you don't fall that far."

Occasionally they approached a dark rise of mountain that shone with the scattered lights of houses. You couldn't see the mountains at night and the lights looked like stars hung low in the sky.

"Give me your hand," Jana told Wyatt. He did. She tried Michael's number on her cell one more time. He still wouldn't answer. She guessed she didn't blame him.

"Most jumpers do the waterfall," Wyatt said. "You stand over to one side and just step off. It's easier."

Lookaway Rock was a much longer drop. It was over three hundred feet of vertical granite left over from the movement of glaciers during the Ice Age. The cliff marked the steep end of a mountain gorge and was shaped like the inside of a horseshoe at the top. From the bottom it looked like a waterfall itself, but Lookaway was pure rock.

"You can jump off anywhere and not feel a thing until you hit bottom," Wyatt said. "It's tricky, though, because the entire curve of rock slopes off at the top, toward the open sky. You get vertigo standing there and that's how it got its name. To keep your balance on the rock, you have to look away."

It sounded scary to Jana. Truly, awfully, dreadfully scary. She hoped Michael appreciated what she was about to go through.

"Tell me why you do this again," she said.

Jana had a goal. She was jumping so she could become a Slider. Mars and Wyatt were jumping just to jump.

Wyatt laughed.

"It's the ultimate extreme," he said. "It's the absolute most, like standing in front of a freight train. Only your body parts don't get dragged all over the place when the slam comes. You don't understand adrenaline until you've jumped. You'll never feel more alive. It's beautiful."

Jana doubted that jumping was beautiful.

"And the slam. It is so total, Webster. There's nothing like it you could ever do in real life. Well, not twice, anyway. You're crushing every bone in your body all in one rush. It's . . . it's total."

"It's definitely suicidal," Jana said. "Why isn't it suicide?"

"Because we're not doing it to quit. When you give up, when you kill yourself to quit, they don't repair you. That's suicide. We're just killing our bodies, because eventually when you're dead, you figure out you can. It's a loophole."

"I don't get it," Jana confessed.

"Okay, if I cut off my finger in Dead School

either on purpose or by accident, it heals itself. We keep the body we died with, remember? So the rest of it, the suicide part, is intent. We're not killing ourselves to give up and quit the whole show. We're taking our bodies to the maximum for the thrill of it, Webster, because we know beforehand we'll get our bodies back."

"What if you jumped as a way to, like you said, 'quit the whole show'?"

"Then it would be suicide. Suicide is intent. You throw yourself into a raging river in order to end the misery of your pitiful existence and you drown, that's suicide. You throw yourself into the same raging river at the same spot at the very same time, but you're doing it to escape a forest fire and you think you might have a chance to survive . . . well, it's not suicide, even though you drown."

Wyatt paused. "Got it?"

"I got it," Jana said. "I'm not an idiot or anything. But it's a tricky distinction, you have to admit."

"That's why you have us, Webster. We've done all the moral groundwork of being dead for you. Sliders are good for that. It's on our minds a lot once we get here."

They'd reached the turnoff from the highway.

Mars drove the car on to a dirt road, then crossed a one-lane bridge over an expanse of rushing water. The rise of trees and mountains on Jana's side of the car blocked the sky.

"They give us our bodies here for I don't know how long," Wyatt said. "They make me drag this mangled leg around and talk out of half my mouth. I don't even care why. I just want to know for how long."

Neither Mars nor Jana suggested an answer.

Wyatt kept talking. "You've got a lot of time to kill here, Webster. You can't just sit around paying attention to all that bullshit in school. So we do something. And if you're going to do something . . . it might as well be the most you can do. We don't do this to quit. We do this to get a jump on life."

He laughed at himself.

Mars pulled the car into a small turnout alongside the road. Two guys stood in front of a pickup truck parked back into the tall weeds. They both came over. They were Sliders from school. One of them leaned by the driver's window to talk to Mars.

"All clear," he said.

"There're no campers up there tonight? Nobody parking?"

"No one but you. And your sidekick."

"Hey, don't call me that," Wyatt said from the backseat. "You're making fun of the way I walk."

The guy from the pickup glanced at Jana.

"How is she getting down?" he asked.

"We have to go back and get the car anyway," Mars said. "She'll keep an eye on it for us."

The Slider looked at Jana one more time and let it linger. "Cute dance you did today," he said to her. "You should come up to the third floor again and show us how you do that."

CHAPTER TWENTY-SEVEN

"ARE THERE SNAKES?"

Jana needed to know. She also worried about putting her hand on a spider in the dark, or having one shimmy up her leg as she walked by.

"Snakes only come out at night if you build a fire," Wyatt told her. "The things to watch out for are nighthawks and owls. Owls are bigger than you think."

Jumping off a cliff was one way to test her resolve and her devotion to Michael, Jana thought. Getting there at night was another. And on top of that, she now had to worry about getting an owl in her hair.

"Do they land on your shoulders or what?"

"Nah," Wyatt drawled. "They just fly by and peck your eyes out. I'm surprised you didn't ask about panthers. They say they're extinct in this mountain range, but people who live up this way say they still hear a panther scream now and then at night."

The trails along the top ridge and highest slopes of the mountain followed old, overgrown logging roads. Pieces of the trails were washed away by weather. Fallen trees crossed the rutted paths here and there no matter which way you chose.

"Turn on your flashlight, Webster," Mars said. He touched Jana on the shoulder. "It's just a path. There aren't any panthers."

Jana switched on her light and moved the beam across the face of the woods they were about to enter. It looked dangerous.

"I'll go first," Mars said. "Webster, grab my belt loop with one hand and come behind me. Wyatt will bring up the rear. Just hold on to my belt. When we have to climb over a log or something, I'll stop and help you."

It was pitch black under the trees. Jana kept her flashlight on her feet. She only let go of Mars's belt once, when she slipped clambering over a fallen tree.

"Hoot," Wyatt said behind her. "Hoot, hoot."

"Not funny," Jana said.

The long, curving expanse of Lookaway Rock seemed to glow in the darkness as they neared. The giant slice of granite caught what light there was from the stars and the waning moon. Shadows moved across the rock as swirls of mountain fog opened holes to the night sky, then quickly closed them.

"From the bottom, they say you can see pictures on the cliff when moonlight comes through the fog," Mars told her. "It's supposed to be like watching a movie."

Jana directed the beam of her flashlight into the sky beyond the cliff's edge. The light dead-ended in darkness.

"I wonder if they can see you fall," she said.

"Sure they can," Wyatt said. "Hey, Webster, I'm going to be a movie star instead of you tonight. How's my makeup?" He pointed his flashlight at his face, rolling his one eye to make it look straight up. "Is my hair all right?"

The three of them stood at the outer edge of the rock, a few yards back from the sheer drop into the bare darkness of night. The rock was edged with a carpet of juniper moss.

Light gusts of air rode the rise of warmth from the floor of the gorge. Updrafts moved over the rock like water, cutting the legs out from under the fog. Swirls of mist danced over the rock. Jana stood close to Mars. There was enough light in the open air that she could see the breeze move the tips of his dark hair. It shimmered.

Wyatt turned off his flashlight. He handed it to Jana.

"If we're all set, I'm out of here," he said.

Mars tensed as Wyatt moved away from them, listing forward until he was standing on the rock, in the center of the curve of sloping granite that only a few yards out disappeared into the black sky. Wyatt leaned into the mist, into the night.

"Hey, Webster," he called back in a whisper full of ragged breath. "Aren't you going to tell me to break a leg?"

He lurched into an odd-looking run that reminded Jana of the backside of a camel. Wyatt swung his injured leg wildly forward and hurried his good leg to catch up so he could do it again. She watched him disappear.

The distant, falling scream sounded like someone

riding a roller coaster. A roller coaster that didn't come back. The scream grew faint, but it never seemed to stop.

Jana began to tremble. She was afraid. It came over her like a wave. She dropped her flashlight. It pointed nowhere.

"Don't leave," she said. Wrapping her arm around Mars's waist, she leaned against him. As she held him, the night breeze moved across her face. She closed her eyes. Every part of her body was real. "Don't leave me here."

"I won't," Mars said. "I'm here."

Jana dropped Wyatt's flashlight and placed her other arm around Mars and squeezed. She was so tired of being alone, of being dead alone.

She pressed her face against his chest. His arms were around her. Mars was touching her low in the middle of her back. He was holding her. His flashlight dropped to the carpet of moss at their feet. Its beam of light crossed the dimmer glow from Jana's flashlight that lay nearby.

Jana told herself she wasn't going to cry. She felt fully human, fully comfortable and comforted for the first time since she'd died. She wanted to go to sleep like this, and sleep for a very long time.

"It's okay," Mars said quietly.

But it wasn't okay, Jana thought. It wasn't okay at all. She wanted to feel this way with Michael, not with Mars.

"What are you afraid of?" he asked. "Are you afraid of me?"

Mars had asked her what she was afraid of before. "I'm afraid of being dead," Jana said. This time she added, "And I'm afraid of being alive."

"I know." His words were spoken so quietly they sounded like breathing and nothing else. "It's okay," Mars said again. "I know."

Jana didn't say a word.

"I'll go back with you if you want to go back."

Mars was so warm, too warm. Her thoughts wouldn't hold while she was wrapped in the tremors of heat that came from the outside in and then, oddly, rose from inside her own living body. Mars was giving her earthly, physical life when he held her.

She forced herself to push away. She was going to jump. It was the only way she could become a Slider in time to do something about getting Michael back.

"Look," she said. "I'm going through with it. I've thought about it. If you hold me, I can jump."

Mars cleared his throat. His hand touched his hair.

"I want to tell you something first," he said. "There's something I know and I should have told you sooner. I just didn't know how. I didn't know if you would believe me."

Jana waited. Then she remembered. "It's that murder stuff," she said, surprised that she had thought of it. "You were trying to tell me I was murdered since first period, first day. And showing me the lubricant spray on my bowling shoe, is that what you meant? Do you think Sherry murdered me?"

"No," Mars said. "Michael is the one who sprayed your shoe. It wasn't Sherry. It wasn't Nathan. I watched it happen. He would have sprayed the other one if you had looked away a little longer."

Jana considered it. It came down to intent, just like the difference between jumping and suicide. Michael hadn't meant to hurt her. He certainly had no intention of killing her.

What Michael did was a stupid joke, she thought, but nothing more than that. She had made them go bowling. So he was getting even. It was supposed to be funny. Michael just thought she would slide around and look goofy . . . and everyone would laugh. Including Jana.

"He didn't mean to kill me, Mars," she said. "He didn't want me dead. He just . . . he was just being a boy."

Mars listened carefully. Her response was what he had feared it would be. Her love for Michael was that strong, that big. When someone loves someone else that much, you don't try to kick holes in it. It wouldn't do Jana any good not to love Michael. It was all she had. It was everything.

"He killed me," she said more brightly, "so I'll kill him."

Mars didn't think it was funny.

"To do that, I have to jump," she added.

Her plan was in place. She was in the seventh maze. The one that Mr. Skinner hadn't drawn yet. You didn't turn left. You didn't turn right. You turned an entirely new way. One you had never tried before.

"I know it's not written down in that antique book word for word like this," Jana said. "I know it's not certain, but it's pretty clear to everyone—to you, me, and Jameson. If I jump, I'll come out of it a Slider."

"Do you really want that?" Mars asked. "To be a Slider?"

"Of course I do. I want Michael. And I want me. It's why I'm here tonight, Mars. You keep saying we're here to learn something. That we have to find out things for ourselves. Well, for me, being a Slider is the way I'm going to learn. I know that sounds backwards to you, and that Wyatt thinks I'm a total ass clown. But being a Slider is my chance. It's my chance to be me again."

Mars couldn't argue with that. Jana was always smarter than he thought she was going to be.

"I can't do it without you," she added. "If I jump alone, it will only be my spirit. If you jump holding me, I'll have my body back. You make me real, Mars."

"You have to ask me," he said quietly. "You have to ask me to hold you when you jump, or I'll be interfering in your fate."

"Will you please hold me, Mars? All the way down?"

Jana took his hand in hers.

"Run with me," she said. "And when we're off the edge, put your arms around me."

As they ran, Jana grabbed as much bodily life from Mars as he had to give her. But falling was not flying, no matter what they say. It was much faster than that. Her body locked against Mars, Jana forced herself to breathe to keep from passing out.

The two Sliders who made up the retrieval and recovery team loaded Jana's broken body into the bed of the pickup, next to Mars's.

Wyatt didn't feel like talking yet. He stood next to the truck and leaned over them. Mars was still unconscious, but moving his hands.

Jana was dead still. Wyatt realized that she had managed a legitimate jump. She'd felt the slam.

Mars had to have been holding her for her body to be such a bloody mess. A Riser couldn't be damaged like that falling alone. They could barely touch the earth at all.

She'd felt every wisp of the fall, from start to finish. It seemed impossible what they had done.

The moon had risen above the roving layer of clouds and mist along the mountaintop. Wyatt watched Jana's left hand, crossed over her chest at the end of a broken wrist and a shattered elbow. As pools of fresh blood were sucked back inside her body, beads of blood rolled from the surface of the large class ring she wore, leaving the metal of the ring glinting in moonlight. Because the ring and the clothes she wore, the cell phone in her pocket, were items she had died with, they would all be good as new soon.

Clothes taken in trade by Sliders from the Planet stayed damaged, stained and torn, when you wore them on the Planet. Wyatt changed into a fresh shirt from clothes stored in the cab of the pickup. He selected one for Mars, who had rolled onto one side already and had drawn his legs up.

Mars would be sitting soon. Jana would take longer to recover. First-time physical recovery was always slow. They wouldn't know whether or not she was a Slider until then.

Jumping, for a Riser, was an act well beyond those that merely earned demerits, Jameson had said. He'd told Mars and Wyatt that the chances were good that Jana would shift status if they could figure out a way she could jump physically, torturously in touch with earth, and not as the lighter spirit body that a Riser usually occupied on the Planet.

If a Slider jumped holding her, there was a good chance Jana would change status at the end of the fall. But they wouldn't know for certain until it was over. No Riser had ever jumped before.

Mars sat up. Wyatt reached across the tailgate to give him a hand. Soon, Mars had changed shirts and was able to stand. He and Wyatt leaned on their elbows on the side of the truck bed and watched Jana.

"Did you tell her?" Wyatt asked.

"Part of it," Mars confessed. "She knows her boyfriend did it. It didn't change her mind about anything."

"Her heart, you mean. It didn't change her heart."

"I didn't think she really wanted to kill her boyfriend."

"Now you know."

"I thought she was going to turn back at any point," Mars said. "Even while we fell, I thought she was going to let go."

"Juliet never let go," Wyatt said. He shrugged. "It's love, man, what can I tell you?"

Jana moaned.

Wyatt and Mars shot glances at each other. Still unconscious, Jana's body felt the pains of recovery, the residual internal bruising and incomplete mending from the jump.

Then she moved. Her arms first. One leg. The other.

Like Mars, she rolled onto her side and curled up as blood rushed through her body, feeding oxygen to her muscles, her brain. She coughed. Jana rolled onto her back and stretched her legs. Her knees worked, her ankles, her toes. "Ow," she said, opening her eyes. She looked at the two faces looming over her in the moonlight. The pain in her head was rapidly speeding away.

"Why is it so warm?" she asked.

CHAPTER TWENTY-EIGHT

MARS WAS GRIM.

The hardest part was now. He and Jana stood outside her door. Mars had asked her to wait before going in. He had to tell her. It was going to be bad.

"I can't do much out there, can I?" she asked.

"Not yet," Mars said. "You sort of have to naturalize yourself to the Planet. Concentrate on it. Focus. Practice. It will come."

"You'll show me, won't you?"

"Knowing you, you'll be fully interacting in no time."

Jana smiled. The thrill of falling, even the horrific bolt of the total slam, kept running through her memory and her body. Jana shuddered involuntarily from time to time as her bones remembered it on their own. Her skin danced with ghostly touches of physical memory. The fine hairs on her arms lifted at the thought of the long, empty night opening under her.

It was everything Wyatt had said it would be. And more. Because of Mars, it had been more. More purely physical than she could have imagined. Still, it wasn't Michael. It was Webster and Dreamcote, not Webster and Haynes.

"I have something I have to tell you," Mars was saying. "It's something you've been overlooking. It's important."

She looked at his blue eyes. His face was tired, but his eyes remained intense. Mars turned his gaze away from her.

"I didn't understand how serious you were about killing Michael, about wanting him here. I thought you would change your mind."

"Oh, he's dead," Jana said almost cheerfully. "Count on it."

"That's the thing, Webster. You can't kill him."

"Yes, I can. And I will."

"No." He held up his hand to stop her from

talking. Mars looked into her eyes. "If you kill anybody, here or on the Planet, you're an instant vacancy. If you kill Michael, he'll be here, but you won't. If you kill him, it will just be murder, nothing more than that."

The inside of Jana's chest felt like wasps were stinging her. She breathed fishhooks and thorns. There was nothing to say.

Jana was tired of it all.

She was tired of trying. She sat on her bed, back against the wall. When she lay down, the night would be over. Jana didn't want the night to end. She wanted it all to end.

Arva hadn't waited up. Both halves of Pauline were dead asleep. Darcee had the best of it, Jana thought. She wasn't waking up.

Jana had forgotten Michael's birthday. What else had she forgotten?

Had they made love? No, she didn't think so. Had they come close? She couldn't remember. She should be able to look at the inside of her hand and see his face there.

She was a Slider now. Jana had always been one, she supposed. Deep down, she'd always wanted

Earth, the coarser touch of life. Deep down, she'd always wanted real life. Just as Christie had when she'd climbed on the back of the four-wheeler. Just as Beatrice had when she gave her bare breast to Brad. Jana had always wanted life and now that was exactly what she didn't have. Or if she did, she had only the small portion of it that hurt.

Michael hadn't saved her. He hadn't tried. He'd stood and watched her die.

That was the part that hurt. Not that he had sprayed her shoe with lubricant. That didn't matter. It was that some ghost had been there with her, doing what Michael should have done. Michael should have tried. Jana hated him for not being Romeo. She loved him with all her heart and hated him just the same. He should have killed himself over her.

"Dammit, Michael, love me!" Jana said out loud. The words flew from her heart. They were the color of blood. "Love me, love me, love me!"

Yes, he should have killed himself over her. That wouldn't have worked either. He would be a Gray. But he should have anyway. And now, if Jana killed him, she wouldn't be here at all. It was a maze with no exit. The last box that Mr. Skinner ever drew would be like that. Dead end. No way out. You just stood still inside the box and let it hurt.

It hit her like a hammer. Michael and Jana were no longer Romeo and Juliet. Jana was both. She was Romeo because Michael wouldn't be. She was Juliet . . . because she just was. She was both parts since she had died. It wasn't written that way. It would never work.

They were on the bus again.

"I can tell," Arva croaked in her usual feather-and-beak whisper. "You're one of them."

The emotion in her voice was either grave disapproval or ardent disgust. Jana looked at her hands in the lap of her school uniform, stared at Michael's class ring, and simply nodded in reply.

"You smell funny," Arva continued. "You smell like a pine tree. When we come back, your room will be on the third floor. And so will all your stuff."

The bus began to move. Jana swallowed the taste of strawberries and watched the houses out the window, wondering who lived there. And why. She wondered what people lived for. She hoped they lived for love. Love could be a good thing. Even if it hadn't been for her.

"You're like a heater now," Arva complained. "I don't know why you're sitting here."

"Because I still need a friend," Jana said quietly.

Arva started to say something in reply, then stopped herself. She and Jana finished the bus ride in silence.

When they arrived, Jana let the bus empty without looking up. She didn't budge. At one point the driver was gone. She could talk to Michael now, but what good was that? She couldn't have him. It would only hurt more.

Jana could swallow a bird, if she could find one, and it wouldn't be as painful as seeing Michael again. Being sliced in half in a tornado didn't hurt at all compared to being torn to little ragged pieces by love. Jana couldn't put the pieces back together again. Her fingers, like her thoughts, were useless, awkward things.

She was an empty house with the windows broken out. Jana stayed on the bus.

"Look, we told him," Nathan said.

"*We?*" Michael said into his cell.

"Me and Sherry," Nathan told Michael. "My mom went with us, and her dad. We told the detective how it happened. It was no big deal to him. He just wants to talk to you. He knows it was an accident and all, just a prank. You know, like hazing."

"Hazing? Did he say that? Did he say *hazing?*"

"Yeah, I think so. You know, like no one intended anything bad to happen. It wasn't murder or anything."

Michael cursed. Nathan was such an idiot. Hadn't he seen what happened to those other college fraternity guys when one of them died during a hazing? No, it wasn't murder. It was manslaughter by reckless disregard or something like that. They went to prison.

"Oh, and Sherry told her dad about the photos on your cell phone. Well, you know, kind of what they are. They asked the detective about them. He told them you couldn't show the pictures to anyone without her permission, that it would be a violation of her civil rights or right to privacy or something like that. Anyway, he told Sherry she could sue you in civil court and win if you showed the pictures to even one other person."

"Listen to me," Michael said slowly. "It's your word against mine. I'm telling them you did it. They got nothing on me. You better think this through,

Nathan. Tell them you were lying because Sherry's dad was there. We'll both say that Sherry did it. Either that or I will tell them you did."

"I don't know," Nathan said. "I already signed the paper that had my statement on it."

"Think it over and call me back. I mean it. I'll tell them you did it and that you and Sherry have this thing and she'll say anything you tell her to say. She's just a sophomore. They'll think she's lying. And it will all go away. They don't have anything on you or me."

"I don't know."

"I'm getting a lawyer, you little prick." Michael seethed. "And I'm telling him you did it. We'll see what happens, Nathan. I'm Ivy League, you got that? You're nothing. We'll see what happens."

As she stared at her empty hands, pieces of Jana's broken hope slowly gathered into a plan. There was one thing left to do.

She got off the bus and walked into Dead School. She walked by the Grays who monitored the halls. She walked by the closed classroom doors. She walked by the library windows.

No one was at the swimming pool this hour.

She found the switches. She listened to the pumps come on. She turned on the underwater lights. Jana wanted to see where she was going. She left the overhead lights turned off. The water looked prettier that way. It looked pretty and deep.

There was nothing to think about. There was nothing left to consider.

She took off her clothes. Her body felt different than when she'd been a Riser. She was warm now, for one thing. Her body also felt a little heavier. Jana could feel the weight of her skin, her muscles, her blood. Gravity wanted a piece of her.

Considering carefully what she was about to do, Jana left Michael's class ring on her left hand instead of nesting it safely inside one of her shoes. She was taking what she had left of Michael with her. As she walked to the edge of the pool, the Virgins appeared. One after another, they showed up out of nowhere and formed a line above the pool. In front of her. Facing her.

Others appeared behind the first line of Virgins until they were four or five deep. There were dozens of them in their white translucent gowns and their white translucent skin. The Virgins reflected the light from under the water. Flashes of iridescent lavender and silver danced across their gowns and faces.

Jana pushed her toes over the edge of the pool and the Virgins came closer, as if they could stand on water. Jana could see the looks in their eyes, the pale colors of their eyes and hair. The Virgins held out one arm each and waved their hands, left to right, in front of them. They sang a harmony of one word. It was dull and flat and low.

The word was *No*.

Jana closed her eyes and jumped in.

Just under the surface of the water, she leaned back and let out all her air. Her eyes open, she could see the Virgins hovering above her.

She let herself sink. She turned her body over and pulled herself through the water with her arms, following the current at the bottom of the pool until she found the drain. As she reached for it, the suction grabbed her hand and jerked it down until Michael's ring was against the grate covering the drain. Jana could not lift a single finger from the drain. It held her hand like a jealous lover and would not let go.

A Slider came into class from across the hall and walked to Wyatt's desk at the back of the room.

"She's not there," he said. "She got off the bus."

"When?" Mars asked. He stood up from his seat behind Wyatt.

"Another guy saw her. He said she walked into the school a few minutes ago, but she's not in class."

Mars pushed the Slider aside as he rushed toward the classroom door. Wyatt knocked over his desk getting out of it to follow as quickly as he could. He'd nearly caught up to Mars when Mars jerked open the library doors and shouted at Jameson to ask if Jana was there.

She wasn't.

CHAPTER TWENTY-NINE

TIME WAS SHORT.

"Turn off the pumps!" Mars yelled to Wyatt as the two of them burst into the room.

Mars didn't have time to take off his shoes. He ran toward the pool, leaped as soon as he could, as far as he could, and was in the water like a knife.

Wyatt hit the switches, swung his bad leg around, and cursed when his weight caught it wrong. Despite the pain, he kept from falling over and kept from slowing down. His bad arm wouldn't allow him to swim well, but he could try.

Mars surfaced with Jana supine and limp in his

arms. She was more buoyant than he'd realized. She'd always said so.

"Stay there!" he shouted to Wyatt just in time. Mars managed to bring her body to the edge of the pool, pausing twice to blow air into her gaping mouth. Her mouth tasted like strawberries, but he barely noticed.

Jana's body came up the ladder between the two Sliders, one pulling from above and one pushing from below. Wyatt clutched her body to him as if she were standing.

"Use your arm," Mars was shouting as he clambered out of the pool. "Grip her diaphragm in your arm and jerk! Hard!"

Wyatt managed it. Water poured from Jana's mouth as Wyatt lost footing and fell backwards with Jana on top of him.

Mars's arms ached and he could barely pull himself from the pool. But soon he was over her on his knees, pulling her chin up in his hand, opening her mouth. Jana's eyes fluttered and she breathed out a short, hard burst of air. Mars touched her chest and felt it fill with a short gasp of air.

She breathed in on her own. Jana still existed.

• • •

They dressed her in the locker room.

Jana did nothing to help. She sat on the floor as if drugged from surgery.

Mars took off his clothes and wrapped himself in towels. He sat on the bench and kept one towel draped over his head. Wyatt remained standing. His clothes drip-dried where Jana had been against him, on top of him. He'd taken the cell phone from her skirt and now carried it in the back pocket of his jeans.

"It hurts," Jana finally said without looking at either of them. Her socks and shoes and bra were in a pile next to her.

"Shut up, Webster," Wyatt said angrily. "One of us wants to throw you back in."

Mars trembled inside the towels. He couldn't get dry enough, warm enough. He chewed his lower lip to keep it from quivering.

"It's cold in here," he said.

Jana sat for the rest of the day at the back of the empty bus.

Wyatt stayed with her. "I don't give a rat's ass about what you did," he said. He sprawled across the seat in front of and across from her, his leg blocking the aisle. "You make your own choices and you can make that choice again."

He pulled himself up with his good arm, his hand on the back of the seat. With his remaining eye, he stared at Jana's head of wet hair, her slumped shoulders. She wouldn't look at him.

"Before you do, there's one thing I want to show you. Tonight."

Jana didn't respond.

"Tomorrow you can go right back and jump in that pool again. But tonight, you're with me. You got that?"

Wyatt dropped back down in the seat.

"Okay, we've got a deal, then," he said.

Michael didn't go to school.

The detective called after Michael didn't show up for their appointment. Michael didn't answer the phone. When the unmarked police car rolled to a stop in front of his house, Michael hid beneath the windows. He didn't answer the door.

As soon as the car pulled away, Michael moved his car out of the driveway. He wore a baseball cap that covered his eyes from the side or whenever he ducked his head.

They were after him, he thought. They had a warrant by now. His license plate number would show up on the computers in police cruisers and county sheriff cars. Michael had to leave the county. He was careful to drive the speed limit, to signal every lane change and turn.

Mars didn't live on the third floor anymore.

Still wearing her school uniform, Jana sat on his old bed and waited for Wyatt. She had her own room at the other end of the hall, with Slider girl dormmates waiting to tell her how they'd died. Jana didn't feel like meeting anyone dead tonight.

She thought about that old movie from the 1960s, *Bonnie and Clyde*. Warren Beatty. Faye Dunaway. Jana had always hated that movie, hated the way it ended. Now she thought getting riddled with bullets together was what should have happened to her and Michael. The together part, anyway. If they had died together, Webster and Haynes would have lived forever.

Wyatt slipped through the hole in the fence behind the dorm. He talked on her cell phone while he tramped through the vacant lot to the street out front.

"Check it out," Wyatt said. "You call that butthead right now and tell him to answer his phone when I call."

"Yeah, sure," Nathan stammered. "I will, I will."

"Right now. And I know you will. I've got something you want. I've got something *he* needs."

The drive to Lookaway Rock was a sullen one.

Wyatt's good side faced Jana. He had to keep turning his head to look out the driver's window. Once they were on the state highway, he handed Jana a stick of gum.

"It's from the Planet. Open it. Take the wrapper off without thinking about it too much. That's your first test."

Jana slipped the gum out of its green paper sheath and unwrapped its foil covering. She put it in her mouth.

"Chew carefully," Wyatt warned. "You'll bite your mouth if you aren't careful."

It wasn't all that difficult. The flavor sluiced over her tongue, rich and sweet, almost choking her. She hadn't eaten since she'd died. She wasn't supposed to.

"And don't try that on campus. You'll choke. You stay out of the pool, we'll go get pizza in a week."

The paved highway wound into the mountains, into the night. The sky was clear and the air was warm. Jana's bottom fit snug against the car seat. She was no longer fearful of falling out when she leaned against the inside of the passenger door.

"He'll be there?" Jana asked. "Are you sure?"

"He was most agreeable to the arrangement," Wyatt said.

The aerosol canister of silicone lubricant that Wyatt had taken from Sherry's house rode in the backseat of the borrowed car.

"I told him to bring a flashlight for the trail," Wyatt added. "He said he'd been to the rock before and knew how to get there."

Jana's hair was a mess. She still wore her school uniform. It would have been ghoulish to show up in the clothes she'd worn the night she died, she'd decided. She remembered her death and decided not to go over it again. She would think about someone else's instead.

"How did you die, Wyatt? Will you tell me?"

Wyatt took a breath, then began. "It was a hot, sultry day," he drawled. "The sun blazed down through the trees, trapping the little birds in their nests under wave after wave of glistening heat. . . ."

He broke out laughing. Jana managed a grin and almost swallowed her gum.

When Wyatt stopped laughing, he told her the truth.

The old man wore a paper hat.

He sat in a plastic chair next to his bed at the nursing home. His grandfather's large frail hands shook in his lap.

Wyatt held out a small sack and said, "Happy birthday, Granddad."

The old man smiled. He wasn't wearing his teeth.

Wyatt tried not to notice how red his grandfather's eyes had become. Removing the saltwater fishing lure from the sack, Wyatt held it out so his grandfather could see it. He carefully set the large shiny lure on the dresser next to the bed.

Stories of fishing off the coast were the ones his grandfather still told with excitement in his voice. But Wyatt knew his grandfather would never cast lures into the ocean again.

"How's your car going, boy?"

"Like new," Wyatt lied.

His grandfather had given him his car when they put him in the nursing home. It was a 1972 four-door Chevy Biscayne and Wyatt was lucky when he could get all four doors to close right. If he turned off the engine after the car had been running a long time, it wouldn't start again until the motor cooled down. No one knew why.

He told his grandfather the name of the lure and the type of big-game fish it was designed to catch.

Wyatt was going to be late for work. He'd left the car running in a parking space at the nursing home. His afternoon job three days a week, for which he received vo-tech class credits, was filling in on various job crews with a local construction company.

He parked the Biscayne at the side of the building and turned it off. He grabbed his work gloves and rushed inside the employee entrance only to find out that the crew had already left for the job site. The receptionist gave him the address.

"Hurry on out there now," she said. "They're ready to let you go if you're late again more than a few minutes."

Wyatt's car wouldn't start. It might be twenty minutes. He couldn't wait.

There was a motel and restaurant across the parking lot from the construction company. The motel manager's Suzuki 250 motorcycle was sitting there doing nothing.

It was a rash decision and a stupid one. A helmet would have been sensible. There wasn't one. That, and the single-cylinder Suzuki was about the least powerful motorcycle they made. It would barely keep up with old ladies and church buses in the slow lane of I-40. And that was going downhill.

Still, it was a pretty day. The sun was out. The wind blew through his hair and Wyatt remembered how much fun it was to ride a motorcycle. He pretended his work gloves were leather gauntlets. He pretended the little Suzuki was a full-throttle Harley.

In his rearview mirror, Wyatt saw the speeding car top the hill behind him. It felt to him like he'd seen the car top the hill before. The passing lane was full. The car was on his tail in seconds, still coming at a ridiculous rate of speed. Wyatt figured he was done for.

He leaned forward. It was all he had time to do. The car swerved to the right to miss him. The driver had two tires on the shoulder. The speeding car swerved to miss him, but a little too late. It clipped the rear fender of the Suzuki.

Wyatt heard the bark of brakes. Then everything upright sort of disappeared. The motorcycle fell on its side and Wyatt let go of the thing. The pavement grabbed his shoulder, his hip, his legs. The bike spun away from him.

The pavement was hot and hard. And rough. At first, he seemed to be sliding along without damage, without slowing down. Then the pavement grabbed his face. A bone in his leg snapped. His elbow banged down hard and bounced up.

Wyatt's flesh felt like it was on fire. He was engulfed in pain. Then his head bounced and everything went away.

The pavement was gone. The sun was gone. Wyatt was gone. His grandfather wasn't the only one who would never go fishing again.

"It happened fast enough," he said. "But I wish it had been a little faster."

Wyatt left out the part about how hot the highway was, how the searing pavement felt like it was burning him alive. It was like riding fire as he slid at nearly sixty miles an hour on the downhill surface of I-40. Torn-away pieces of his clothing smoked from the heat of friction.

Jana thought about the violence of Wyatt's death. At least she had died quickly. Snap, crackle, pop. It had to be difficult to die more slowly, to die painfully. It had to make you feel things differently once you were dead.

"What were you doing wrong when the car clipped you from behind? You were doing something bad or you wouldn't be a Slider. Were you speeding?"

"No. I could barely keep up with the traffic. If anything, I was going too slow."

"Mars was speeding when he crashed and he was driving drunk," Jana said. "He told me that much. That's what made him a Slider. And that's why he wanted to save a life. Another person died in his wreck, he said. He wanted to make up for it while he had the chance."

"I guess that's it."

"So what were you doing wrong?" she tried again. "Why are you a Slider, Wyatt?"

"Oh, that," he said, tossing it off. "I took the motorcycle without asking. I could get it started without the key. So I did."

He shrugged. "I was going to bring it back. With a full tank of gas."

Jana believed him. It was just like Wyatt to steal things and bring them back.

"Was it his girlfriend?" Jana asked.

"Who?" Wyatt was confused.

"Mars," she said. "Was it his girlfriend who died in the car with him?" She wanted to know if Mars was in love when he died.

"He was alone, Webster. Didn't he tell you that?"

"He said someone else died." Jana watched Wyatt's face, the way his hand moved on the steering wheel, the way it tensed.

"You know who it was," she said.

"Yes."

"Tell me."

"You want me to name it to you," Wyatt said. "The old ladies in my family, that's what they say when they're mad. My grandmother and her sisters. They're from way up in the back hills, like Christie's family. Anyway, they say they'll 'name it to you' if you really want to hear it."

This was the first time Wyatt had talked to Jana about his life. What you remember when you're dead isn't what you think it's going to be. It's dumb stuff. Things you don't really need. Like handkerchiefs.

"So name it to me," Jana said.

"It was me, Webster. Mars was driving the car that came up behind me over the top side of the hill, the car that clipped the bike. He swerved to avoid it, but not quite in time to keep either one of us from dying."

Wyatt pulled the borrowed car into the small turnout where only last night the pickup truck had been. He turned off the lights and took his foot off the brake pedal.

He handed Jana her cell phone. "You can call him here. You won't be able to farther up. The mountain blocks the signal."

Jana didn't open her phone.

"Go ahead, Webster. I know you want to talk to him. Ask him if he's on time."

"I can't," she said. "I ran the battery out last night."

"I put a new one in at the dorm. It's working fine."

Although she was a Slider now, Jana's Earth skills were slim. She flipped her phone open, and pleased to see that her fingers worked the buttons, she punched in Michael's number. His face showed up. And he answered this time.

"Michael, it's me."

He could hear her voice. Michael said hello in reply. He sounded nervous and confused, but he talked to her.

Jana was excited. Hearing Michael speak made her heart race. But something had changed. His voice sounded small. Michael sounded littler now, not quite as tall. He told her he was at the rock. She said she would be there soon.

"Will he be able to see me?" she asked Wyatt after she closed her phone.

"I doubt it," he said. "You're too new to this, Webster. I'll help you when it's time. He'll be able to hear you, though."

Jana smiled for the first time in what seemed like forever. She smacked her gum on purpose.

She watched Lookaway Rock rise above them as they drove into the gorge. The solid granite wall reached to the sky. It was hard to believe that she had jumped off that rock, had fallen that far. That fast. That hard. She smiled at the thought of it. She smiled at herself. High above the top of the rock, there was a star tied to Jana by a tiny string of light. She wanted to climb to that star.

And jump.

Wyatt parked the car in the clearing at the top of the switchbacks. Michael's car was there. She and Wyatt carried flashlights to the head of the trail. Entering the darkness under trees at night, Jana tripped twice. She dropped her flashlight. It hit a flat rock and went out.

Wyatt came back for her.

Jana banged the flashlight against her hand. It wouldn't come on again.

"It's broken," she said.

"Leave it," Wyatt told her. "Grab my belt. We're almost there."

His awkward gait jerked her arm to the left with every step, but she held on. Jana walked through what seemed like a hundred separate strings of spiderwebs she hadn't felt the night before.

Leaves brushed her skin. She could feel and smell everything the Planet had to offer. The air was heavy with the scent of balsam and hemlock. Little dabs of perfume, the fragrance of moon vine and wild briar rose, hid in the darkness alongside the trail.

Michael stood at the juniper-moss edge of Lookaway Rock, the treacherous slope of mountain granite drifting off behind him. Michael was a tall silhouette in the darkness when Jana first saw him. The stars sparkled over his shoulders and to either side of him.

She stepped from the trail behind Wyatt, who turned his flashlight on Michael. The updraft of air that swam over the rock, from the bottom of the gorge to the top, bathed Jana like gentle hands lightly combing her hair.

"Michael," she said. He looked left, but not at Jana. He couldn't see her.

"Turn her voice off," Michael said to Wyatt. "That game is over. I'm not putting up with it."

Wyatt leaned close to Jana and whispered for her not to talk.

The circle of light from Michael's flashlight found Wyatt's face in the darkness.

"*Oh!*" Michael said. He saw a monster. "Who are you?"

Wyatt closed his one eye slowly and opened it. "Blind date," he said. "I hope you're not disappointed. I like walking on the beach and summer picnics."

Jana laughed. Sometimes you had to love Wyatt.

Michael looked to the left again, moving the

beam of his flashlight. He saw nothing where Jana stood. He moved the flashlight back to Wyatt, and when he did, the half-face monster was standing closer. Wyatt's full Earth body was there looming in front of Michael like a threat.

"You're the guy from Sherry's house," Michael said. "The police are looking for you."

"That's not the way I hear it," Wyatt growled. Nathan had told him that Michael was on the run, looking for a way out of the mess he was in.

"Look, I don't care what you think. I didn't kill that stupid bitch. She killed herself. Now, where's the can of locksmith spray?"

Jana was stunned by what Michael had called her. His words repeated themselves over and over in her head.

Her heart was ice.

Stupid bitch.

Then it shattered.

"The one with your fingerprints on it?" Wyatt said. "It's right here." He cradled the flashlight in the crook of his bad arm and held up the aerosol can so Michael could see it.

As far as Wyatt was concerned, the date was over. Michael had said enough. Jana had heard him. It was up to her now to take in the truth and accept it or to stay trapped in her love for Michael for eternity.

"Give it here," Michael said. "Give it to me now."

Instead of setting down the canister, Wyatt sprayed the air in front of him with a fine mist of dark gray silicone particles. They sparkled in the light from Michael's flashlight like dust mites in bright sun.

"Why don't you hand me one of your shoes for a second?" Wyatt suggested. "Then put it back on and take a walk on that rock behind you. You know, as a joke. A prank. It would be kind of fun."

"Set the can down and leave," Michael said. "I have a gun."

"Sure you do," Wyatt said. He stepped forward, leaning into it and straightening up quickly. His flashlight beam brightened a circle of empty sky to the side of Michael.

Wyatt held the can inches away from Michael now. He sprayed it again.

Michael fired from the hip, accidentally. Nervous and scared, he'd only meant to lift the gun, to show it to Wyatt. To keep the monster from coming closer. Jana saw the bright flash of light before she heard the loud report.

Wyatt wobbled. His stance faltered in his own teetering sideways fashion. He lurched somewhat forward, like he was going to walk but couldn't. He folded to the ground on one bent knee. His flashlight fell and went out. Wyatt rolled on his side then his back, his good hand gripping his stomach where the bullet had entered. His head rested on granite rock. The aerosol can was under his leg.

Jana screamed. Michael moved his flashlight beam in frantic jerking swings, looking for the canister of silicone spray. Blood covered Wyatt's hand. It soaked his shirt.

Conditioning from life on the Planet told Jana one thing and one thing only.

"He's dead!" she screamed.

Jana rushed to Wyatt without a thought but to comfort him, to help him, to touch him before he was gone for good.

Michael stepped back. Jana fully naturalized as she focused her entire physical and emotional existence into urgently tending to Wyatt. She bent over the fallen monster and Michael saw her as plain as day. Jana looked up at him, her face contorted by rage and pain and fear.

"You killed him!" she yelled at Michael. She tore the words from her chest. "You bastard!" A piece of gum fell from her mouth. It looked to Michael like her teeth were falling out.

Michael stepped away from her. He moved his flashlight over Wyatt's lifeless form on the ground. He saw the blood from the bullet wound. He hadn't meant to fire the gun. It had fired on its own. He searched Wyatt's body for hope. There was none.

He dropped the gun. It clattered to the surface of Lookaway Rock, bounced, then slipped away along the slope of granite on which Michael precariously stood. The gun soon disappeared.

Wyatt slowly lifted his good arm, stretching it out above him until his blood-soaked hand was straight up in the air. His fingers spread as if to grab life itself. As Wyatt's arm moved, Michael jerked back another step.

"Damn, that hurt," Wyatt said.

Staggering backwards from the shock of seeing Jana, of seeing the dead guy lift his arm, Michael lost his footing on the deceptive slope of smooth granite under his feet. His flashlight shone straight down, then the beam of yellow light swung into the darkness behind him as he bent forward from the waist to gain his footing. Jana heard a distant gunshot from the bottom of the gorge.

Michael cartwheeled his arms forward then back. He was falling, being pulled toward the darkness against his will. He danced on toe and heel, his shoes slipping on the granite floor.

He lifted one leg and lost his balance entirely. The only way to keep from falling on his face was to step backwards again. It was one step too far. And then it was too late. He held the flashlight high over his head, as Jana had held the bowling ball over hers. Michael looked like the Statue of Liberty when he went over the edge. He let go of the light.

He started to scream, then stopped. Michael fell quietly into darkness.

"I'm not kidding," Wyatt said. "That really hurt."

CHAPTER THIRTY

"WHAT'S THAT?"

"It's a newspaper, Webster. Surely you've heard of them."

"I meant what are you reading?"

"A little something about your boyfriend." Wyatt handed Jana the local newspaper. He'd had to stay up all night to sneak off campus early to get it.

She sat next to Wyatt at the back. Other than the Virgin in the front seat, they were first on the bus. She had folded the top of her high-waisted uniform skirt down inside itself and tied the tails of her school blouse into a knot in front. She smelled a little less of Ivory soap this morning.

Michael's fall had made the front page. The paper headlined Lookaway Rock as a new Lovers' Leap.

The article reported that Michael Haynes of Asheville, distraught over the recent death of his girlfriend, had launched himself from the granite precipice late at night. His body had been found near a gun that had been fired twice.

"Suicides are like that sometimes," a county detective was quoted. "They have more than one way to kill themselves in mind and decide which at the last moment."

In county documents filed by the coroner, Haynes's cause of death was ruled as coronary asphyxiation.

"The boy was dead before he hit the rocks," the coroner stated in a telephone interview with the newspaper reporter. "When you fall that far, it is possible to stop breathing. In this case, the trauma of beginning the fall stopped the boy's heart. He was dead of a heart attack in midair. It was fear, maybe. Or shock."

Nathan Mills, of Asheville, a close friend of the deceased, expressed the more popular theory circulating among students at Central High School in Asheville, where Haynes was a senior preparing for early college coursework this summer.

"Broken heart is more like it," Mills said. "His girlfriend, Jana Webster, died in a freak bowling accident and he couldn't handle it. They're burying him next to her at the cemetery. Everyone in school is calling him Romeo Haynes now."

There was a new student on the bus.

"How come he gets to sit up there?" Jana stared at the back of Michael's head, where he sat near the front in a seat next to Henry Sixkiller.

"Maybe it was self-defense," Wyatt suggested. He draped his crooked arm over Jana's shoulder and leaned back. "Or maybe he didn't mean to shoot me."

"Why does he get to look so good? He should be all broken up."

"He died before he hit the bottom, Webster. Remind me to do that the next time I'm on a motorcycle."

"It's not fair," she complained.

"Now you're catching on," Wyatt said. "Brains *and* beauty, what's to become of you?"

"I don't have beauty, Wyatt. I wished you'd quit saying that."

"Well, see, there's something for you to learn yet. You're the most beautiful girl in Dead School, Webster. And you were the prettiest girl in your real school too. It's hard to believe you never noticed."

Fart, fudge, and popcorn. Wyatt had made her blush.

Mars turned around from his aisle seat right behind Arva's and looked at Jana once. He started to smile. She flipped him off. He looked silly with his hair combed and his school clothes ironed. Mars smiled anyway before turning to look front. Jana tasted strawberries every time she looked at him.

"You got that boy wrapped around your little finger," Wyatt said.

"Which boy?" Jana grinned when she said it.

"All of them. All of them except one."

"You mean you?"

"That I do, Webster. That I do."

Beatrice and Christie sat together on the bus. Jana looked at Christie's hair and wondered if she could get her own hair to look like that. Beatrice got out of her seat, as if Jana's looking at her had been a cue. She walked to the back of the bus to talk to Wyatt. She wasn't supposed to.

She stood right next to Jana and grinned like a

watermelon cut in half. Beatrice wore less makeup than usual. She lightly touched the top of her head where her hair was combed over the sawn-off inch of yard dart tip still in her head. Only the portion that killed her had to stay with her after death.

"I just wanted to thank you," Beatrice said to Wyatt.

Sliders weren't allowed to talk to Risers on the bus. Wyatt nodded and winked his only eye.

"And thank the others too," she added before walking back to her seat.

"Talk about wrapped," Jana said to Wyatt, shaking her head.

"I am a handsome devil, aren't I?"

Sliders left the bus first at Dead School. Jana had a crazy thought. The aisle between the bus seats, the aisle they walked to file out, could be the aisle in a chapel. The Virgin up front was dressed for a wedding, after all. Jana tugged Michael's ring from her finger and buried it in her fist.

With her empty hand she touched the back of Mars's seat as she walked by, trailing two fingers gently across his shoulder. She knew the warmth he was feeling when she did that. She had kissed him once.

She paused next to Henry's seat. Jana reached her arm across in front of him. Palm down, she opened her fist. The heavy class ring dropped into Michael's lap. He looked up at Jana with his mouth open and blinked. It didn't mean anything, his mouth being open. It was always like that now. Michael's mouth was a permanent circular cave waiting for the scream to come out. It probably echoed when he talked. He looked like an idiot, Jana thought.

She glanced back at Mars and smiled. Even as a Riser, his blue eyes blazed under perfect brows when he smiled in return. She had kissed him once and she would kiss him again.

Jana had the jitters. For Mars.

She'd fallen for him.

ACKNOWLEDGMENTS

The author thanks the following talented individuals for all sorts of hard work, and for many other things:

My editor at HarperCollins, Erica Sussman, and assistant, Tyler Infinger; my agent, Merrilee Heifetz, and assistant, Jennifer Escott, Writers House; agent Sarah Self, the Gersh Agency; my favorite movie producer, Mason Novick; and Jenna Block, creative executive, Escape Artists production company.

Lifelong writer friends Robyn Carr, Sally Goldenbaum, Judith Kelman, Lia Matera, and Nancy Pickard. Colleague authors Shawn Goodman, Marissa

Guibard, Kathy McCullough, and Ruta Sepetys. First readers Janet Barnett and Cat.

And, of course, my family: Janet, Gracie, and Honey Bunny.

DEMCO